# A DARK AND STARLESS FOREST

## SARAH HOLLOWELL

Houghton Mifflin Harcourt
Boston   New York

For Mom and Dad and Aunt Teri, and
all the stories you gave me

hmhbooks.com

The text was set in Sabon LT Std.
Cover design by Mary Claire Cruz
Interior design by Alice Wang

Library of Congress Cataloging-in-Publication Data is available.
ISBN: 978-0-358-42441-3

Manufactured in the United States of America
1 2021
4500830252

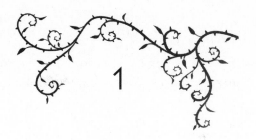

# 1

THE SNOWDROPS IN the gardening book are mocking me. Their white blossoms hang from vibrant green stems, all huddled together in a bunch. Laughing at me, probably, as I try to defy nature.

I press my hand into the patch of dirt cleared just for this test. It's been baked by the high summer sun until it nearly radiates heat, and now I have to grow a winter flower out of it. The flower's primary season is January to April—May at a stretch—and we are quite solidly in August. The snowdrops are all asleep and they don't want to come back just because some sixteen-year-old alchemist asks them nicely.

I wish Frank had given me any other task except for growing a real flower. *Real* is always so much harder. When I ask the earth to bring plants from my imagination into being, it responds eagerly, like we're playing a game. But with anything real, it hesitates. It seems to purse its lips and look me up and down, and find me wanting.

Wanting for what, I don't know. I've read absolutely every book on gardening and botany that we have in the lake house. I know all about snowdrops. *Galanthus nivalis*. Incredibly common. Native to more places than I can name, but one of them is Indiana. I've seen them bloom here every winter. I know that this earth knows these flowers and can grow them.

I sneak glances away from the book, toward my audience. "Audience" is a generous term, since that would imply more than a few of them were paying attention. Only Jane and London are actually watching, with London in Jane's lap. Winnie's lying on her stomach, too busy tearing blades of grass into pieces to look up. Brooke and Irene are having an animated conversation in sign language that I think is about a movie we watched recently, but it's hard to tell from this angle. Violet's reading while Olivia braids their hair, and Olivia's hair is being braided by Elle.

My siblings.

Seven sisters and Violet, who came out as nonbinary after being with us for a year. Frank couldn't exactly kick them out by that point. *Wouldn't* have, I think. Irene is trans and that's never been a problem, so Violet shouldn't be either. Any gender welcome except male, because Frank thinks male alchemists are prone to either being less powerful or burning out faster or both.

Frank's my primary source of information on alchemists, so I can't really say if he's right or not. Considering how much he's helped us all grow and learn to control our magic, I'd say he knows his stuff, but . . .

I shift my eyes toward him. Frank's a tall white man

somewhere in his thirties or forties—he's never said, and I'm not good at ages. His lean frame towers over all of us, and when we're outside he wears reflective sunglasses that hide his green eyes. I can still always tell when he's looking at me. His gaze has a weight to it. It settles onto my shoulders first, then worms its way up my spinal column into my brain until the world is both too fuzzy and too sharp.

It's not a good feeling.

Frank's pacing behind my siblings, holding the iPad he uses to take notes during tests. Chatter descends into whispers or dies altogether whenever he draws close, then rises as his pacing takes him away.

He nods at me to begin.

I snap back to the book. I stare at the snowdrops so hard my vision begins to blur.

*Please,* I think into the earth. *I know this is all wrong, I know it's too hot—it is for me, too. But could a few of you come out anyway?*

"Remember to breathe," Frank says. "Squares. Straight lines."

Right. Breathe in, that's the base of the square. Breathe out, and draw the left side. Steady, now. Build a box for the spell to grow in. Breathe in, form the top. Feel the magic and harness it. Breathe out, close the square.

It's not working. The earth is unimpressed. What does it care for straight lines?

I risk another glance at Frank. He's frowning. Anxiety bursts into my veins like a thousand microscopic bombs. I don't want to disappoint him. Another peek toward Jane, seeking a last boost of strength, because at every test she's there, she's watching, and she's smiling like she knows I can do anything.

But Jane's not looking at me. London still is, with those serious eight-year-old eyes, but not Jane. She's looking over her shoulder, across the lake and toward the forest. When she turns back around, her expression is worried. My heart stutters. Is she thinking about what happened in there? Is she reconsidering our deal? Is she—

"We don't have all day, Derry," Frank says.

*PLEASE, GROW.*

The magic square in my mind shatters. What comes out of the ground isn't the blanket of snowdrops I'd imagined, the kind of dense thicket that looks like actual snow from afar. It's no more than a dozen scattered flowers. They stand too rigid, as if they're too proud to droop in front of us, but the blossoms are bell-shaped and white, and it's close enough.

It has to be close enough.

The magic I sent into the earth flows back into me. Tiny gray flowers bloom on my shoulder and descend across the thick fat of my upper arm. It doesn't hurt. It's a gentle push under my skin, a tug from somewhere above it, and then

I'm growing my own flowers. I barely register them in the moment. I brush them off, leaving no trace, and wait for judgment.

"Good," Frank says. He smiles, but it's not a real, true smile. It's a consolation prize. I did *enough*, but I wasn't *impressive*. I think he knows I didn't try hard enough to exert control with the square breathing.

I collapse on the ground between Jane and Winnie. London reaches outside the boundary of Jane's lap to pat my head.

"You were great," Jane says.

"You were fine," Winnie says, pulling several more strands of grass apart at the middle. Her face is almost entirely shrouded by her long blond hair. "Better than me."

I can't do much to comfort her there, because she's right. Her test didn't go well. They rarely do. Out of all of us, Winnie's magic is the least reliable. When it decides to show up, it's usually fine, but it rarely decides to show up when she wants it to. She's supposed to be telekinetic, but it primarily manifests as a breeze that hangs out near her. We call it her little pet poltergeist, because it mostly just messes around. It's the poltergeist that's forming her ripped-up pieces of grass into a tiny whirlwind.

"You were also great," Jane tells Winnie. "You improved from last week, and that's what matters."

Anyone else would have earned a glare from Winnie for

that, and probably prank-based retaliation later. One time Winnie used all the plastic wrap in the house to individually wrap every piece of my clothing, and that was just because of some stupid fight I don't even remember the genesis of now.

*Genesis.* Good word.

Winnie got time-out for like an hour for wasting so much plastic wrap, which had to be hell. She dutifully apologized once she got out, but the way her poltergeist whipped around my face told me she wasn't sorry at all.

But you don't do that kind of thing to Jane. Instead, Winnie smiles at her, and the shreds of grass settle back onto the ground.

Jane looks over her shoulder again. It's so quick, I doubt anyone else notices. Before I can say anything, the next test begins. Jane turns her attention full force to Violet.

I look across the lake, toward the forest.

We weren't supposed to be in the forest that day. We're *never* supposed to be in the forest. If Frank knew even that much—if he knew what I did—

I lie down on my stomach, mimicking Winnie, and press my face into my hands. They're sweaty and my face is sweaty and it's too goddamn *hot,* Frank had to know I'd never be able to grow snowdrops in this heat. Maybe he already knows what I did. Maybe that's why he set me up to fail.

Winnie nudges me. I raise my head to glare at her.

"Stop," she hisses. "Whatever you're freaking out about, stop. You're practically vibrating, and it's distracting."

"Distracting from what? All the rapt attention you're giving Violet?" She glares, and I sneer, and Jane clears her throat. Moments later, Frank's shadow falls over us.

Neither of us look up at him. He doesn't say anything. Winnie and I just stare straight ahead at Violet as they glamour their own hair from brown to purple to silver.

Eventually, Frank walks away. Winnie sticks her tongue out at me. I return the favor, feeling like I'm ten years old but also feeling entirely justified.

Pretty sure we only have like half a roll of plastic wrap right now anyway.

~

Tests and what comes after them take up all of Monday morning, every week. The testing part is over and we're painfully close to lunch, but first we must deal with the flowers.

Nine glass flowers sit on a shelf in the living room. There's one for each of us. They glow a rainbow of colors — some more brilliantly than others. They're meant to represent our magic. The tests are important to see *what* we can do, but it's the flowers that tell us and Frank if our magic has truly grown.

My siblings and I line up across from our flowers while Frank stands by the shelf with that ever-present iPad.

Jane steps forward first. She takes a glass camellia from the shelf. Its pink glow is steady and strong. Dependable. She holds it with two hands, and waits.

Jane is the oldest of us at nineteen. She's a slender Black girl who spent the first ten years of her life on a farm in Ohio. She wound up here, like the rest of us did after her, when her magic became too much for her parents to handle.

The camellia flashes and settles back to the same pink glow. The flash is a good sign. It means that the flower sensed some kind of growth. From the size of the flash, it's only a little growth, but that's normal. How much can you really grow in a week? The size doesn't matter as much as the fact that we continue advancing.

Frank lightly taps notes into his iPad. He beckons Winnie to come forward next. She's anxiously braided a small portion of her hair while waiting her turn. The braid falls apart when she drops her hands and steps up.

Winnie arrived at the lake house a few months after Jane. I don't think she changed much from that point to when I met her two years later, or even to now. She's still a chubby white girl with pigtails, a temper, and a Minnesota accent.

Her glass amaryllis glows with faint swirls of red and white that refract through the glass as if a piece of her little pet poltergeist is trapped inside. She glares at it as she picks it up, as if she can threaten it into flashing.

If anyone could, it would be Winnie. That's probably not why her amaryllis gives the gentlest of flashes, but her triumphant smile says that she thinks it is.

We continue on down the line. The third-oldest, Brooke, is a Deaf Mexican American. Her flower is a cluster of blue forget-me-nots that outshine anything else on the shelf. This morning during her test she signed 'I cast Sacred Flame,' and scorched a circle out of the grass.

Surprising no one, her flower's flash is bright enough to make us shield our eyes.

Elle and Irene are twins, but not identical twins— they're both tall white girls, but there are a million little differences, like Elle's honey-blond hair versus Irene's dark blond, or Elle's face, with its thick smattering of freckles, versus Irene's face, which tends to go red more than it freckles or even tans.

Elle's flower is a vivid pink snapdragon, and Irene's a coral-red hibiscus with deceptively delicate petals. Both their flowers flash when held, but while Elle beams at Frank and waits for his approving smile before stepping back in line, Irene doesn't even glance his way.

My turn. The poppy near the middle is mine. Seven years ago, I sat on the floor of this living room with Jane. We held the glass poppy together until it filled up with red light.

9

She's the one who did all the magic to make the flowers ready to sense our magic. It's something to do with her affinity for inanimate objects. Usually she can only physically manipulate them, but Frank said the glass is special. It allows Jane's magic to reach a little farther.

I take my poppy off the shelf. It's solidly middle of the road—nowhere near as bright as Brooke's, not as faint as Winnie's. After my unimpressive display with the snowdrops, I'm half-expecting it not to flash at all. Maybe it'll even weaken. That's happened before, once to Elle and twice to Winnie, and it's not an outcome you want.

It doesn't happen to me today. I get a little flash, comparable to Winnie's. I'll take it.

Next is Violet. They're a couple years younger than me, but already taller. I'm not that short or anything. Violet just sprouted up over the last couple years. They're five-foot-ten, with shaggy brown hair and huge gray eyes behind plain black glasses, the same kind I wear. They're Mexican American, like Brooke, though their skin is a little lighter than her deep brown.

Violet came to us at eleven, and by then they'd already spent enough time researching on the library internet to figure out that the word for their gender is *nonbinary*, to learn that *pansexual* best described why their crushes spanned across and beyond gender.

Between Violet and the big twins, we all got a chance

to learn more about ourselves. To put labels on our feelings that we hadn't learned before we came here, and certainly never would have learned from Frank. Words like *bisexual* and *asexual* and *demiromantic*. Words we never knew we needed until we heard them. Words to make a person feel whole and understood.

Like every week, Violet's patterned an item of their clothing—today a T-shirt—to have a sunflower pattern. It matches their glass flower. A good luck charm.

Not that Violet tends to need it. They may not have the strongest, brightest glow, but their magic is rock-solid. The yellow light never wavers, and it never fails to flash after a test. This week is no different.

Unlike the big twins, London and Olivia *are* identical. They're two little Black girls with the same inquisitive brown eyes, same broad noses, same round chipmunk cheeks. They're the youngest in the house by six years. They're the babies of the house, and we all dote on them, but being young doesn't get them out of our weekly tests.

London's apple blossom is a pale pink, but it still glows brighter than most. Olivia's sweet pea is a vibrant, flickering fuchsia. London's flash is always small, where Olivia's tends to be brighter, because London isn't as fierce about practicing her magic. Her powers are . . . difficult. She had a bad history with them before she came to the lake house. I wouldn't want to practice very much, either, if I were in her shoes.

All through the flower tests, I keep sneaking glances at Jane.

Jane keeps sneaking glances out the living room window to the forest.

I don't get a chance to talk to her alone until after lunch.

We're in the back, watering the large garden. We grow a lot of our own produce. If I could ever master growing stuff out of season, we'd be able to grow it *all* for ourselves.

I could be valuable, then. I could make my siblings safer by limiting our dependence on the outside.

I've got the hose out to spray down the vegetables while Jane uses a watering can on the flowers and herbs. I direct the spray on a batch of zucchini, trying to find the courage to say something to Jane. I want to know what she's thinking, but I don't want to talk about what happened. I've spent days now trying to pretend that *nothing* happened. Jane and I took the secret and buried it deep inside ourselves, never to resurface, never to be known by anyone, not even our siblings.

But if she's already struggling to keep the secret, then I need to know. We need to talk about it.

When I turn to Jane, I find her once again staring at the forest.

The forest circles the lake and the house, with only the one road out. There's a lot of tree line. Earlier, she was looking in the direction of the clearing, where the *nothing* happened. Now, she's squinting into the trees nearest us, as if she sees something there other than trees.

"Jane?"

She keeps her gaze on the forest, but goes, "Hmm?"

The words are right there. *Are you okay?*

She finally turns to me and smiles. Her forehead is smooth again, clear of the creases from her worried squinting. The moment's erased.

I say, "What about *conjurer?*"

Frank calls us alchemists, and as a word on its own it's pretty good, but applying it to ourselves feels like wearing someone else's too-small clothes. I've had an ongoing project to find a word we all like a little better. *Witch* would be the most obvious word, but Frank's made it clear that where a witch goes, death follows. Burning. Drowning. Crushed with rocks. Buried alive. We can't be witches without risking the same fate, so the search continues.

*Conjurer* is one I've already rejected, but it's the first thing I think to say.

"It's not bad, but doesn't really click with me," Jane says. "Are you done with the zucchini? The peppers could use it next."

Something twists in my gut and tells me to ask her. Just ask her. It's probably nothing, but what if it's not?

I don't ask her. I water the peppers and when Jane keeps looking back to the forest, I keep not asking.

I don't ask when we're done in the garden, or when we go inside to play Monopoly with our siblings. Brooke handily beats us all, as usual. If anyone else notices Jane sneaking glances out to the forest through the kitchen window while she helps with the dishes after dinner, they don't say so. Maybe they think she's a little off, but that can be explained by a million things. Test day isn't easy for anyone. Jane has depression, and it can manifest in nights like this, or her ADHD meds wearing off could have caused an energy crash.

And I can't talk to anyone about it, because I can't explain why I'd be so freaked out about Jane just looking at the forest. Yeah, we're not allowed *in* the forest, but we're allowed to look at it.

So I don't say anything, and I don't ask Jane anything. I go through the motions by her side. I eat dinner, I clear up, I pretend to concentrate on reading a book about black holes and other terrifying space phenomena.

At the end of the night, I sit cross-legged on the floor of our dark bedroom with the little twins and Violet. Jane places two thick white pillar candles on our windowsill and lights them. She kneels. They all look out the window, up to the stars and the moon. It's a ritual for wishing, or praying, or thinking about everything you've lost and everything you'll never have.

I stare at the flickering flames until my eyes start to burn and go blurry. I long for the mother who left me here. She and my dad didn't want me anymore, but I want her to brush my hair and braid it before bed. I want to hear her humming and know that I'm safe.

But I can't. All I can see is blurry flames and blood in a forest clearing.

After she blows out the candles, Jane puts the little twins to bed and Violet returns to their room. I stay up with the black hole book, but I'm still not reading it. I'm waiting for Jane to return. There are words built up in my throat and I'm going to get them out. When she comes back, I'm going to say, *What do you keep looking at in the forest? Does it have to do with what happened?* and I'm going to listen to her answers, and whatever's wrong, we're going to solve it together.

I hear her footsteps coming up the stairs. I'm going to ask. As soon as she's in the door, I'll ask.

But the words don't come out, even though she's standing *right there* and I've never struggled to talk to Jane before. Jane's the only one I can *always* talk to.

"Do you mind if I stay up a bit with a book light on?" she asks.

I close my mouth, and shake my head. She smiles and settles at her desk.

*Just ask.*

I don't. I decide that I can ask tomorrow, if anything's even still wrong. Maybe she's just distracted today and I'm overreacting. Tomorrow she'll be normal, and I'll laugh at myself for letting my anxiety take control, and we'll keep our secret.

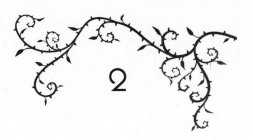

# 2

## JANE IS GONE.

I was having one of my regular nightmares. Just a few weeks before they left me with Frank, my mom showed me one of her favorite movies. It included a scene where a car falls off a bridge into water and the couple inside dies. It's a funny movie after that—one of them's a ghost, I think there's basketball involved—but I could never get rid of that image. Once I ended up at the lake house, it started showing up in my nightmares. I'm trapped in a car, unable to scream, unable to move. The car sinks into water hazy with blood. Sometimes I'm alone. Sometimes my parents are in the front seat, but they're unconscious and I can't wake them up.

That nightmare often makes me cry out, and it wakes Jane. Instead of turning over and going back to sleep, she comes to me. She rubs my back in circles. She talks in a low, soothing voice about the farm she lived on in her other life. I inhale the same unscented lotion we all wear but that still smells uniquely *Jane,* and eventually drift back to sleep.

But Jane isn't in her bed, and she's not in mine, either.

I sit up. I squint across the room, wondering if I'm not

seeing her bed properly without my glasses. "Jane?" I whisper. The only answer is the steady hum of cicadas outside.

She could be in the bathroom. I put on my glasses, get out of bed, and stick my head out our door. The bathroom door down the hall is open, and the light is off.

"Jane?" I whisper again, even though I know she's not there. I slip down the stairs to check the living room. Sometimes Jane has trouble sleeping and she'll take to wandering. She'll work on whatever puzzle is taking shape on the living room floor, or get a midnight snack.

The nine flowers on the wall shelf glow enough for me to see that the puzzle of a sunny cliffside on the floor is half done, and that Jane isn't here. I pause at the flowers, and briefly touch Jane's warm camellia for comfort.

I try hissing her name again—quieter, now. I'm too close to Frank's part of the house. Even the small noise of her name rasping off my tongue brings anxiety close to the surface, vibrating just under my skin. Subcutaneously.

That's a good word. *Subcutaneously.*

I only know one place left to try. I don't know why Jane would risk it alone, much less on a night when Frank is home, but where else could she be?

I move away from the living room on mouse-quiet feet to the little twins' room. London and Olivia are asleep, and they're *deep* sleepers, thank god. I don't want to have to explain that Jane is missing, and I have to go down through our secret tunnel to the lake to try and find her.

The little twins are smart, but too brave. They wouldn't let me leave them behind. They'd scrunch up their faces in determination, hold hands, and refuse to budge until I let them help me find Jane.

I tiptoe across the room, on the way nudging one of Olivia's many makeshift terrariums more fully under her bed. What Olivia really wants is a cat, but that's not going to happen, so last year she began her collection of moths and spiders. Her prized pet is a shiny black beetle named Gabriel. She found him on her recent birthday, and took it as a sign that he was her familiar. Gabriel gets his own elaborate terrarium, and Olivia likes to hold and play with him.

I'm here for the wall nearest London's bed. I glance at her as I pass. The foot of her bed is covered in books—a pretty good sign that she definitely stayed up even after Jane tucked her in. In sleep, her brow is unfurrowed, erasing that little worried frown she often has.

The wall seems like nothing. Lavender and polka-dotted, it could be in any bedroom anywhere.

I put my hands on two dots spaced just far enough that the little twins have to stretch when they do it. If you didn't know what you were looking for, you'd never find it—but

I do. The dots are soft and warm, as if someone has just been here.

I want to believe that means Jane's fingers touched these same dots only moments ago. It doesn't mean anything, though. They're always warm.

But she *was* here. She has to have been. I can't be far behind.

I push on the dots. Not with physical strength — with magic.

Just a little.

Just enough.

The wall parts; silently, like fog dispersing, a space appears.

No one knows who made the passage, and I don't know who found it first. When I arrived at the lake house, there were already three girls here, and it was just a Known Thing. *In this bedroom, there's a wall with old painted polka dots, and in the wall there's a secret door, and behind the door, there's a tunnel that shouldn't exist, and the tunnel goes down, down, down, and you can only open the door with magic.*

Which means Frank can't open it.

We're not allowed outside past sunset, and technically not allowed outside at all without Frank's supervision or permission. It's for a good reason. If we strayed too far,

Frank might not be able to protect us from people who would kill a "witch" on sight.

*No going past the tree line, no going out after dark, no going out when Frank's gone.*

The rules exist for our safety, but we still bend them from time to time. We all know the alarm codes to the doors, but we can't use them to leave when Frank's gone because they keep a record. He'd know. Same if we want to go out at night while he's asleep.

So we use the tunnel when we want a better view of the stars, or we want to swim in the lake, or we just want to be out of the house. We never go out alone, and we don't go into the forest.

Usually.

I close the bricks behind me and I'm engulfed in darkness. My anxiety is momentarily soothed. I've always found darkness comforting.

I need at least a little light to walk by. Luckily, light's always been my job in the tunnel. Once I arrived, the three sisters I joined no longer had to rely on flashlights.

I touch the wall and push a thin ribbon of magic through the cracks and crevices in the brick. White flowers bloom out of the shadows. The petals open, revealing pistils and stamens that glow as bright as any electric light. The rim of my left ear tingles. Tiny green flowers have sprouted along it in response to my magic. I pull them out absentmindedly, long since used to the tugging sensation as they release from my skin, and I let my eyes adjust to the flower light.

Jane's worry is etched into the walls.

When Jane is anxious, she reaches out. She takes hold of whatever she can find and fiddles with it, reshapes it with her magic. There's a toy chest in every bedroom, and hidden deep at the bottom of ours are Jane's favorites. Her mutated little darlings.

Frank took the rest away. For research, he said. No matter how much Jane loved her creations, the research came first.

Now, here, on the walls of our secret passage, I see the lines her fingers traced. They sank into the wall as her magic leaked out and left it looking like putty. When we went out a couple days ago, the walls were smooth. These marks are new.

My heart beats faster. I was right. Jane went this way.

I walk down, down, down. I keep my fingers in the grooves Jane left. The walls start to take on a wetness. It's humid. The path stops going down and turns, leading me around the lake to the far edge.

Finally, the path slopes upward. At the top, I don't meet another brick wall—I meet the hot and humid air of a summer night that has refused to turn cool. There's nothing physically blocking the passage on this side, only an illusion.

I'm on the other side of the lake from the house, close to the forest. I can't be seen from the house. Not at night.

Still, I've never been out here alone. I've never been so aware of the forest, dark and looming, the shadows blending all the trees together into one hulking leviathan. I've never been so aware of the lake, so conscious of what I don't know about its depths and what could be lurking in them.

There's that subcutaneous anxiety again. It's like the blood in my veins has been injected with helium and it's all rising up to the surface of me.

I peer into the water. Violet has a book detailing creatures of the deep—bioluminescent fish waiting to strike, aquatic dinosaurs that never died but only went into hiding, squids bigger than ships. Violet's book is about the ocean, not a lake, but I still squint into the water for a faint glow or writhing tentacle.

Nothing.

I swallow hard. The longer I stay, the more I'm sure that some monster could surface.

"Jane?" I follow the edge of the lake. If she was in the tunnel and didn't come back into the house, she has to be out here. The tunnel doesn't let out anywhere else.

All I hear is the drone of cicadas. This close to the forest, they're deafening. A pulsing, vibrating hum that's been the ambient noise of summer nights for as long as I can remember.

They all go quiet at the same time.

My legs jerk, like when you're on the edge of sleep and something somewhere misfires. Elle told me what causes it once, but I can never remember what she said. To me it feels like a last gasp for survival. Your brain mistakes sleep for death, and it desperately, uselessly kicks out into the night.

That's how it feels now, wide awake, heart slamming into my rib cage, all at once sure I'm being watched and sure it's by something I'll wish had never noticed me at all.

Somewhere in the forest a branch snaps underfoot. I try to call Jane's name but my throat's gone dry and whatever took the cicada's voices must have taken mine, too.

I dig my nails into my palms and approach the tree line.

I haven't been back in the forest since that day. We were never supposed to be there to begin with. The forest is too risky. It's too far from the tunnel, too far to see if Frank has come home early. It's too close to the outside world. But we went in, Jane and I.

I swallow, attempting to wet my throat. "Jane?" I hiss. "Are you in there?"

There's no response. The cicadas and Jane keep their silence.

I dare to speak a little louder. "Jane? We have to go back." Every moment I'm out here I'm viscerally—*good word*—aware of Frank and the possibility that he'll wake up, do a bed check, and find us missing. Or worse, that a stranger could find us and recognize us for what we are.

I'm going to have to go into the forest, aren't I? We swore we'd never go back, but I *have* to.

Step by step, I make my way through the trees. With each step, I breathe a little easier. There's still no Jane, but there's also no blood splattered across trunks. Just me, bare feet on grass, sweat drying on my skin. There's nothing writhing out of the shadows to get me.

*Yet.*

"Jane?"

I hold my breath, trying to hear her above the voice in my head screaming GO BACK GO BACK. I don't know what's out here watching me, I don't know why Jane isn't answering, I don't know what the punishment will be if Frank discovers I've been outside. The voice whispers that Jane would want me safe in bed, dirty feet tucked under blankets where Frank can't see, waiting for her to return home.

Because there's no outcome other than "Jane comes home."

A breeze rustles the treetops. I look up. An endless canopy, and beyond it, gently glimmering stars that have no idea my world down here is threatening to fall apart.

Someone runs past me on the left, only a few yards away. I run after them, shouting for Jane.

The person stops with their back to me. I freeze. We're still separated by a few yards, and they're engulfed in shadows so I can't see much. The shape is similar to Jane's. The way they stand, with one foot in front of the other, is one of Jane's quirks.

But Jane wouldn't run away from me.

Their head moves, turns, just barely to the side. They look like they're *made* of shadows, but that has to be a visual trick. I'm not breathing. I don't want them to see me. I'm overwhelmed with the sense that if they see me, I won't exist anymore. I'll disintegrate, or dissolve, or disappear. Their head moves a little more and I take one step back.

They look over their shoulder. A flash of yellow, owlish eyes.

Like a thunderclap right over my head, every cicada bursts back into discordant, vibrating song.

I run.

It's not a voluntary action. It's like the falling-asleep-leg-jerk. This is my body kicking out into the night, desperate to survive.

But I can't leave Jane out here with *that*. I abruptly switch course before my legs take me out of the forest, hooking my arm around a young tree and planting my feet.

I'm already in here. It already knows I'm here. I can't leave without Jane.

Except I also can't *feel* her. I was never aware I could feel her presence before it was gone. Now it's a gaping absence, like a forest of silent cicadas. It flickers back in, then out, then in.

She's here, but she isn't. It's an impossible thing and I can't explain how I know it, but it's true. Jane is here in the forest, but she's also gone. Gone somewhere so far I don't know where to start looking.

"Jane?" I whisper. "Jane, if you can hear me, please. Help me find you."

*Give me a sign,* like a ghost story.

Over the cicadas I'm not going to be able to hear her voice or hear anyone running. I can, however, see the shadows growing darker in the depths of the forest. They're advancing, like lights turning off down the length of a hallway. They climb and climb until I can't see the stars anymore.

I can't stay here alone. I can't leave Jane here alone.

*Irene.*

Irene's magic has to do with sensing emotions, and Frank's been having her learn to use it to track people. She hasn't gotten good at it, but it's worth a shot. It could be the only chance we have.

How do you find a girl who's here but not here?

"Jane!" I yell, no longer bothering to hide from whatever's in the forest. There's no point. "Jane, I'm coming back for you. I'm getting help and coming back. Wait for me!"

When I run this time, it's with purpose. I'm going to get Irene. She's going to find Jane. It'll turn out all the shadows I feel chasing me are just part of my imagination. The way they slam into the tree line, apparently unable to follow me into cleared land? You think and see all sorts of weird things when you're alone in the dark.

Maybe Jane was sleepwalking. That's why she didn't respond to me. Irene will find her curled up under a tree, and we'll all laugh, relieved. We'll go home and Frank won't know we ever left. It will become a whispered funny story between siblings. *Remember that time Jane sleepwalked out to the forest and Derry became convinced something evil lived there?*

I slow once I reach the little twins' room. I try not to breathe too loudly even though my lungs burn from the run. London and Olivia can't wake up until we have Jane back.

It's the lack of light that catches my eye as I make the turn to go up the stairs. The flowers on the shelf are a little dimmer than they used to be. I don't understand why until I get closer.

Only eight of the nine are glowing. Jane's has turned into clear glass without a trace of pink.

I've never seen this before. I don't know what could cause it. Dread pools in my stomach as the idea forms, then grows, then spreads through me like shadows through the forest. If the flower isn't reflecting Jane's magic anymore, then the connection is severed. If the connection is severed, then Jane . . .

My knees buckle, my feet slip out from under me. I forget about finding Irene. I barely register the sound of footsteps behind me, heavy, surely Frank's. I'm breathing too hard and too fast, hyperventilating until the corners of my vision go dark.

I'm too late.

Jane is gone.

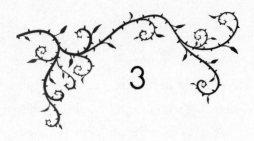

# 3

IT'S QUIET NOW in the living room. The remaining eight of us are huddled together on and around one of the two couches. We don't say it, but no one wants to spread out too much. No one wants to risk another sibling slipping away.

Only Winnie is standing. She paces in front of the flower shelf, looking from the camellia to me and back. Occasionally the flowers tremble as she passes.

'Derry, again.' Winnie signs this in ASL instead of speaking it, both for Brooke's sake and because none of us want to call Frank with our voices. Winnie's fingers move again, then her face scrunches up. She waves her hands, starting over. 'Describe what happened again.'

'I woke up, and Jane was gone.' I've already told this to Frank and to my siblings, but Winnie isn't satisfied. I feel flat. I feel numb. 'I went outside. Followed her into the forest. I couldn't find her. I thought Irene might have better . . .' I can't remember the sign, so I fingerspell. '*L-U-C-K*. I came back, and when I saw her flower . . .'

Winnie's little pet poltergeist ruffles her hair. 'She's not dead.'

'What else could she be? What's another reason for her flower to be like that?'

'Maybe she got too far away.' Brooke's hands seesaw in front of her. 'We don't know how far the magic can stretch before it breaks.'

'Exactly!' Winnie signs emphatically.

I shake my head. Jane and I went farther into the forest on that day two weeks ago.

Can't say that, though. No one knows we were in the forest at all.

The tears are coming back. I snake my fingers under my glasses to rub at my eyes.

'Frank will find her,' Elle signs, her lips set in a hard line. She sits on the arm of one of the couches, with Irene at her side. Her blue eyes are red-rimmed and her pale cheeks are blotchy from crying, but still she tries to sit straight with her shoulders back.

'He's been out there for hours,' Irene signs. It was around one a.m. when I got back, and now it's nearly four. 'Either she doesn't want to be found, or . . .'

Elle's eyes go wide and wounded. She shakes her head, and sets her expression into something wholly determined. 'He'll find her.'

'She's probably hiding.' Desperation shows in every twitch of Winnie's fingers. 'Waiting until Frank gives up so she can run.'

'No,' Olivia signs, her face screwed up in that stubborn way only eight-year-olds can muster. London is curled against her twin, silent and crying, while Olivia is all certainty that her eldest sister *has* to be okay. 'Jane wouldn't leave us.'

Winnie shrugs. Her pacing increases, bare feet slapping against the hardwood.

'We'll only hurt ourselves guessing,' Brooke signs. Her left side is to me, the side with a constellation of freckles and moles traveling from cheek to neck to shoulder. 'Let's wait for Frank to come back.'

'Why can't we go out and look for ourselves?' Violet asks, their gestures precise, careful.

"It's too dangerous to send you out," Frank says. He stands in the doorway.

Frank is lean, but so tall and with limbs so long that he seems to take up the whole space. He always stands in doorways like that, filling them. None of us would be able to get past him if we tried.

I inch closer to Brooke, who's stiffened in her seat next to me. Winnie freezes, her head down, her poltergeist silenced. London's sobs stop with a small gasp. She's holding her breath.

Elle brightens as she looks at Frank, turning her whole body toward him and waiting for confirmation that Jane is okay—that Frank, as always, has kept us safe.

"You know why it's dangerous, don't you, Violet?" he asks, coming around the couch to look directly at them. He doesn't sign. He knows enough to watch us talk, to catch most of what we're saying, but never uses it himself.

Violet shrinks. So do I, and he's not even looking at me. I'm just close enough to feel the energy of him staring Violet down. Frank doesn't have magic, but his presence takes up all the air in the room. Brooke calls it his *aura*.

Frank continues talking. I watch Irene signing translations for Brooke behind his back. That aura is so suffocating I can barely breathe. Irene's pale hands blur in my vision. "What if you got lost in the forest? What if you ran into someone other than Jane?"

Violet grabs for my hand and I take it. We squeeze, hard, trying to prevent tears from coming.

"What would happen if you ran into someone else, Violet?"

"They'd kill me," they whisper.

"If you were lucky."

Bile rises in my throat but I swallow it down. Violet's fingernails dig into my hand and I welcome the sting.

The world outside doesn't understand magic. They fear it so much their fear has turned to fury. They call us *witches* and they hurt us. Torture us. *Kill* us. It's why, no matter what, we're safer with Frank than we are without him.

Frank may be strict, but he doesn't hurt us. He doesn't take pieces of us as trophies.

It's better here.

It has to be better here.

"Did someone find Jane?" Olivia asks.

"I pray they didn't. She might be scared and hiding. But I'll find her. You know that, right?" Frank puts on his Fatherly Face. A firm but gentle smile. A voice like honey and morning coffee and late summer afternoons with the grill going in the backyard while big hands guide me through shucking cob after cob of corn.

Even abandoned by my parents, I still miss them. I still miss my dad.

It's not just me. We all lean in. We're drawn toward him. *Inexorably.* There's a good word. We wait for the pat on the head, for him to tell us he's proud of us.

"But Derry, I'm curious," Frank says. His brow furrows in apparent confusion. "The alarms are all still armed, and I can't find a record of you leaving or returning. How did you get outside?"

I flinch away from him. "Just through the door," I say. Is my voice shaking? I can't let it shake. I can't show too much weakness. Or should I be showing more? Crying might lead to pity and leniency, or it might lead to accusations of manipulation and being thrown into time-out. I can't know.

The rules change too often. "I wasn't thinking, and the front door was open."

"So you went through it?"

"Yeah, to follow her."

"Why didn't you come get me?"

"I wasn't thinking," I say again. "I was worried about Jane."

He's nodding but I don't think he fully believes me. He just hasn't figured out where the lies are yet. He's missing the tunnel-shaped piece of the puzzle.

I hate the way I have to lie to him. He's trying to protect us, and we betray him by sneaking out any chance we get.

"You've been doing well, haven't you, Derry? You haven't had a time-out in—what, four months?"

"Five." The word comes out in a cracked whisper. Olivia, already sitting beside me, puts a small hand on my back. I feel her magic flow around me, forming an invisible, impenetrable shield, run on her own energy.

"I would hate for you to break that streak." Frank crouches in front of me, bringing the father-smile back to his face. "You're not hiding anything, are you, Derry?" he asks. Olivia's shield flares. Frank can't see it, but I can feel it. She can't protect me from his words, but she's trying so hard.

"No." His eyes flick over me, examining my face, body language. Looking for lies. Looking for truth.

Frank straightens back up. Olivia moves her hand away and the shield falls. "All right. Listen up. I had a trip planned for tomorrow. Over the past couple hours, I've considered rescheduling, but . . . well, perhaps you can all use it as a chance to reflect. Think about what you've lost, what you still have. What you could still lose."

Elle nods like he's preaching. Winnie's hair is ruffling like she's in a storm, and I know what she's thinking. *We haven't lost Jane, she's alive, she's just hiding.* I feel like my insides are rotting. I desperately want to believe Jane's alive, but every time I look at her drained camellia, I can only fear the worst.

But I felt her in the forest. Even if it was that weird "she's here but she's not" feeling, the "she's here" has to mean something, doesn't it?

"I'll resume the search for Jane at dawn, then again when I return," Frank says. "Elle, you're in charge while I'm gone." Winnie and Brooke are older, but no one argues the chain of succession. Frank would never leave Winnie or Brooke in charge, not when there's Elle. Not when there's someone less willful. "For now, I think it's time everyone gets back to bed."

It's not a suggestion. Frank watches us until, together, we stand. He's still watching as we walk out of the room. That walk becomes a scurry just past the doorway, like when you turn off the bedroom lights then try to jump in bed before the monsters get you.

We split up, and once Winnie, Brooke, and I reach the top landing, I realize I'm the only one who will be sleeping alone tonight.

I haven't slept alone in seven years.

Brooke nudges me and signs, 'Do you want to stay with us tonight?'

I shake my head. 'Nah. I'm a big girl.'

I regret saying that almost as soon as I close the bedroom door behind me. Jane's bed is still unmade. The first thing she does on any morning is make her bed, so seeing it with the blankets thrown back adds to the sense that she could be just down the hall. She got up in the middle of the night to go to the bathroom, but she'll be back.

Any minute now.

I curl up on top of Jane's unmade bed, and I wait.

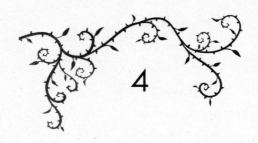

4

SHE DOESN'T COME back, of course. It's not a fairy tale. Jane won't return if I clap my hands and believe.

I still stay up until dawn waiting, and when that fails, I go downstairs to beg Frank to let me search for Jane with him. Naturally, he refuses. The forest is too dangerous. All I can do is pull the smaller couch up in front of the living room windows, which face the lake, and squint across to the forest.

At some point Brooke finds me lying on the couch. She nudges me into enough of an upright position that she can sit, and I can rest my head in her lap. She's fat like me, her thighs generous and cushy pillows that nearly put me to sleep.

Maybe they do put me to sleep. It's that weird liminal space where you're dozing so lightly that you think you're awake, until something actually wakes you up and for the space of a heartbeat, your entire concept of reality is a jumble. One moment, Brooke is stroking my hair, and the next, Frank is back.

"Anything?" Elle asks. How long has Elle been hovering

nearby? For that matter, when did Olivia and London join us? They've curled up against me and Brooke and fallen asleep.

Frank shakes his head. "I found a few tracks, but I'm not sure if they were Jane or Derry." His voice is tight in a way I've never heard before. Even when he gets angry at us, his voice usually stays calm and level, almost disinterested.

Did losing Jane shake him that much? He takes care of us, and I think that's the same as caring about us, but . . .

Maybe I imagine it. Maybe it's just me. But . . . sometimes when he looks at us, there's nothing behind his eyes. No love, no pride. Barely even recognition. All these little moments when he looks at us as if we're not really here.

If Jane going missing has affected him like this, then I have to be wrong.

I sit up, untangling myself from Brooke and the little twins. London takes my place in Brooke's lap and rests against her.

Brooke and London have a bond no one else can understand. All magic can be dangerous, if it's twisted and prodded and pushed the right way, but some magic is dangerous *unless* you twist it the right way. You have to work at not letting it hurt someone.

Brooke's magic is nature-based, like mine, but with fire and air. She didn't always know how to control them or how they feed off each other. She's never told us exactly what happened before she came here, what prompted her to be left on Frank's doorstep, but I can imagine.

The trigger that brought the little twins to us was an incident with London. She had a tantrum and their babysitter grabbed her by the arms. She yelled at her and shook her. London was only six. She was scared. Who can blame her for lashing out? London's magic mangled the babysitter's hands, twisted her elbows back the wrong way and too far.

Like Jane, London can manipulate matter. But for London, it's anything with a pulse.

Or maybe anything that once had a pulse. We've never tested it on something dead. As it is, Brooke and London both avoid using their magic unless it's for lessons and demonstrations with Frank, where Brooke keeps her fire and wind as soft as Frank will allow, and London tries not to cry when a sibling is placed in front of her as a test subject. Winnie usually volunteers. The one emotion her pet poltergeist actually lets her hide is pain, and it's less scary for London if she's testing her magic on someone who will smile through it.

I join Frank and Elle. "What now?" I ask. "We can go look for her while you're gone—"

Frank turns on me and snarls, "NO," with so much ferocity that I stumble back a step. His face quickly smooths

40

back into normalcy. "No one is leaving the house until I get back," he says.

"But when will that be?" I demand. "She's already been gone for *hours*. We can't lose another whole day. If we stick together in groups, we'll be fine."

Thinking of the shadow-creature from last night and the thundering of the cicadas, I'm not sure that's true. Maybe it would be better if I went alone. Kept the rest safe.

"You won't be fine, you'll get lost. You don't know the forest and we don't know what happened to Jane," Frank says. He lowers his voice until only Elle and I can hear. "She's probably dead. That's the primary reason her flower would react like that. I won't have you endangering yourself and your siblings to find a body."

With that, Frank retreats to his rooms. I stay rooted to the spot, digging my fingernails into my palms, shaking. He knows the forest, he knows the world outside this place, he's the one who always knows what's going on. If he thinks she's dead, then she must be.

One word echoes in my mind over and over. *Primary*. If it's the *primary* reason her flower would be empty, it means there's a *secondary* reason.

Jane could be alive.

Elle clearly didn't focus on that same word, because she's begun to cry. She looks at me with tears streaming out of her wide blue eyes and says, "Do you think he's right?" She claps a hand over her mouth as if she's just said something horribly offensive. "I mean—he's always right—but—you know what I mean."

I nod, but that doesn't seem to help because she just cries harder.

Fuck.

I desperately scan the room for reinforcements. Brooke is still covered by the little twins, who seem to have fallen asleep. She's not looking my way, so I can't get her attention without Elle noticing.

Irene—bless Irene—either has great timing or sensed her sister's distress. Doesn't matter. Either way, she's here, wrapping Elle up in her arms, and I'm given a chance to escape upstairs. I need a moment alone, and in this house, there are only a few places to find that.

The upstairs bathroom is down the hall, across from Violet and the big twins' bedroom at the end. Brooke decorated it, to the best of her resources and abilities. Frank wouldn't buy her anything but the basics, but she painted flowers and clouds on the walls, and Violet glamoured our towels into the teals and creams Brooke picked out.

The toiletries we get are nice. The brushes are sturdy, the shampoo is gentle, the toilet paper is soft, and each menstruating sibling has a cup. Not my favorite, but Frank says it's more sustainable and affordable than keeping us supplied with pads or tampons. Jane, Olivia, and London get their hair oil and silk scarves and wide-toothed combs. A few years ago, Frank finally allowed us sharp hair scissors and clippers.

I'm one of the few who keeps my hair long. Every time I brush it, I remember how my mother would brush and braid it before bed.

There's a doctor that comes about four times a year. More if we need him, but we almost never do. Dr. Sam saw us from childhood. He brings our medications—hormone blocker shots for Irene, antidepressants and anti-anxiety medication for all of us. We get our vaccinations on schedule, including flu shots. He tells us to open our mouths wide and checks our teeth as if we're horses. He takes a million little measurements, then smiles and gives us a sucker.

He never asks too much. For the medications, he needs to know our moods, but he doesn't ask what causes them. If we start to say something like, "My anxiety has been worse because I didn't do well during a test, and Frank got mad," he recommends a stronger pill and changes the subject.

I think Frank pays him a lot. *Exorbitantly*. That's a good word.

Between Dr. Sam's visits, there are first aid kits and Midol and Advil and vitamins, things we need.

But not things we *want*. That's the difference. We don't *need* makeup or hair straighteners or anything but basic black hair ties. We don't need to shave, don't need extensive skin care. We don't need heating pads for our cramps (it was a minor miracle when Violet came along and taught us about putting rice in a sock and microwaving it).

We need to be clean and taken care of, not spoiled.

I keep the lights off and lower myself into the empty bathtub. It's always been a little too small for me. I can sit in it, but it's a squeeze. My thighs press up against the sides. Right now, that's what I want. The gentle constriction of the bathtub around me doesn't feel like a trap. It feels like security. Right here, right now, in the dark, I'm safe and Jane is waiting for me in our bedroom.

The size of the bathtub makes an actual bath feel awkward and unwieldy, though. It's one of the few moments I'm jealous of my thinner siblings. They can be completely surrounded by the water, enveloped. Encompassed. *Pretty okay word.*

I'd be able to do that too if Frank would just install a larger bathtub. So would Brooke. So would Winnie, and Violet.

But we don't *need* it, so . . .

I sit in the dark long enough to not know how long I've been sitting here, and then I sit a little longer. There's a pit in my stomach that's threatening to overtake me if I have to see Frank again too soon. It's a familiar pit. Frank's good to us and everything, but sometimes the anxiety of being around him and knowing he'll be watching and knowing he'll see every flaw, every mistake . . . it can be too much.

It can swallow me whole.

I sit, and I wait, and I hope that when I finally clamber out of the tub and squint at the light of the hallway, he'll be gone.

When I finally emerge, Elle is waiting. Her eyes are still a little red-rimmed but she's not crying anymore. She's picking at her nails in a way I haven't seen her do in years. She stops when she sees me, and reaches out for my hand. She tries to make it seem comforting, but I think it's just to stop herself from picking.

She frowns. "Derry, you're hurt." She holds up my hand. It's covered in little scratches. The blood is dry and they've started scabbing over. There are tiny little wood splinters throughout.

"Oh, I didn't notice. It must have . . ." I pause. Did I scrape it on a tree when I was running? I never even felt the pain.

". . . it's not a big deal," I finish.

Elle shakes her head. "You can't leave even a scratch unattended, you know that."

I bite my tongue to keep from saying *I'm not going to get sepsis from a scrape*. Elle reads all the medical books, which means she diagnoses us with fatal diseases off of vague symptoms. Sepsis comes up again and again, especially with Violet, who's clumsy and prone to scraping their knees or slipping up with a kitchen knife.

On days when I feel charitable toward Elle, I think it's a sign she cares. On days when I don't feel so charitable, it seems like another way to prove her superiority.

Elle covers my hand with hers. There's no visible glow, but I can feel it, warm and a little itchy. Her magic absorbs through my skin. The splinters are pushed out. The skin stitches back together.

"Better than Band-Aids," Elle says. I smile at the familiar phrase—something she's said every time she heals us, for as long as she's been here. "So . . . Frank's gone." I had good timing, then. "And we were talking."

"We?"

"Me and Irene and Brooke." She stands with her shoulders back and looks me in the eye, but she also drops my hand and picks at her nails again. "We want to go look for her."

"For Jane? In the forest?" I ask. I'm about to say *Yes, finally!* because we *should* be looking for her, no matter what Frank says.

Except for those shadows . . .

Elle nods. "Yes. We can't let more time pass without *anyone* looking."

"Frank said we have to stay here," I say. The words are rough and dusty in my throat. *But Frank said we shouldn't* isn't an argument I use. It's even weirder to use it against the daddy's girl/teacher's pet that is Elle—like I walked out of the bathroom and into an alternate universe.

Elle clears her throat. "I know. Normally, I wouldn't agree with this. But it's important. Isn't it?" She searches my face for some kind of confirmation, reassurance.

Uncertainty is as weird from Elle as citing rules is from me. Elle's got this unshakeable moral compass—she knows what's right, what's wrong, and you can't convince her otherwise. Her rules *have* to be right, because they're the same as Frank's, and he's the ultimate authority. He's the one Elle needs to approve of her.

Sometimes I understand so well it hurts.

Sometimes I want to slap her.

Elle's uncertainty is enough to make me nod, though. "Yeah. It's really important."

We'll be fine in the daylight. Jane and I went into the forest during the day last time, and although something terrible happened, there wasn't any sign of a shadow monster. It must be nocturnal. We can search together during the day, and if we still haven't found Jane by nightfall, I'll go alone.

I follow Elle downstairs. I don't know how long I was in the bathroom, but it was long enough for word to spread. All of my siblings are gathered in the living room. I bite my lip, looking at the little twins.

It's safe in the forest during the day, surely, but . . .

Irene smiles when she sees us. 'Awesome! Now we can pair up. I thought I could go with London, Elle with Olivia, Brooke with Violet.' She glances up at me, expecting an objection. 'Which leaves Derry with Winnie.'

'That's fine,' I sign. 'But maybe someone should stay behind.'

'We want to cover maximum ground,' Irene signs.

'Yeah, but it might be dangerous.' I glance meaningfully toward the little twins while they aren't looking. 'We don't know what happened to Jane.'

Irene's cheeks flush. I'm not sure it's occurred to anyone else that there's more than one thing that could have happened to Jane—lost, sure.

But also *taken,* and if *taken* is the right verb, then we can't pretend the little twins will be safe. Maybe we can't pretend any of us will be safe, but eight-year-olds? I refuse to think about the other possibility—the one where someone stumbles upon a body.

'Elle, maybe you should stay with them,' Irene offers. 'I could go with Brooke and Violet in a team of three.'

I don't know if Elle is more scared of the forest than she lets on, or if it's that she's not comfortable disobeying Frank even for something she considers important. Either way, relief spreads across her face.

48

"Great plan," she says. She claps her hands and turns to the little twins with a huge smile. "London! Olivia! We actually have a really important job to do here at home while the others go out to the forest."

Olivia protests, loudly, tears already brimming in her eyes. London squeezes her twin's hand in support, but even as she nods along with Olivia's arguments that it's not fair to leave them out, there's something on her face that looks a lot like Elle's relief.

It's only when Brooke volunteers to stay behind with Elle and the little twins that any kind of peace is reached. Still, Olivia watches the rest of us disappear into the tunnel with her arms crossed and her cheeks streaked with drying tears.

As the wall closes behind the scouting team made up of Irene, Winnie, Violet, and myself, I give us light. Jane's mark is still on the walls. I don't point it out, but I know when someone sees it because they gasp. Winnie reaches out for my hand and squeezes.

We take our procession down, down, down.

In terms of physics, the tunnel doesn't make a lot of sense. London and Olivia's far wall is an outside wall. It's not underground. Some of the tunnel — before it descends — should be visible outside.

It's not.

It also should take significantly longer to walk to where it spits us out at the lake. The tunnel is where it shouldn't be and is shorter than it should be.

The lakeside entrance is weird, too. It's not closed like the one in the house. It's just stairs leading down into the earth. When you're more than a few steps away, you can't see it. You only see grass, and the shore of the lake. It shimmers into reality when you get close. I think you must not be able to see it if you're not magic, because otherwise Frank surely would have found it by now.

We may never know who made it, since Frank certainly didn't. Whoever they are, I love them. Going outside without Frank is *different*. A little scarier, but energizing, too. Irene once described it as what it must feel like for Frank's iPad when it gets plugged in to charge at night. It gets to exist outside of his sight for a few hours, unneeded, untested, and soak up all the electricity it can.

Yeah. It feels like that.

We emerge into sunlight. Winnie, less shaken now that we're out of the tunnel, releases my hand and stomps ahead.

"We'll go this way, if you want to wrap back around toward the house," Irene says. She gestures off in the same direction Jane and I went two weeks ago. My stomach twists. There's no evidence for them to find, and I definitely don't want to go back, but . . .

*It should be me.*

"Well?" Winnie snaps as air gusts in my face. Her poltergeist is in quite a mood today. Irene and Violet are walking away.

I follow Winnie to the tree line. She hesitates, crossing her arms over her chest and hugging herself hard.

"I never liked the outdoors," she says. She stares between the trees, into the shadowy places where the sun can't quite filter through. Her words have gone round, leaning into the Minnesota accent that never quite faded and always gets stronger when she talks about Before. "My parents loved camping, but they also loved telling me scary stories about the things that can live out there."

"Like what?" I ask a little absently. I squint into the deeper parts of the forest. The shadows aren't forming into human shapes. They aren't too dark, they aren't moving too much. We'll be fine. I have to repeat it to myself a few times to believe it. *We'll be fine, we'll be fine, we'll be fine.*

"The usual stuff like ghosts or rabid animals, but the big one was the wendigo. They always told me that if I heard their voices calling to me at night, I should be careful, because it might be the wendigo luring me away to eat me."

"Seems like a good thing to tell a nine-year-old."

Winnie laughs. "I liked the stories. I just didn't like that after they told me the story we still had to go camping." She looks back at me. "Any wendigos in there, you think?"

"Guess we'll find out."

Winnie squares her shoulders against the wendigo threat, and walks into the forest. I follow.

It's cooler in the shade of the trees, more than I think it should be. I can barely feel the summer heat at all. Distantly, I hear Irene and Violet calling for Jane.

Here in the last place I saw her, I have that sense again of Jane being both *here* and *not here* at the same time. I've never had any kind of extrasensory perception. I don't have visions or read minds. I don't magically feel emotions, like Irene does, or even have an overabundance of empathy like many of my siblings. There's no reason for me to trust this sense.

And yet . . .

"Jane!" Winnie calls. "Jane, he's gone! You can come out!"

"Jane!" My voice cracks, and I clear my throat. Winnie is wandering away, but not yet out of sight. "Jane!"

*"Derry?"*

"Jane?" I whisper. I walk in the direction I think I heard her voice, but it's disorienting in the forest.

*"Derry?"*

That time it's Winnie. I look back at her. "Did you find something?" she asks.

I wait a moment before responding, listening hard for Jane to speak again. "No, I don't . . . I don't think so."

Winnie sighs, and keeps shouting for Jane.

*"Derry."*

I whip around. That was right in my ear, but there's nothing and no one there. Except—a flash of movement in the distance. I head toward it, slow at first, then at a jog. I keep calling Jane's name, pausing each time to listen. A couple times I hear her whisper, a couple more, footsteps. I try to follow the sounds.

It doesn't make sense for Jane to play around like this. Why can't she come back to us? It has to be *can't,* not *won't,* because Jane wouldn't do that. She wouldn't run without us, wouldn't hide without us. Wouldn't leave us.

Of course, that means there's something keeping her away. Either there's some reason for her to stay in the forest that's more important than her siblings, or she's a captive.

A captive of who? Of what? We're the only ones out here. The only person we've seen other than Frank in years is Dr. Sam, and—

One other. One who would certainly have reason to want to hurt Jane and me. But he's dead.

"Hey!" It's Winnie, making her way toward me, twigs snapping underfoot. She's got her usual glare on. "Why'd you wander off like that?"

"I thought I heard something," I say.

She perks up. "Jane?"

"Maybe. But I couldn't find her, so . . . maybe I just imagined it."

I didn't imagine it, but I'm not sure how to tell Winnie what happened without her jumping to wendigos. That's not what this is—I'm hearing Jane's voice, her real voice, I'm sure of it.

*They always told me that if I heard their voices calling to me at night, I should be careful, because it might be the wendigo luring me away to eat me.*

I'm sure of it.

*"Derry,"* Jane says, close enough that I should be able to see her.

Winnie has no reaction. She obviously didn't hear it, but I still ask, "Did you hear that?" She shakes her head, confused.

Okay. Jane is alive, and she's out here in this forest, but I can't find her. I can only hear her. More specifically—only *I* can hear her. If Winnie can't, I have my doubts the others would either.

I can't begin to know what that all adds up to.

*"Derry,"* Jane whispers, to me and only me, as Winnie and I carve a path back to the lake. *"Find me."*

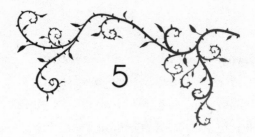

5

WE SEARCH FOR as long as we dare. Frank never says exactly how long he'll be gone, but he tells us if he'll be gone overnight or for multiple days. Knowing he'll be back sometime today—but not knowing if that means in an hour or when we've already gone to bed—we only stay out until the sun starts its dip into afternoon.

The four of us return to the house in defeat. The others murmur, their voices floating through the tunnel, comparing notes. *Did you see anything? No, just trees.*

Elle is waiting for us in the little twins' room. Seeing us, she holds out her arms, and Irene collapses into them. Elle looks between me, Winnie, and Violet. "It didn't go so well, did it?"

"We called and called and called," Irene says, pulling away from Elle. "And nothing."

"I can't imagine her staying in there willingly." Elle wraps her arms around herself, as if against the cold. "It's so scary in there. She has to be dead, right?"

"Or she's not in the forest, dead or alive," Winnie says. "She saw her chance to run and she took it."

"She wouldn't leave us," Violet snaps. "It's not that."

"Oh, so you want her to be dead, then?" There's a beat of silence after Winnie's words, and she clearly knows she shouldn't have said that. But instead of apologizing, she sets her face into a stubborn glare until Violet stomps out of the room.

"Very well-handled," Irene says. She sighs, rubbing at her eyes.

"Well! I'm not wrong!"

I should tell them what I heard. The weight of Jane's voice—*find me*—is so real, so vital and *alive,* but when I try to put it into words, they sound silly. I can't give a voice to them.

"Violet's right, though," Elle says. "Jane wouldn't leave, much less *run.* What is there to *run* from?"

Winnie sends a significant glance in my direction. I shake my head. There's no shaking Elle's conviction that no one could ever want to leave the lake house, even if they've said it directly.

We don't have a bad life. It's just that we don't all love it as much as Elle does, and Jane's been here the longest. She's the only one who ever had to be alone with Frank in this big old house, being tested on her magic. If any of us has a right to be tired of this place . . .

When no one responds to her question, Elle claps her hands together. "Okay then! It's time for lunch. Brooke and

I have had the little twins busy with prep, and it's just about done."

For a few minutes, it all feels painfully, wonderfully normal. In the kitchen, the table is set with plates stacked with French toast. Brooke and Olivia are debating over Gabriel's right to eat with us. Brooke argues beetles don't belong on the table, Olivia insists he's not doing anything wrong, and eventually Olivia sighs the kind of put-upon sigh that says Brooke is ruining her life and takes Gabriel back to his place under her bed.

We all settle into our regular seats. Elle tells Winnie she's using too much maple syrup, so Winnie pours on more. The only fruit we have is raspberries, which Violet keeps thinking they like, but as soon as they try one their face screws up unhappily. They transfer the rest to my plate. I pop one in my mouth and make an exaggerated "Mmm," sound while Violet fake-gags.

For a few minutes, I can forget the empty chair and the spaces in conversation that should be filled by Jane.

*Find me.*

The front door opens. We turn as one toward the sound, tense, waiting to see which version of Frank has come home—or if, by some miracle, it could be Jane.

It's not her.

Frank stumbles into the living room, leaning against the

door frame. Elle gasps. Frank is bloody and bruised. He wipes a hand across his face and it smears red.

"Bad trip," he says, before collapsing on the couch.

Elle is the first out of her seat, rushing over to him. Irene follows close after. The rest of us stand, but hesitate and hover, not getting too close.

"What *happened?*" Elle asks in a horrified whisper. She holds a hand over a cut on his forehead. *Better than Band-Aids.*

"Some rumors have been getting around," Frank says. He winces as Elle heals a black eye. He still manages to look at each of us individually, as though to be sure we're listening. Winnie is translating for Brooke. She can read lips a little, but only if she can focus and the person is speaking very clearly. "I don't know how or who. But some men in town had heard I might be hiding—well, they used the word *witches*. They were . . . quite determined to find out if that was true."

Violet whimpers, and Frank gives them one of his fatherly smiles before Elle passes her hand over his split lip.

"I didn't tell them, of course," he says. "I've taken many precautions over the years to make sure no one knows where this house is."

*Not enough to stop people from stumbling upon it,* I think. I shake the memory out of my head before it can form.

"So, they won't . . ." Elle bites her lip, then continues. "They won't come here?"

"No. I'd never let them. As long as you're here, you're safe."

She breathes a sigh of relief, and I find myself sighing with her.

I understand why Jane would want to run, if that's what she did. Frank takes care of us, but his watchfulness can be oppressive. His moods can be unpredictable in a way that can mean "extra movie night, as a treat" or "time-out for asking for an extra movie night."

You never really know where you stand with him.

We know where we stand with everyone outside this house, though, and it's not good. The lake house is the only place in the world where we can be alchemists out in the open and not end up as bruised and bloody as Frank after his run-in with those men—or worse. Frank may be moody, but he never touches us, and instead of squashing our magic, he encourages it to flourish.

My magic first showed itself when I was seven. Ivy grew up through the floor in my bedroom and twisted into a canopy across the ceiling. My parents didn't know what to make of it. They were prepared to help me through bullying and illnesses and The Talk. Nothing could have prepared them for their little girl to be magic.

They'd tear down the ivy, and every night, it grew back.

It reflected my dreams. When they were good, the ivy filled with honeysuckle and light. Nightmares brought tangles of poison ivy and flowers with scorpion-stingers.

And then there were the flowers growing on my body. I would wake up in the morning with tiny flowers blooming along my hairline, or circling my belly button. I hid that from my parents pretty effectively until one day, when they were fighting. I sat in the backyard listening to them through an open window, and I cried, and wood sprouted through the earth. A tree grew up around me, shielding me. When my father pulled me out, my long brown hair had become red-flowered vines that my mom had to shave off.

Children can hardly be expected to control their magic that young, especially when no one is there to teach them. Sometimes their parents get confused. Scared. Angry. They drive four hours to give up their ivy-growing nine-year-old to a man who says he can help. They, I imagine, move out of their old house and resign themselves to never having had a daughter at all.

I loved my parents. I needed them to love me, and instead they dropped me off like an unwanted pet.

We all have stories like that. Brooke and London have their tragedies. Irene and Elle's single mother could handle twins and a trans daughter, but not when one turned out telepathic and the other, in a desperate burst of powerful magic, brought a run-over cat back from the brink of death with the touch of her hands. Jane's parents grew weary of her trying to fix things around the house and disfiguring them beyond repair instead.

For all of Frank's flaws, at least he *wants* us.

Frank gets up and goes to the sink to wipe the blood off his face. It reveals clean, unbroken skin. As always, Elle has done a remarkable job.

"I was thinking," he says, turning back to us as he swipes a damp washcloth around his ears for any stray drops, "that maybe we could have a movie night."

That makes all of us pay attention. "Really?" Violet asks.

Frank laughs at our eagerness. "Really. I know it's not the usual circumstances, but I think we could all use it." He points the washcloth at us. Once white, it's now stained with his blood. "*If* you can finish your chores, and I know at least a few of you have worksheets you didn't finish yesterday. If that's all done by dinner, then after, we can watch a movie."

There it is again, that sense of normalcy, that ability to forget Jane isn't here. She could be up in our room, making her bed while the rest of us scatter to our own duties.

I don't get far before Frank calls my name. "Derry. One moment." His voice is grave.

My siblings leave, giving me worried looks, but not

intervening. They all know they can't help me right now. Only later, when we're out of his sight.

Carefully, the way you would with a wild animal, I raise my eyes to Frank's. I can only hold the contact for a second.

"Take a seat," he says, gesturing to the table still covered in the remains of our lunch. He sits across from me, in the seat that's usually Winnie's.

He doesn't say anything, not for a long time. I stare at the syrup-sticky plate in front of me, and he watches. I know because every few seconds I glance up to find him still watching with that passive, patient face.

"Did I do something wrong?" I ask.

"Did you?"

Every rule I've ever broken runs like a film reel in my mind. Every transgression. *Good word.* I've put off chores, I've cheated on assignments, I've taken too-long showers, I've fought with my siblings, I've kept secrets from Frank, I've gone outside without permission.

"I don't think so," I say.

Frank nods, tapping his fingers on the table. "I had some time to think while I was gone, and there's this one little part of last night that I can't quite . . . reconcile." Here, he pauses again and waits for me to make eye contact.

He smiles.

"You trust me, don't you, Derry?"

I hesitate. I grip the sides of the chair, fingers curling

up under the seat. "Yes?" It comes out like a question, and his eyes narrow. More confidently, I say, "Yes. Of course." I hold the eye contact until his face settles back into a calm smile.

"Then why didn't you come get me as soon as you realized Jane was missing?"

He asked me that last night. What did I say then? "I was just thinking I had to find Jane."

"And you thought you'd be better equipped to do that than I would?"

"No—"

"I'm still not sure how you got out, either."

"The front door was open."

"With no unusual activity on the alarm record?"

I shrug. "I don't really know how that works. I just know it was open."

Frank leans in across the table, searching my face. I want to school my expression into something he'll believe, but I don't know what that expression *is*. I don't know if it makes more sense for me to be scared or confused or vulnerable or defiant.

"You know that lying only hurts you, Derry," he says. His voice is soft. Gentle. Asking me to trust him with all my *secrets*. "Everything I've built here is for you. For your siblings. The world out there doesn't understand you. It doesn't *want* to understand you. Here, without their fear,

63

without distractions? Your magic can grow into something beautiful and powerful." He smiles, and I find myself leaning in like a flower toward the sun. I want him to be proud of me and my magic. "Lying only hurts this home."

I recoil. *I'm* the one hurting our home? Jane's been taken or lost or run away, but I'm the one who's doing the hurting? This isn't fair. I *didn't* do anything, not this time—all I did was look for my sister. So what if I didn't come get him first?

My grip on the chair tightens, fingertips tingling with pins and needles. Magic courses out of them, into the chair and out. Something grows out of the underside of the chair and around my fingers. A familiar dizziness buzzes at the edges of my skull. Not like I'm going to faint, but like I'm going to explode if I don't *scream,* if I don't reach across the table and shove Frank's face into the wood—

"You can and *should* talk to me," he continues. "Any problems you have—I can fix them, but only if you tell me. There's nothing I can do to save you if a problem I don't know about gets out of control."

He smiles one last time, raps his knuckles on the table twice, and leaves. Once he's gone, the oxygen rushes back into the room. I can breathe again.

With some effort, I unlock my fingers from around the edge of the chair. I brush away the purple flowers that sprouted out of my right thigh, just below the hem of my shorts. I'm still a little shaky from the rush of anger, so it takes me a moment to get on the floor and check the underside of the chair.

It's covered in small, twisted snowdrops.

Figures.

If I found my siblings right now, they wouldn't mean to crowd me, but they would anyway. They'd want to know I'm okay. They'd want to hear everything Frank said. Elle would pace and flutter about, alert for the possibility that we might not all be thrilled or in agreement with Frank. Even if no one else said anything against him, Winnie definitely would, and Elle would chide her, and they'd fight and Brooke would step in, and—

It's exhausting to even think about.

Instead, I clear the table. Elle and Brooke believe in cleaning as you cook, but the little twins don't, so I toss eggshells in the trash and rinse out a bowl that held the milk-egg-vanilla mixture for French toast. I get the dishwasher started.

Then, using the sound of their voices and chores as a guide, I avoid my siblings all the way up to my bedroom. I close the door behind me and sink to the floor, wishing I could sink *into* the floor.

I've always struggled more with anxiety than with depression, but sometimes . . .

Someone knocks. I don't scream *FUCK OFF*, and good

thing, because when I clamber to my feet and open the door, it's London. She's holding a huge, battered dictionary.

"Do you want a word of the day?" she asks.

I smile. London couldn't know this is just the right thing. I hadn't even known, until she was here and looking up at me with those big brown eyes, not asking for answers. Just asking for a word.

"Let's do two," I say. "I still haven't found a good replacement for *alchemist*." I sit on my bed, and London climbs up with me.

"How do we find a word for that out of the whole dictionary?" she asks.

I'd been doing it the way we do word of the day — pick a random page, look for something that sounds magic-y. That can take forever, though. "Go to *magic*," I say. "Tell me the synonyms."

London flips to *M*. She runs one finger down the page until she finds *magic*. "*Bewitchery. Conjuring. Devilry. Sorcery.*"

"Tried *conjurer* already," I say. "Not into *devil*. How would we make *bewitchery* work? *Bewitcher?*" London wrinkles her nose, and I nod. "Yeah, agree. So, *sorcerer?*"

Even as I say it, I don't like it. London shrugs, more neutral on it than she had been on *bewitcher*, at least.

"Well, worth a try," I say. "Find us a word of the day."

London closes her eyes, flipping back and forth through

the pages. After a few seconds, I say "Stop!" Eyes still closed, she points at the page she stopped on.

We lean in together to read it.

"*Senescent*," London says. "*Growing old; aging.*" She purses her lips. "Couldn't that be *anything?*"

"Maybe it means something that's already old and is *only* getting older," I suggest. "Like how as a kid, you aging means you're developing, not getting old. But Irene said that after a certain point, the cells in our bodies don't develop and grow—they age and die. So someone past that age would be senescent."

"Is Frank senescent?" London asks.

I pause. I don't know how old Frank is, but he's always looked . . . not young, exactly, but not old, either. He's never changed. Even as we lost baby teeth and grew taller and wider, Frank stayed the same.

But everyone is senescent in some way. Like Irene said, at some point, your body just starts the process of dying and never looks back. She'd know—she's read every biology book that Frank has ever given us. I think she said it starts earlier than you'd think, too. In your twenties, maybe?

Frank's *got* to be older than that. Surely that death process has started in Frank's body by now. Even if he was only twenty when Jane first came here, he'd *have* to be near thirty now. Or older.

How much longer could he have? What would it mean

for us, if he died? Sure, we can grow a lot of our own food, but we'd have to start going into the world for everything else. Frank can barely do that without being attacked, and he's only *rumored* to associate with "witches." What they'd do to *us* if our secret was discovered . . .

But maybe we'd figure it out. Keep each other safe. Get a chance to try everything Frank calls wasteful or dangerous, and learn for ourselves.

London is fiddling with the edge of the page, not looking at me. Frank might be the closest thing to a father she'll ever remember, and here I am, saying, *Oh well, he's gonna die, don't worry about it.*

Cool. Very cool. Very helpful, especially with one of her sisters missing. The thing London needs to worry about right now is definitely losing another piece of her family.

"He might be," I say carefully. "But if anyone could convince their body not to age, it'd be Frank."

She smiles and nods. Her smile is bright, but I think I've still managed to plant one more fear in her young brain.

London scans the dictionary for another magic-y word. I lean back, resting my head against the wall.

He *is,* though. Everyone's senescent. One day, Frank's going to die, and . . .

I don't know why that makes me a little happy.

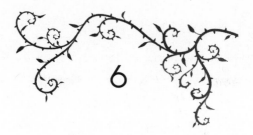

# 6

AFTER DINNER, FRANK wheels the TV out into the living room. It's usually kept in his quarters. Too much screen time, he says, is bad for the growing mind, so he has to regulate it strictly for our own good. That's why we don't get our own iPads or internet access, either. According to Frank, that way lies addiction.

He also brings out a little bowl with nine slips of paper in it. He closes his eyes and dramatically fishes around before pulling out a paper, unfolding it, and saying "Violet!" like they've won first place at the county fair.

We clap as Violet stands and walks over to the shelf containing all twenty-seven DVDs. They clasp their hands under their chin, examining each title with care, even though they must have each movie as memorized as the rest of us.

After a few moments' consideration, Violet picks a DVD case colored blue and silver and teal with a flash of red hair. *The Little Mermaid.* Violet hands the case off to Frank, who nods in approval—as if each movie wasn't already chosen and approved by him—and he puts it in. We're all piled onto the two couches and the floor in front of them with blankets and pillows and popcorn.

The movie opens on a flock of seagulls in a cloudy ocean sky. I know every beat, every line, every song, every flip of Ariel's tail. When you only have twenty-seven movies to watch, they tend to sear into your brain. I've even memorized how my siblings will react to certain parts of a given movie. When the huge fluff of a dog is on screen, Winnie's eyes never stray from him, because the one thing she misses more than her parents is her dog. Elle sings along with every song in every musical we have, but none more passionately than "Part of Your World." Frank does a perfect Sebastian impression during "Under the Sea" that never fails to make us all dissolve into giggles. Olivia and London both hate the part where Sebastian is in danger of being cooked and eaten, and will usually cover their eyes. Brooke is more likely to cover her eyes during "Kiss the Girl," overcome by second-hand embarrassment. As much as she devours any book with a romance plotline, she can't deal with it on screen—*especially* if there's a pretty girl involved. Brooke has a crush on a minimum of one girl in every movie we watch.

Personally, I'm a sucker for Ursula. She's expansive in body and power, she has the best song, and a little part of me thinks she kinda deserved to win.

Frank's favorite is King Triton. He likes to point to the pain Ariel goes through on land as proof she shouldn't have left her family behind, and firmly believes she would have had an even happier ending if she'd only listened to her father. It's a little heavy-handed, as messages go, but he's not entirely wrong. I couldn't leave my family for anything.

Tonight, I can hardly focus on any of it. The TV is set up with the window behind it, and with the lights off for the movie, I can see out to the front lawn. It's silly, but I can't look away.

There's nothing there.

There's *something* there.

Even in the empty space I know there's *something* there, outside the house, waiting.

For me?

The movie's over before I know it, and Frank's shooing us off to bed. Brooke stays downstairs with the little twins long enough to make sure they brush their teeth and get settled. The rest of us head upstairs, change into pajamas, and take turns in the bathroom. I go through the motions of washing my face and brushing my teeth, but I'm still outside that window, in the dark.

Brooke's coming upstairs as I leave the bathroom. She smiles at me. 'Do you want to stay with me and Winnie?' she asks, just like she did last night.

Just like last night, I shake my head. 'Thank you,' I sign. 'But I want my own bed.'

I spend almost an hour lying awake, staring at the ceiling, unable to sleep. It's too quiet. I like the quiet, but this is the kind of quiet that's so inescapable it's *loud*. I briefly consider seeing if anyone else is awake and asking them to come stay in my room, but I don't want anyone in Jane's bed—and I doubt they want to be in hers.

I sit up, grabbing a notebook and pencil from my bedside table. Sometimes, if I can't sleep, it helps to do train-of-thought journaling or doodling. Distract the part of my brain that can't sleep until my body can do it.

In a cursive so lazy no one else would be able to read it, I write *Jane is gone. She's alive but she's gone and I think she's still in the forest but I don't know how to find her and I don't think I can tell anyone and*

I trail off, my eyes drawn to the window. The forest. My hand keeps moving, shifting into drawing. If she's really out there, then why am I here? My breath comes in a little faster, a little more shallow. Anxiety is building and if I don't get control of it, it's going to be a panic attack, and how can I be allowed to have a panic attack if Jane is the one who's out there, in the forest, alone—

*Find me.*

My hand stops moving. On the page, without thinking about it, I've drawn the messy but clear shape of something that stands on two legs and has no face. Its antlers reach up to the top of the page and disappear.

I throw my blanket off and stand up. I pause, listening to the house. No movement. No sounds. I go into the hallway and pause again. Every few steps down the hall, down the stairs, I pause, I listen — but everyone else is asleep. There's nothing blocking me the whole way to the tunnel, and then inside, and down, down, down, all the way to the tree line.

I close my eyes, and all I can see is blood, and shadows chasing me. I hear the roar of a thousand cicadas.

When I open my eyes, I see light. Hundreds of slowly blinking lights. The forest is full of lightning bugs.

Lightning bugs have long been my favorite. I'm not a huge fan of bugs in general — I get the appeal of Gabriel, and from a distance they're all fine. Lightning bugs, though, are the only ones I'll willingly touch. As a kid, their glow always seemed impossible and magic. I'd catch dozens of them every summer night in the backyard, and wish on each one. I wanted a little bit of their magic for myself.

That wish came true, I guess.

I step into the forest and, imagining that I'm six or seven years old and standing under the big oak I remember in the backyard, I gently close my hands over one flashing little bug.

Its legs are so small, so delicate, that I barely feel them as more than a faint tickle. I open a space between my fingers *juuust* wide enough to see the glow, but not enough for the lightning bug to get out; not yet. You can't let them go until you make a wish.

*I wish for Jane to come home.*

I open my hands. The lightning bug doesn't fly away

immediately. It crawls up to the tip of my finger and pauses, as if making sure I'm paying attention.

When it takes flight, I follow. Hope rises in my throat, but it's a hope I'm scared to have. It doesn't feel like joy. It feels like nausea and bile. It's a hope that whispers, *You know it's not taking you to her, so you shouldn't even think it.*

Unless?

I follow the lightning bug deep into the forest. The hundreds of other lights have politely parted, making my lightning bug easier to follow.

Eventually, it lands on a tree. It stays there, flashing, as I approach.

"So . . . a tree," I say, aware that I'm talking to a bug. "In a forest, of all places." This is obviously not a wish-granting lightning bug, since Jane isn't a tree.

The lightning bug rises off the tree, circles me, and lands again. Okay. Maybe it wants me to copy it. Sighing, I spread my hand across the trunk.

I've been talking to plants for as long as I can remember, even before I knew about magic. At some point they started to respond. When I asked them to grow, they did. I couldn't *hear* them, though. I just knew they were listening because they grew.

When I touch that tree, I hear them. They *want* to grow. They want me to tell them about a dream and make it real.

I ask them to cover the tree with a dozen giant flowers, bulbous and glowing yellow like lightning bugs. They rush up to the surface. I laugh, and they laugh with me. They're proud of what they can do. They're proud of what *I* can do.

I pull away from the tree, dizzy, still laughing. Blue flowers bloom up and down my arms. They fall thickly to the ground as I brush them away. I don't remember the last time magic felt like this. Like I'm tapping into something wild and splendid and sparkling. Frank taught me to control my magic. I memorized a million pictures of plants and did his breathing exercises and made the magic orderly. Even when my siblings and I go out to the lake and Frank's nowhere to be seen, I always try the square breathing method before anything else. I try to bend myself to his theories, his way of doing magic.

*This* way feels like freedom.

It's intoxicating.

"Thank you," I whisper to the lightning bug. But it's gone. I turn in a slow circle, scanning the forest for its light.

I clap my hands over my mouth to muffle it, but I can't stop the scream that escapes.

A girl stands in front of me. She's pale and dark-haired with huge dark eyes. Her gray dress has buttons from the high white collar all the way to the calf-length hem.

The shadows around her are a little too deep.

Her lips move as if she's speaking, but nothing comes

out. Not for a moment. After she's already closed her mouth, upturning it into a smile, I hear the "Hello." It's like when one of the too-often-used DVDs skips and lags.

"Uhm," I say. I feel faintly dizzy. Every sound is impossibly loud. Tree limbs creaking. Leaves rustling as something scurries through the underbrush of a forest where I've never seen an animal. My own shaky step backward, my own too-quick breathing.

The girl makes no sound at all. She doesn't move, either. She's eerily still. She doesn't shift her position the way people do when they're just standing around. There's no movement in her chest that might indicate the movement of lungs. Her eyes dart curiously over me, but she doesn't blink.

Everything about her is subtly wrong. It could be imperceptible if all the little wrongs weren't compounding on each other, or if fear hadn't honed my sense of her. Some deep-buried survival instinct is telling me to examine her, catalog everything for weakness or strength in case I need to fight, only there is nothing to find.

The one thing I know is that I'm not about to turn my back on her.

I struggle to swallow with a mouth gone dry. "Hello," I say.

It happens again. Her lips move, but there's no sound until her mouth is closed. This time, it doesn't even sound like speech. It's scrambled and garbled. Hearing it is like an itching in my brain, and I shudder involuntarily.

I don't have a chance to say anything else because the girl disappears into thin air.

"Cool," I whisper, backing away. "Cool cool cool."

When the low hum of cicadas starts to build, I don't wait. I run. I run until my legs and lungs hurt and I have to collapse halfway through the tunnel to drag in big, ragged gulps of air.

I stay in the tunnel until I can breathe quietly again. Eventually, my lungs stop hurting. Eventually, the fear fades away.

There's this thing that can sometimes happen when you're removed from a source of fear: you forget why you were scared. The adrenaline is gone, and you feel a little silly for freaking out, and you decide it can't have been *that* bad. I know this, and I know I should hold tight to the fear and the way just looking at the girl hurt, but instead all I can think is:

*I want to go back.*

The girl scared me, but it's not like she did anything. Yeah, the whole lagging-speech thing was unpleasant, but not dangerous. She's obviously magic. Her magic might just be different than anything I've seen before. That doesn't make her dangerous.

Maybe she's even here looking for help. She heard about

Frank, however it is that people hear about him, and she knew she'd be safe here. Maybe her magic is some kind of out-of-control teleportation. That's why she disappeared. The speech—that could be like the flowers that grow when I use my magic. I probably overreacted. Fear isn't always a reliable indicator of whether or not you're really safe.

And . . . these are all justifications I'm making because I want to go back and hear the plants again. I want to have that actual two-sided conversation again. I want to hear them laugh and feel their pride in me.

I press my hand into the floor, and glowing flowers spring up. Their light dips into the grooves Jane carved into the wall.

My heart sinks. I should have done more to look for her. A wish on a lightning bug is nothing. I got distracted by the magic and the strange, glitching girl, and I didn't even look for Jane.

That's just more of a reason to go back. I can talk to the plants again, but this time I can ask them if they've seen Jane. The girl may have seen her. If we can get her talking coherently and staying in one place, we can work together.

It's not just that I *want* to return to the forest. I *have* to. For Jane. Tomorrow night, after everyone's asleep—that'll be my chance.

I stand. My pulse is still racing and my throat feels scraped from the panting, so once I'm out of the tunnel I go right into the kitchen. I chug a whole glass of water, and then fill it again to sip at more slowly. With each drink, I tell myself this is the right path. This is how I find her.

A whisper in the corner of my mind reminds me about the too-deep shadows around the girl. I can ignore my fear all I want, but didn't those shadows rustle a little unnaturally? Didn't they seem familiar?

A floorboard creaks behind me, followed by a yawn. "Derry?"

Violet's in the doorway, rubbing their eyes. Their hair is tinted blue, and when they open their eyes, they're green instead of gray.

We call them sleep-glamours. Violet's a vivid dreamer and an active sleeper—they flop and mutter and half the time their blankets are on the floor by morning. They do a lot of things in their sleep they can't remember, and the big one is sleep-glamours.

"Hey," I say, grinning as they yawn again and dark freckles populate their cheeks. "I was just getting a glass of water. Want one?"

They nod and flop onto one of the stools, draping their torso across the kitchen island while I pour a second glass. "I had this dream that we were living under the lake," they say.

Violet's rambling dream stories are such a perfectly normal part of life that it grounds me here, to the kitchen. The forest and its lightning bugs and its strange girls seem very far away, as if I'm the one who was dreaming.

Violet continues. "And you were there and Winnie was there but Winnie was also kind of my mom? And you were a mermaid, and there was another mermaid who wasn't Brooke but also was, you know? Like she didn't look like Brooke but she was Brooke, I could tell. And she was teaching us to play the accordion, but you kept wandering off into the deep water, and Winnie would scold you and say 'no, that's where the snakes are' but you wanted to see them. And I was really good at the underwater accordion, and I wanted you to come listen, but you kept going deeper and deeper until I couldn't see you, and I was kind of scared but figured you must know what you're doing, and anyway the accordion contest was coming up and if I didn't win then the snails—oh yeah, there were all these snails—they'd hate us. And then I woke up."

I don't say anything for a long time. I feel cold all down my throat and into my stomach. Violet doesn't seem to notice. They yawn so big their jaw cracks and their hair streaks blond.

"Let's go back to bed," I say.

I don't know if prophetic dreams are a thing. I'm pretty sure, though, that dreams aren't magic. They're brains making a mess of things while we sleep so that maybe our waking lives are a little tidier. Violet's dream was *The Little*

*Mermaid* getting all mixed up with stress over Jane's disappearance and a million little things in their head and that's what came out.

Except that I can still see bursts of yellow flowers on a tree trunk, and hear the laughter of plants, and feel the tug of the forest that stole my sister. I wonder if it's trying to steal me, too. I wonder if I'm heading into the deep water.

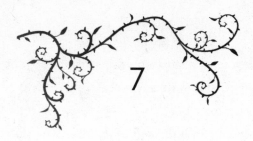

# 7

THE FIRST TIME I met Dr. Sam, I thought that he would save me.

I'm not special in that regard. Each one of us was desperate to be saved in our first months at the lake house. It wasn't our home, and these weren't our siblings, and Frank wasn't our guardian—this was a strange house full of strange people. We didn't want to be magic. We wanted our parents.

Then came Dr. Sam. He's friendly and warm. He looks a little bit like my dad. He never asks us to perform magic; he doesn't scold or yell. His jokes are bad, but in that nice, normal way. A dad way.

He listened solemnly during our first visit when I told him about the headaches I'd been having. *Stress headaches,* he said. *From the crying,* he said. *It'll get better,* he said. *And we'll check the prescription on those glasses, just in case—sound good, kiddo?*

He gave me a sucker at the end of my exam. It felt like a promise.

I waited for him to make his move. He probably couldn't whisk me away right then. It needed to be the right moment, when Frank had been convinced to let me go, or when he wasn't paying attention.

It took a year for me to stop believing that my parents were going to come back.

It took another six months after that to stop believing in Dr. Sam. I remember the moment it happened. I was having my usual exam, and he asked how I was doing. I described my anxiety and depression, how hopeless I felt. As always, he listened with a furrowed brow and a slight, encouraging smile. His eyes were kind.

And distant. Distracted.

It surprised me. I lost my train of thought. His eyes didn't look any different than they had in all the other exams. It just took me a year and a half to recognize that he wasn't actually listening. He put on the right face, he nodded. He upped the dose on my meds.

I got a sucker at the end of every exam. He'd tell a corny joke. He'd smile and ruffle my hair.

Each time, he'd leave me in that house with Frank and never look back.

I know that he never carried me out the door like a rescued princess because I never needed rescuing at all. I was just a scared kid in a new place. I've grown up enough to see that.

I still don't like Dr. Sam. I don't know why I can't grow out of the sense of betrayal, but I can't. No matter how warmly he smiles, no matter how pleasant his behavior, I know I can't trust him. I know that he's not seeing me, and he's not really listening.

Today is one of those regular checkups. We're all gathered in the living room, waiting. Frank comes through first, carrying the cases Dr. Sam brings with him to every appointment. Then, the good doctor himself.

Dr. Sam would be handsome if I didn't hate him. He's a little older than Frank, I think. His brown hair is graying, and there are small lines around his mouth and his blue eyes. His cheeks dimple when he smiles, and he smiles a lot.

"Hello, girls and Violet!" he says. His voice is deep and boisterous. "Let me get set up, and then we can get going."

The first thing that goes up is a set of screens to partition the living room from the kitchen, where Dr. Sam does his tests. Even if we couldn't hear everything happening, we'd tell each other everything, but there's something comforting about the illusion of privacy.

We start getting called in, oldest to youngest. Winnie. Brooke. Irene. Elle.

While we wait, London snuggles against me on the couch and flips the pages of the dictionary, looking for a word of the day.

"*Per-AM-bu-late,*" she says, pronouncing each piece of the word carefully.

"Isn't that just a fancy word for *walk?*" I ask.

"*Walk or travel through or around a place or area, especially for pleasure and in a leisurely way,*" she recites. She peers up at me through long lashes and round glasses. "One more?"

I laugh. "Okay, one more."

She flips through the pages again. "*Tenebrous.*"

"Hmmm. I don't think I've heard that one."

London opens her mouth to read the definition, but Frank calls my name. I'm up.

"Tell me after," I whisper to her.

"Derry," Dr. Sam says as I round the screen. His smile is smaller than Frank's, less like he's going to eat you and more like he's actually trying to get you to like him.

*Well, Dr. Sam, that stopped working on me somewhere around age eleven.*

I climb awkwardly onto the stool. Frank stands off to the side, not speaking or interfering, just watching. Dr. Sam picks up the blood pressure cuff first, getting my least favorite out of the way. He's considerate like that.

"How have you been doing?" he asks, ripping apart the Velcro and wrapping the cuff around my upper arm.

I just stare at him. Frank has to have told him that Jane is missing.

"Right." Dr. Sam slips the stethoscope into his ears and starts pumping. I try not to hold my breath even though I really, really want to. He pumps until it hurts, until I think I can't take it anymore. I glare at Frank and fill my mind with good words.

*Disembowel. Exsanguinate, decapitate, defenestrate.*

Then the blessed hiss of releasing air. I break eye contact with Frank and images of his blood disappear. Dr. Sam doesn't tell me what my blood pressure is. He just nods and writes on his clipboard.

He presses his fingers against the veins in my wrist and feels my pulse. He looks at his watch for a few moments and he nods, satisfied. He also presses his fingers against my neck and temples, feeling for who knows what. He listens to my lungs, uses a light to look in my eyes and my ears. Looks in my throat and at my teeth. Says the same thing he always says—"I'm no dentist, but that's a good pair of chompers on you."

If I was still nine and starry-eyed, waiting for him to rescue me, I would have laughed.

Dr. Sam puts a weird clip on my finger, takes my temperature, takes the clip off. He has me get up and stand against a screen. It's taller and wider than me, white and blank, but I've seen him fold it back down into something portable at the end of his visits. Dr. Sam sets up his laptop on a high stool and begins the directions.

I look left, right, up, down, move my arms out, then in. I feel like I'm being conducted. Sometimes he squints at me, and then at his laptop. Frank turns off the overhead lights, and Dr. Sam tells me to look at the little red light on top of his laptop. I do. It pulses in a gentle rhythm. He's squinting at the screen of his laptop again, and the white expanse behind me grows strangely warm.

Frank and Dr. Sam don't tell us what it's all for or what it's measuring. They don't tell us what numbers get spit out, much less what they mean. I think these are the ones that tell them something about our magic.

But I don't know anything for sure. I just follow directions until Frank turns the lights back on.

Last but not least, I sit in a chair. Dr. Sam ties a tourniquet on my arm. I stare right at the spot where the needle goes in and watch my blood drain into tube after tube.

Dr. Sam says the blood is just for "the usual tests," whatever that means, but we're pretty sure it's for Frank, too. We think he's trying to find the magic in our blood.

It's hard to say if magic is genetic or not. Sure, we have two sets of twins who have it, but are they statistical anomalies? Or is it *because* they're twins? Violet has two sisters, and by the time they left at eleven, neither one had shown magic. Same for Winnie's brother, for Brooke's siblings.

I'm an only child.

Or, as far as I know. I guess my parents could have moved on and had other children by now, unless they were scared to have a repeat of me.

Anyway—we think Frank might be trying to crack that particular code.

Now for my least favorite part. Frank leaves, and Dr. Sam pulls up another stool for himself. He puts on that face. Serious. Concerned. Brow furrowed, eyes kind and distant.

Dr. Sam isn't a therapist, but he's had "some training"—that's what he says—and Frank likes to give us time to talk to him privately. Give us a chance to bare our souls and get our meds adjusted.

"Frank told me what's been happening," Dr. Sam says. "I wanted to see how you're coping."

"Coping?" I ask dumbly.

"You've been through trauma. I want you all to be equipped with proper coping mechanisms. Frank worries about how Jane's . . . passing might affect you."

So Frank told Dr. Sam that Jane is dead. Does he really believe that, or is it just a story?

"How it might affect us?" I ask, trying to tease out what he knows.

"Frank said you were the last person to see Jane."

"I guess I was."

"And considering the . . . well, the manner of her death." Dr. Sam clears his throat. "There's concern about imitation."

"Imitation," I repeat.

"Yes."

Dr. Sam and I stare at each other. The cogs turn slowly in my head, sliding each word into place until I can see a whole picture.

"Oh! You're afraid we're all going to kill ourselves." Frank must have told Dr. Sam it was a suicide. Again, I have to wonder if it's because he really believes it, or because it was a better story than *She disappeared into the forest and I haven't been able to find her.* Can't imagine it's easy for Frank to admit he lost one of us.

Dr. Sam chuckles, which is not what I expected. "I should have known better than to try and sugarcoat it with you, Derry. You're a practical girl. Yes. Frank has concerns that one suicide could set off a chain reaction, and obviously we don't want that happening."

"So you're evaluating us."

"Yes. I'm hoping you'll tell me if you're suicidal, so that we can talk about it. Have you been feeling any desire to hurt yourself?"

"No," I say, and that's true. I don't want to hurt myself.

I sometimes want to hurt *others*. But that's not what he asked.

"Do you think anyone else has been?" When he sees my eyes narrow, Dr. Sam smiles. "Please don't consider it tattling, or anything like that. If you're worried about any of your siblings, it's better to know now so we can help them before it's too late."

"I'm worried about everyone," I say. "None of us are okay. Do I think any of them are going to kill themselves? No. But I didn't think Jane was, either." It's always wiser to follow whatever story Frank has constructed for Dr. Sam. Contradict him, even on accident, and you may find yourself in time-out.

"But no one has said anything concerning?"

"No. We're all just upset and scared and angry."

He leans in, still with that serious, furrowed brow. "Angry? At who?"

"What?"

"Are you angry at Jane?"

"Of course not," I say incredulously. "She didn't do anything wrong."

"What about your other siblings? Are you upset they're still here when Jane is gone?"

I wrap my arms close around myself and lean away from him, feeling suddenly dizzy. "Well—no, I don't think so—"

"Then Frank? Do you feel that he should have been able to stop this from happening?"

The dizziness reels around and around until it solidifies into frustration. "Yeah, he should have!" I snap. "He keeps us under such close watch, but Jane got lost? And he doesn't know how or why? He lost her and he doesn't have *any* answers! Yeah, I'm angry!"

I don't realize I'm shouting until Dr. Sam tells me to calm down.

That just makes me shout louder.

"*Calm down?* Are you *kidding me?*"

Frank comes back into the room. I can see by the look on his face that shouting at Dr. Sam is a time-out sort of infraction. My heart drops.

"Frank, it's really okay—" Dr. Sam is saying.

"It's not. I think Derry needs some time to think about what she's done." Frank is practically *snarling* and I can't quite breathe.

"I'm sorry—"

Frank points. "Go. Wait for me."

I don't need to ask what he means. I stand up, swaying just a little from the combination of blood loss and high emotion, and hurry off. Brooke reaches out as I pass her but I flinch away. Part of me wants nothing more than to curl up with any or all of my siblings, warm, safe, protected, but *most* of me knows that if someone touches me I'll lash out, and I won't be able to take it back.

I walk obediently to the time-out room. It's on the first floor, down the long hallway. After the entrance to the basement, but before the door that leads to Frank's rooms.

*Room* is a nice word for it. It's more like a walk-in closet. In the center, there's a stool, tall and narrow. I hate it. My legs are short and my butt is way too big for the seat, so I have to hook my ankles around the legs of the stool to stay steady and try to ignore the sharp corners digging into my flesh.

Frank's going to expect to find me sitting on that stool when he arrives, so I do. My ankles and thighs hurt almost immediately. I don't move. Frank can be incredibly quiet when he wants to be. I won't be able to hear him coming and get back on the stool in time.

When he finally comes in, I don't look at him. If I do, I'll cry, and I don't want him to see me cry. Whenever we cry, Frank gets this strange, satisfied glint in his eyes, and the corners of his mouth turn up in a way that makes my stomach hurt.

Not even Elle lets him see her cry if she can help it, and she loves him the most.

"Twenty minutes," he says. "That should be enough time for you to calm down."

He closes the door. The overhead light clicks off.

For a few blessed moments, it's dark. A deep, soothing darkness. I slip off the stool and shut my eyes tight because I know what's coming.

The lights flicker on. Fluorescents covering every wall, bright and white and blaring. I cover my eyes with my hands, but the light still seeps in.

The humming begins. Low at first, then louder, then

low, low, loud, the pitch rising and descending — there's no rhythm, no predictability. The sounds layer one on top of the other, discordant, impossible to block out.

The time-out room isn't like this for everyone. Frank customizes it for each of us. A lot of the others hate the dark and the quiet, and sticking them in a tiny room where light doesn't even come in under the door . . .

But for me, it's the light. The heat. The noise. It crowds around me and into me until I can barely breathe.

It's the way time distorts, making it impossible to know if my twenty minutes are almost up or if it's only been thirty seconds.

I try not to cry. I always try not to cry.

I always fail.

It's worse this time, too, because Jane's missing, and she won't be there to hug me when I get back to our room, which she'll have made dark by shutting the curtains and turning off the lights.

Eyes closed tight, I wrap my arms around myself in a boa constrictor hold.

Vines grow out of the floor beneath me, black, poisonous vines, wrapping around my ankles. They hiss like snakes, their thorns are fangs. They inch up, up, up, swallowing me.

They reach my knees. Another flock of vines grow up across the lights, not making it dark, but making it dim.

If only they could break through the walls, seek out a heartbeat like bloodhounds, tear into Frank—

Maybe my magic could be powerful, but not beautiful, no more beautiful than a monster. Something with fangs. With claws. Something no one can stick in a room, because it is simply too big to be contained.

I used to dream of something like that back when I was in elementary school, back when I saw people other than Frank and my siblings. The other kids would laugh at me for being fat, and even as I shrank with shame, I wished to grow into something so huge that it couldn't be moved or hurt, like a monolith—*good word*—or the planet Jupiter.

The vines are winding up my thighs, and *they* are huge and powerful, if the rest of me could be the same—

A particularly high-pitched hum breaks through. The vines disintegrate into dust. The light floods back in. I cover my mouth with my hands, and at last, I cry. I *sob,* giant, wracking sobs, wailing into my palms and knowing no one can hear me outside this room. I cry because Jane's gone. I cry because she needs me to find her and I don't know how. I cry because the light and the sound are too much, too much, and I'm going to shake and shake until I shatter into a million pieces.

What's worst is that I *could* leave. Frank doesn't lock the time-out room door. There are no locked doors in the house, and each one is a test of our obedience and loyalty and faith in him to tell us what's right. He's told us what doors not to open, and so we don't.

We're not ever supposed to open the door during a time-out.

But I *could*.

But I *can't*.

I've managed to stop the tears by the time Frank opens the door. Maybe it's been the promised twenty minutes, maybe it's been a hundred years. I'm no longer sure. My eyes must be puffy and red when I look up at him.

He smiles.

Something rushes into the place inside me that the sobbing hollowed out. Something with teeth. Something that could leap forward and rip out his throat.

For one wild moment, I taste copper.

"There, now," he says. He holds out the red-wrapped sucker I'd usually have gotten at the end of my exam. "Calmer?" I'm not, but *he* is. Somewhere in the last twenty plus minutes he cooled down and tucked his anger away.

I nod, swallowing the copper taste. I take the sucker, like a good girl. Frank crouches until he's a little below my level.

"It's been a long day," he says. "Dr. Sam is finishing up with your siblings, and after that it'll be nearly time for dinner, but I was thinking after we've eaten and everyone else has gone upstairs, maybe you and I could have some ice cream and talk." He taps his own temple. "I can tell there's something going on in there, Derry. You've got to talk to someone."

He's not wrong. I do need to talk to someone. I'm not used to keeping so much bottled up, unsaid, left to mutate into wilder and wilder thoughts.

I usually talk to Jane, who's obviously not an option. Winnie and Brooke get a lot of my brain-vomit too, but every time I imagine their faces when I say *I saw someone in the forest,* or *I keep hearing things that aren't there,* or *The forest is calling me back,* or, worst of all, if I tell them what happened two weeks ago, what I did—

They aren't an option either. Not just because I don't want them to think I'm crazy.

If Violet's dream was right, and I'm heading into some kind of metaphorical deep water, I can't drag anyone with me. Isn't that what I did to Jane? And look what happened to her.

Maybe I *should* talk to Frank, then. Maybe I've been selfish to expect my siblings to shoulder those burdens when Frank is right there, older, stronger.

Besides, while I'm so scared of how everyone else might react to hearing my secret, I kind of suspect that Frank might be . . . proud. I think he'd understand what I was trying to do, and he'd be proud of me for taking action. He'd be proud of the innovative use of my magic.

Frank's watching, waiting for my answer. I nod. "That would be nice," I say. My veins get that anxiety itch, my middle seems painfully hollow with the idea of telling him the truth about any of this, but I swallow it all down.

I need to tell *someone*.

Frank leads me back to the living room. I gravitate automatically toward Elle on the couch and sit at her feet — for her healing, or maybe because I want to absorb her love for Frank. It seems so much less complicated than mine. I'm forever on a precipice, loving him, hating him, wanting him to love me, wanting to kill him. Elle just looks at him like he hung the moon. She probably tells him all of her secrets, even the ones we don't know. Not about the tunnel, or how whenever he leaves she and Irene can't wait to dive into the lake. Other things, though. I bet Frank knows secrets about Elle that I'd never even suspect.

Maybe if I sit close to her, I'll learn to trust him with my secrets, too.

"You okay?" she asks. Her fingers brush my shoulder. I almost feel the itch of her healing magic.

"I think so," I say. "Just a lot happening at once."

"It's a really stressful time. I'm sure Frank understands. He knows how close you were to Jane." She pauses. She lowers her voice. "He shouldn't have put you in time-out."

I look up at her sharply. For Elle, that might as well be blasphemy.

Elle clears her throat. "But he's stressed out, too. To lose Jane, when he's supposed to protect us? It's a lot of pressure, you know. Taking care of all of us. Imagine the guilt he's feeling."

"Yeah," I say. "Right."

Elle brushes a hand softly through my hair. "He'll make it all okay, Derry. He will."

I badly want to believe that. I let Elle's words carry me through the rest of the day, through dinner, until I'm sitting awkwardly at the kitchen table while Frank digs in the freezer for ice cream. After dinner, he told everyone else that they could read or do assignments or whatever they wished, but he wanted everyone in their rooms the rest of the night. He asked me to stay behind.

Frank scoops out ice cream into two bowls—rocky road for him, plain chocolate for me. He slides the bowl of chocolate in front of me and sits across the table.

"So, what's been on your mind, kiddo?" he asks. I snort, and before I can regret it, he laughs. "Dumb question, I guess. I'm assuming your mind has been on mostly one thing."

He looks out the kitchen window. For a wild moment, I

think he already knows about the forest. He already knows I've been out there and that I'm connected to it and—

"Jane," he says. Oh. "You probably can't stop thinking about where she is."

I hesitate. There's a question I need to ask, but haven't dared to. There are two reactions I can think of—Frank thinking my question is reasonable curiosity, and Frank thinking I'm accusing him.

*Find me.*

I can't be the only one searching.

"Why did you stop looking for Jane?" I ask. "You haven't been back to the forest since the first time."

He's mid-bite. He pulls the spoon slowly out of his mouth, and swirls rocky road on his tongue thoughtfully. I hold my breath. I can't tell yet which Frank I'm going to get.

He swallows.

"When I left, before, I went to see some friends of mine. I'm not sure I've ever told any of you about them." He looks to me, and I shake my head. I didn't know Frank had anyone other than Dr. Sam that he could call a *friend*. "They're not as magic as any of you," he continues. "You couldn't call any of them a full-fledged alchemist . . . but they have some . . ." He waves his spoon about, searching for the word. "Sight. Psychic abilities. They can use tarot cards, scrying mirrors and water, bones, tea leaves." He laughs. "A few messier ones you wouldn't want to hear about. I usually use them to find alchemists who might need my help. I had them all looking for Jane. They all said she was gone. Lost."

"Lost? Not dead?"

He hums, curious. "You think there's a difference?"

I shove ice cream in my mouth to give me a moment to think about how much to say. Then, "Yeah. I do. I feel like she's gone, too. But not dead. Just . . ." I shrug. "Lost. Like she needs finding."

"Feel it how?" He leans in, peering at me. "Does it feel like sisterly intuition, like something you just want so badly you believe it? Or like premonition? You've never shown psychic tendencies before."

I wish I could tell him that when I felt it, I was *in* the forest. It changes things, I think, for me to say that I feel Jane being alive when I'm in the forest where she disappeared. It sounds more real than, *Yeah, when I'm huddled in my room, staring at her unmade bed, I feel like she has to be alive.*

*That* just sounds desperate and wanting.

"I don't know," I say, slouching back in my chair. "I don't know how to tell the difference."

"Fair enough. You know, at one point I considered teaching you all a little bit about psychic talents. A primer, at least. It's a slippery kind of magic. There are people who can always tap into it, and others might only be able to do it once or twice in their lives, or never at all." He shrugs. "I decided that it wasn't necessary, not unless one of you started showing signs. But maybe I should have anyway. Just in case. Maybe then you'd know."

Frank finishes off his ice cream and stands. "I'm more than willing to look for Jane again. I don't want to believe she's dead any more than you do. Maybe tomorrow we can go out together. You might feel something stronger in the forest."

I stare at him, shocked into silence. He's offering to take me out into the forest with him?

"Would you like that?" he asks.

I nod vigorously. A chance to go to the forest *without* having to sneak, without fear of being caught? Yes, obviously, absolutely.

To look for Jane, of course.

Not to feel that magic again.

"Yes," I say. "Yes, I would. Thank you."

That night, I lie awake telling myself that I don't need to go to the forest tonight. There's no reason to go other than to look for Jane, and Frank is taking me with him tomorrow to do just that. It'll be safer with him.

I've nearly convinced myself to stay when there's a quiet knock on the door. London peeks in.

"Can't sleep?" I ask. She shakes her head. "Do you

want me to come read you a story?" She shakes her head again. "Then . . . ?"

She glances toward the window, and I understand. I smile. "Of course. Is Olivia already asleep?" London nods. "Then it can just be us."

Jane keeps the two candles in a box under her bed. Candles are the only thing she ever asks for on her birthday. Her strongest memory of her mother is that she *loved* candles. She owned them in a thousand shapes, sizes, and scents. When she needed to relax, she lit candles and breathed in the scent.

Frank only gets Jane plain, unscented white candles. A couple years ago, he gave her a set that smelled faintly of vanilla. We were pretty sure it was an accident, and no one mentioned it.

The scent doesn't matter. The candles are a symbol, and symbols aren't exact recreations. All that matters is that the flickering flames send Jane back in time to the family she misses, and now they can send London and I back in time to Jane.

I place them on the windowsill, in the faint rings of wax left behind by many nights of this ritual being played out. London kneels. I light the candles, sitting cross-legged next to her. We stare past the candles up into the night sky, and I imagine we have the same wish.

*Please let Jane come home.*

Afterwards, I walk downstairs with London. I sit on the edge of her bed and she puts a small chapter book in my hands. I read in a soft voice that won't wake Olivia, and minute by minute, London's breathing slows. Before she falls asleep, she whispers, "Do you want to know what the word means?"

"What word?"

"*Tenebrous.*"

I'd completely forgotten. I smile. "Tell me."

"I memorized it. *Dark; shadowy or obscure.*"

Goosebumps rise in a line up the side of my body facing the tunnel.

"Good word," I whisper.

I sit with London until she falls asleep, and then I open the wall and head back to the tenebrous forest.

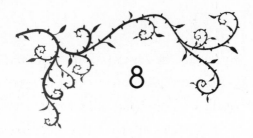

# 8

THERE'S NO HESITATION walking into the trees this time. I'm where I'm supposed to be. I press my forehead against a tree and magic sings in my veins.

"Hello." I'm not startled by the voice this time.

The girl is back and instantly, so is the fear. Why the fuck did I think I was overreacting before? Looking at her is like looking at a hole in the universe and the only thing you can do with a hole in the universe is run and hope it doesn't catch you.

I squeeze my eyes shut. *Come on,* I admonish myself. *Get over this. She hasn't actually done anything to you.* If being kind of spooky but harmless was a reason to abandon someone, my siblings would have left me, Winnie, and our absurdly vast combined mental library of ghost stories and urban legends a long time ago. Me especially, considering the way I can't stop myself from saying the scariest thing that pops into my mind when we're trying to sleep. One of the first sleepovers we had in the living room involved me, lying in the dark, whispering, "Doesn't the ceiling fan kind of look like a body on the ceiling?" and Irene whacking me with a pillow.

I do a round of square breathing. Mediocre results for magic, much better ones for anxiety. When the adrenaline of pure terror fades, I carefully open my eyes.

The girl is still there, still a little too motionless. This time, though, she cocks her head to the side as she watches me. It would be like a confused puppy, but her neck bends too far and it's more like an owl.

I remember the shadow and its owlish eyes from the night Jane disappeared, and I have to close my eyes again.

"I'm sorry," I say.

"I'm sorry," she says.

Eyes still closed, I shake my head. "No, it's me. I don't know what's wrong with me." There's got to be *something* wrong with me—why else would I be so scared of her when there's no real reason to be?

"I don't know what's wrong with me," she says.

I open one eye. Her mouth keeps moving for a couple seconds with no sound. The jolt of fear isn't as intense. I'm getting used to her. *Acclimating.* That's a good word. Frank has this book about climbing Mt. Everest, and it talks a lot about how important it is to get acclimated to higher elevations. It's a slow process. You climb to a higher camp, spend a little time there, then go back down. You repeat it until you're ready to go to the next highest camp, and then you go back and forth.

That's what I'm doing. Acclimating.

I look at her with one eye and ask, "Can you use your own words?"

"Own words?" she repeats.

I open the other eye. With slow, careful steps, I circle her. Her head swivels to follow me until she has to turn her body. At least *that* part isn't like an owl. If she turned her head all the way around, all that acclimation would be ruined. I'd be gone in a flash.

"I'll take that as a no."

"No."

"Okay, well . . ." I stop circling her.

"Okay, well . . ." She stops her swivel, and watches me.

"I have to find my sister," I say.

"I have to find my sister."

"I'd ask if you've seen her, but I'm guessing . . ."

"I'd ask if you've seen her—" I wave my hand, interrupting, but she finishes the sentence anyway. It's like she can't control it. She's compelled to repeat my words.

"Find me."

It takes a moment to realize what she's said, because I'd tuned out when she started repeating me. But it was her—the girl who only repeats words—and *I* didn't say that.

Screw acclimation. I get up close to her. "Have you talked to Jane? Have you heard her?" I demand.

"Have you heard her?"

I shake my head, flexing my hands in and out of fists to

fight the anger surging up through my gut. It's not her fault she can't communicate the way I want her to. Chill out.

"Okay, you can't talk to me, but maybe you can show me the way?"

"Maybe you can show me the way?" she repeats, nodding. She gestures for me to follow her. I do.

There aren't many parts of the forest that look familiar. I haven't spent that much time in here. There's just one area that's seared into my brain. Once I realize what path we're on, I can feel the warmth of blood on my hands. I can feel Jane shaking as we walk away from the clearing. I can hear her promise no one will know.

"No," I say, stopping in my tracks. "She's not going to be that way. The only thing that way—"

"Is dead."

My throat tightens until I can't breathe or move.

The girl turns to me. She's learning her own words and she's moving more naturally. She's got a crooked sort of smile that reminds me of Winnie's—closed mouth, almost more smirk than smile. She looks past me, over my shoulder, at whatever's footsteps I hear now.

I don't look. It's not a person. I know it's not. It's going to be that shadow with the owl eyes.

I close my eyes tight, as if not seeing it will mean it doesn't see me. The footsteps draw closer. They aren't quite footsteps, though, more like the steady rustle of leaves.

An image flashes into my mind—tall, standing on two legs. Antlers reaching up to the sky. Made of shadows and lightning bugs. It should be insubstantial—*ephemeral? Better word*—but I know it's solid, solid, solid. Solid enough that if it reached out, I'd feel it.

It doesn't. It only stands behind me. It inhales deeply, and so do I. We exhale together.

Its breath is hot on my neck.

I turn, and there's nothing there.

"Run," the girl says. She hasn't moved. "But come back." She glances toward the clearing, then to me, that crooked smile still in place. "She's waiting."

I don't need to be told twice. I run.

I'm already shaky when I get back to the house. I need to go to bed. I need sleep.

I *don't* need to walk into the little twins' room and find Elle, hands on her hips, a glare on her face. She looks me up and down, pursing her lips, then spins on her heel and walks out.

Well.

Fuck.

I close the tunnel and follow her out into the living room. Her arms are now crossed over her chest and she's looking at me like a mother about to scold her child.

"What in the world were you thinking?" Elle hisses.

"Oh, please, like we don't know how you and Irene sneak out to night swim," I whisper angrily.

Elle pales, then shakes her head. "We've only done that a few times, and at least we went together. You went out *by yourself*. What if something had happened to you? What if you got injured and you couldn't get help and the wound got infected? What if—" She puts a hand over her mouth, and her eyes sparkle with tears. "We already lost Jane to . . . *something* out there. What if it had taken you?"

I soften. "It won't."

"How can you know that?"

I shrug. I can't answer that, because the honest answer would be that I don't know. What I do know is that no matter if I'm scared, no matter if I'm not safe, I'm going back.

*She's waiting.*

"What were you even *doing* out there?"

"I thought I saw something from my window," I lie. "I thought it might be Jane, so . . ."

Elle looks doubtful. "I'm guessing you didn't find her."

"I must have imagined it. I don't know about you, but I'm ready to go back to sleep."

She opens her mouth as if to push the subject, then closes it and shakes her head. She follows after me. As we cross to the stairs, Elle glances down the hallway toward Frank's rooms.

'You won't tell him, right?' I ask, signing because we're a little too close to his door for comfort.

She looks back at me, startled. She shakes her head.

She was considering it, though. I can tell. His trust means everything to her, and she's told on siblings in the past to stay on his best side. Not on big things. She'd never purposely get us sent to time-out. She tattles about the little things, like having windows open, or neglecting to practice our magic. Things that prove *she* knows the rules.

She won't tell Frank I snuck out. She'd have to tell him about the tunnel, and that would implicate her.

So I nod, holding her gaze until she turns away first.

"Let's go to bed," I whisper. I hold out an arm, indicating for her to go ahead of me. She glances back down the hallway, but quick, so quick I almost miss it before she raises her head high and ascends the stairs.

I pause, staring down the hallway the same way she had, thinking about Frank asleep in his rooms. He's lived here for a long time. Long enough to make this house into a self-sustaining home and raise us.

The forest has always been off-limits, because it's too easy to get lost, too easy to stray from his sight and into the sight of someone who would hurt us. Those are the reasons he's always given. I don't doubt them, exactly, but I wonder.

Does he know what really lives in the forest?

9

"SORRY, YOU'RE WHAT?" Winnie asks, except she has her toothbrush in her mouth, so it's muffled and takes me several seconds to translate.

I don't answer right away. I continue brushing while Winnie glares, and I give her a look that says I'm too dignified to talk with my mouth full of toothpaste foam. We take turns spitting into the sink. I reach for my pill caddy, and Winnie nudges me hard enough that it's almost a push. Her little pet poltergeist rattles the other toothbrushes on the bathroom counter. I reach out to steady their holders.

"No, seriously," she says. "You're what?"

"Frank's taking me out to the forest." I successfully claim my pill caddy and pop open today's box. Two pills sit inside, both white, one a thin oval and the other a thick circle. The orange bottles Frank uses to refill our caddies every week say *buspirone* and *bupropion,* and one's for anxiety and the other's for depression, but I always mix up which is which. I fill my mouth with a handful of water from the sink and swallow the pills.

Winnie, a show-off, swallows her pills dry.

"Or at least he says he is," I amend. It feels a little too good to be true that Frank would really take me out to the forest with him, so I don't want to act like it's a sure thing. I think he'd take it away if he knew how badly I wanted it.

"Why?"

"To look for Jane."

Winnie frowns. "I thought you both thought she was dead."

"I did," I say. "I don't anymore."

For that, Winnie smacks my arm.

"Ow!"

She rolls her eyes. "That didn't hurt. I barely touched you. Why didn't you tell me you think she's alive? I've been over here feeling like I'm the crazy one for hoping."

"Sorry," I say. "I kind of feel like the crazy one, too. I don't . . . I mean, I don't have a good *reason* to think she's alive. I don't have proof or anything, so don't get your hopes up too high."

"Too late. Hopes up. Hopes in the stratosphere. What changed?"

"Well." I lean back against the sink. "We all searched the forest and didn't find a trace of her." That's a good place to start, I think. With facts. "No body or anything. Surely someone would have stumbled on her."

"Unless she ran away and isn't in the forest anymore."

"I *know* you don't believe she'd do that. None of us do."

"Fine. Then maybe someone took her."

"Who would take her? No one comes here."

"Do *you* know how far the forest goes? We never reached the other side of it while we were searching. For all we know, the forest goes for miles and miles and miles and has campsites eventually. Hikers."

*Blood on the ground, Jane's hands over her mouth, my hands held out in front of me, trembling.*

I scoff in a way that I hope is believably incredulous. "I think we'd know if hikers ever got this far. Besides, if one did, why would they take Jane?"

Winnie holds up her hands defensively. "I don't know about you, but I feel like if anyone would have the bad luck to encounter the one serial killer among whatever hikers find our forest, it'd be us."

"She's not dead," I say firmly. "It's not just the lack of a body. I can . . ." I groan. It feels even sillier saying this to Winnie than it did to Frank. "I can feel it. When we were in the forest, I felt it. She's alive. She's out there. We just have to find her."

Winnie doesn't respond immediately. She stands there, looking at me as if she's trying to figure me out.

"You mean it?" she asks. I can hear it now, the hope in her voice. "You feel her?"

"I do."

Winnie nods. "Okay. You're not usually one for intuition

and crap, so, if you say that you *feel* she's alive . . . I don't know." She needlessly rearranges and neatens the lines of toiletries on the counter. "I believe it."

My heart squeezes. I'm not used to a Winnie that's this kind of vulnerable. Even the Winnie who lay in my bed with me a couple years ago and confessed that she was asexual hadn't been what I'd call vulnerable. She was excited, maybe in part because Brooke had already claimed the word. It made the identity more accessible, made claiming it for herself feel safer. The only nerves I saw were in little glances my way, because, well, she told me right after kissing me.

That was back when we were more like two girls living in the same weird boarding school, not sisters. Becoming sisters took *years,* and there was a brief crush phase on the way. Never serious, never more than a few awkward kisses.

When I reacted positively to her announcement— because what other way is there to react when someone tells you a profound way to understand them better?—she launched into eager babbling, and any hint of that vulnerability dissipated.

I should tell her what I've been doing in the forest. I should tell her I've gone out by myself more than once, and tell her about the girl, and about the antlered *something* whose breath I can still feel on my neck. She believes in me. She trusts me. I should return that. I *want* to return that.

But my vocal cords are paralyzed, and instead of join-

114

ing Winnie in that frightening vulnerability, I smile and take her hand and we walk downstairs to join the others for breakfast.

Frank is at the head of the table with a newspaper. It's one of the things he comes back with every time he leaves — a stack of newspapers to catch up on. They stay in his rooms for the most part. He doesn't think we should read them. It would be too stressful, he says, to worry about what's happening in the wider world.

So all we see are glimpses when he brings one to a meal. Headlines that we have no context for, pictures of people we don't know. There was a time when it felt like torture, being so close to knowledge of the life I left behind and yet unable to access it, but now? Now I barely glance at it. He's right. I have enough going on without taking on the troubles of people that would hate me for being an alchemist.

Brooke and Elle are cooking. When Frank isn't here for breakfast, we tend to default to cereal, but when he *is,* it's a full home-cooked meal. I walk over to the kitchen island to get a peek at what they're making. Elle is chopping her way through a cantaloupe. Brooke is at the stove, making what smells like eggs.

Brooke turns, sees me, and purses her lips. Elle remains uncharacteristically silent, but with a very characteristic smug smile on her face.

After making sure Frank has his back turned to us,

Brooke starts signing angrily. 'Are you *very* stupid?' she asks. 'What were you thinking?'

Great. I was right that Elle wouldn't tell Frank I snuck out. I just didn't think about her telling Brooke.

'I thought I saw something from my window,' I sign, giving the same excuse I gave to Elle. Brooke, however, wants the explanation more than she wants to have caught me, so that's not enough. She just stares at me, eyebrows raised expectantly. 'I couldn't sleep. I was at my window and I thought I saw Jane or someone in the forest. I didn't think. I just ran for it. It was reckless, and I'm sorry.'

Before Brooke can scold me further, Frank says, "How's breakfast coming?" He hasn't looked up from his newspaper.

"Almost there," Elle says. She piles the cantaloupe into a bowl and sets it on the table. "Over easy on the eggs, right? Toast well-done?" She knows the answer. We all know the answer. He's never changed it. It's almost a compulsion for her, wanting the pleasure of Frank knowing she knows.

"Yes, thank you," he says.

"Derry, will you finish up the toast?" Elle asks. The toaster chimes, signaling that the latest batch is done. Because it's Elle who asked, I almost say no.

But Brooke is still glaring at me. I need to get back in her good graces as quickly as possible. I take on toast duty, carefully extracting the slices and putting them on plates already stacked with a dozen pieces. A last round of four and we'll be good to go. Once I've pressed down the levers—the dial on the right turned almost all the way up for Frank—I'm just standing awkwardly at the counter while Brooke angrily scoops out the scrambled eggs that will be for me, Winnie, Violet, and the little twins, and checks on the eggs in other pans. Elle, humming, pours drinks. Coffee for Frank, tea for Brooke, Irene, Violet, and herself, orange juice for the rest of us. I spring into action to carry glasses of juice to the table.

"I have to go to the bathroom," I say, then scurry out.

Maybe if Brooke just can't see me for a little bit, her anger will tone down. Brooke doesn't get angry often. She doesn't start fights, she inserts herself calmly between the fighting parties and de-escalates.

Not often being angry doesn't mean she's not skilled at it. On the rare occasions Brooke *is* angry . . .

Well. That's why I'm trying out my own de-escalation.

Even though I don't actually have to pee, I sit on the toilet and count slowly to ten. I wash my hands. When I return to the kitchen, Violet and the little twins are helping to load and distribute plates, and Frank's put his newspaper down. I take my seat. I don't look at Brooke. I don't look at anyone.

Who else did Elle tattle to? Did she just go to Brooke, or did she gather everyone for a little meeting to detail my indiscretions? I know she didn't tell Winnie, because Winnie sure wouldn't have been that nice in the bathroom.

After everyone has had a few minutes to eat, Frank takes a piece of paper out of his pocket and places it on the table. "Today's schedule," he says. "Who wants to copy it onto the whiteboard?"

Following our own private chore wheel, Violet raises their hand.

"Wonderful. Once you're finished eating, of course." He clears his throat. "I think a good deep clean of the house could really help us clear our minds. I've written down everything that should get done today, and some suggested assignments." Not really suggestions, of course. If he wrote that I should do the dishes and found Irene doing them instead, we'd both be on his mental bad list for the day.

Next, Frank points a finger at me. "Derry. After breakfast, we're going to go out into the forest." A few eyebrows shoot up around the table at this announcement.

"Can we go?" Olivia asks immediately. "We can help!"

Frank smiles at her. "Sorry, kiddo, this is a special assignment." He winks at me, like we have a true partnership. "Derry, don't think it gets you out of doing chores. We should be back by lunch, and afterwards I want you on linen duty."

We pass the paper around to see our part in the day's

schedule, to see who has dishes, who's on sweeping and vacuuming, who's stuck with the bathrooms.

"Look good?" Frank asks, as if there's an option other than smiling and nodding.

I eat fast. Frank won't leave any sooner than he wants to, but I'm feeling eager to get away from Brooke's accusing stares and Elle's quietly smug smile and the growing confusion among the rest of my siblings. It's becoming clear that Elle only told Brooke. Everyone else just gets to be concerned about what's happening between us.

The moment my plate's in the sink, I sprint upstairs to change. I'm not alone. Brooke is close behind with Elle and Winnie.

'Did you really see something?' Brooke asks as soon as we're in my room. 'Is that why you went out?'

'Went out?' Winnie asks. 'What's going on? What were you talking about before breakfast?'

'Derry's been sneaking out to the forest by herself,' Elle answers.

The wounded expression on Winnie's face makes my stomach twist with guilt. She hides it quickly behind her usual scowl, and that only makes it worse.

'You make it sound like I do it all the time. I did it once.'

'Plus the night Jane disappeared,' Elle adds.

'Yeah, because I was following her. Like last night, except last night, it was nothing. I thought I saw something from my window. I was tired and wasn't thinking straight. For all I know, it was just moonlight and trees rustling around in the wind.'

'Why didn't you tell me?' Winnie asks. I know now that I wasn't the only one feeling the opportunity for us to trade vulnerabilities. She'd been waiting for me to answer her call, and now she's finding out just how much I ignored it.

I throw up my hands, that stomach-twisting guilt coming out as exasperation and anger. 'It was nothing!' I sign *nothing* particularly vigorously, my loosely closed hands pulling apart and punching the air on either side of me. 'I thought I saw something, I went outside, I was wrong. There's nothing to tell!' I jam a pointed finger toward the door. 'Interrogation time is over. Please, leave me alone.'

It takes real effort to ask politely instead of screaming *GET OUT*. It's what I want to do. I want to scream and I want everyone to just leave me alone and give me a second of silence.

But whatever's happening, I can't take it out on my sisters.

Brooke whips around and leaves with the sharp slaps of her bare feet on hardwood. This is definitely not the last I'll be hearing from her on the matter. Elle follows her. Winnie hangs back. Our eyes meet. The vulnerability is gone from her eyes. I've brought the anger in. With each heartbeat, her little pet poltergeist rustles her hair with more force. I look away first.

"Have fun in the forest," she says, making it sound like a curse. Then she's gone.

I close the door, and slump against it. I cover my eyes with the heels of my hands, pressing in until the black becomes polluted with pinpricks of light and color.

I'll have to apologize. The pestering still makes me want to explode, but I know *why* they were pestering me. They're worried. I would be, too.

I'll have to apologize, and I'll have to tell the whole truth to everyone so that they can stop worrying. It'll be easier on them if they know the details. I'll tell them.

Later. After the forest.

I put on my customary outside-with-Frank outfit. It's different from what I'd wear on my own. Frank likes us to be protected from bugs and sunburn and poison ivy and all the other little harms that live outside. So, jeans, T-shirt, the sneakers that live in the shoe cubby downstairs, a quick slathering of sunscreen over my arms and face.

Frank is already waiting at the front door when I get downstairs. He flashes me a patient smile, as if I'm late but he's gracious enough to forgive me.

"Let's get going," he says. "It'll be best if we can do this before it gets too hot."

He watches as I pull on my shoes. When we go out in

secret, we go barefoot. It's easier to clean feet than it is to clean shoes. The sneakers I'm tying—white when they were given to me, glamoured a deep purple by Violet some years ago—aren't even usually worn when we go out *with* Frank, not unless it's too cold for bare feet but not snowy enough to bring out the snow boots.

I flex my toes uncomfortably inside the sneakers. The shoes still fit, but it's more than a little claustrophobic to have my feet contained by something so unyielding. The most I'm used to is the fluffy socks I basically live in once it gets cold.

Outside, the first thing Frank does is douse me in bug spray. I hold my breath at the first hiss of aerosol, but it somehow still gets in my mouth. It *always* gets in my mouth and makes the whole world briefly chemical.

"I wanted to start where you saw Jane last," he says. He gestures around to the circle of forest around us. "I know that it can be disorienting, especially at night, but do you know where she was?"

I point across the lake. "It was near the dock. I'll be able to tell a little better once we're there."

Frank leads the way. When we're closer, I try to direct him to the exact spot where I followed Jane into the forest.

"So you saw her run in," Frank says as we navigate through the trees, "but that was the last time?"

"Yeah." I walk ahead of him. "I think I was about here when I stopped."

"This is where you had the feeling you talked about, that Jane's alive? Do you feel it now?"

I don't respond because the girl suddenly appears a few feet behind Frank. She only has eyes for him, and those eyes are full of fury.

I clear my throat. Her glower doesn't falter. "Yes," I say. My voice quivers, and I clear my throat again. I look at Frank and only Frank, even as her anger grows in my peripheral vision like a gathering storm. "I felt it as soon as we walked in. She's here, somewhere."

Frank looks over his shoulder. "What are you looking at?" he asks.

It doesn't surprise me that he can't see her. I'm more surprised he can't *feel* her.

I'm about to answer him, but the girl's mouth opens, and she screams. It rips out of her throat like something broken and wild. I clap my hands over my ears as my eyes water with the primal force of her yell.

And then she's not behind Frank anymore. She's in front of me, inches from me, shouting, "Get him out get him out GET HIM OUT GET HIM OUT!"

I grab Frank's arm and I run. It's probably only the shock that makes him follow instead of pulling me back and standing his ground. Once we're back in the sunlight, I let go. In the aftermath, my hand is tingling unpleasantly, knowing I touched something I shouldn't.

"What the *fuck* was that." Frank's face is red and contorted, but his anger can't match the girl's. For a brief moment, I look at Frank, aware that I'll be lucky if I don't get an hour in time-out when we get back, and instead of being terrifying, he seems . . . petty. Compared to the girl's bone-shattering, heart-rending scream, Frank's anger at being dragged from the forest feels so totally inconsequential.

But the moment is brief. It dissipates and leaves fear in its wake.

"I, uhm—I felt something. But . . . bad. A bad something." I close my eyes tight for a second. That sounded so stupid. "I felt Jane, like I said. She's there. She's lost, but she's alive. But there's something else in the forest with her, and it was angry. Violently, violently angry." I shudder. I don't know if the girl would have hurt me or just Frank, or if she could even touch either of us, but I don't ever want to find out. "It hit me like—like a train. I panicked."

The red in Frank's face is fading, but only because his expression is turning stony.

"Clearly, it was a mistake to allow you this much leeway," he says coldly. "I should have predicted that it would be overwhelming for you. Combined with Jane's loss, well . . ." He shakes his head. The look he gives me is still tinged with anger, but there's something else, too — pity? "I'm beginning to think I shouldn't have taken your . . . *feelings* so seriously. Maybe we should be talking to Dr. Sam about new medications if you're having these kinds of—" He rolls a hand in the air, searching for the word. "—emotional hallucinations. Delusions. It's not a good sign, Derry. It could make a person think that you're broken."

"I'm not," I whisper.

Now it's definitely pity on Frank's face. "It's possible to be so broken that you can't see it. Only the people around you can."

I think about how I did something so beyond the pale that Elle even briefly considered telling Frank I'd snuck out, which would require revealing the tunnel. I think about how I worried Brooke into anger, how I betrayed Winnie's trust, how I'm sure I would have actually screamed if they hadn't left my room when they did.

Am I broken?

Frank doesn't speak on the walk back to the house. He doesn't say anything at all until I've taken off my sneakers and stored them back in the cubby. Even then all he says is, "Go change. Get on linen duty."

So I do.

Linen duty is straightforward, but not my favorite. I like the chores where I can stay in one place and really get into a rhythm. Dishes, for instance, or folding laundry.

Linen duty is an all-over-the-house sort of chore. I go from bedroom to bedroom, removing sheets and pillowcases and tossing them out into the hallway. Frank leaves his outside his door.

I spend a long time staring at Jane's bed, uncertain if it's better to leave it unmade so that I can pretend she'll walk back in at any moment, or to strip it and put on new linens so it's fresh and clean when she returns.

*It could make a person think that you're broken.*

*Find me.*

I don't have it in me to make that choice. That's a job for Future Derry.

All of those linens then have to be taken down to the basement, where the washer and dryer are, and the process of cycling through the multiple loads it will take to clean them all begins. Meanwhile, I go back to the ground floor and the linen closet and distribute clean sheets and pillowcases for everyone. I don't have to put them all on, at least—just leave them neatly folded by their beds—or, in Frank's case, outside his door.

Depending on Frank's mood, whoever's on linen duty can sometimes spend the rest of the afternoon in the basement with a book while everything's going through the machines. It's my favorite part of my least favorite chore. There's something peaceful about sitting on the cold stone floor with a book in my hands and the washer and dryer rumbling beside me. It requires a good mood from Frank, though, because otherwise he'll get upset at you for being lazy.

I'm guessing that, considering how everything went in the forest, Frank's mood will not be on my side today.

Instead, after each load switch, I go back upstairs and check the whiteboard. It takes up a huge part of the kitchen wall it's mounted on. Down one side, magnets spell out MORNING, AFTERNOON, and EVENING. More magnets line the top, giving us each a column labeled with our name, and one "Miscellaneous" column. Each chore from Frank's paper has been recorded in Violet's neat handwriting. Violet separated them by his suggested assignments. Any leftovers go in "Miscellaneous."

Linen duty was my only assigned chore, so, to stay under the radar and to get back on Frank's good side, I tackle the "Miscellaneous" column between laundry loads — organizing the Tupperware. Checking the pantry for anything that's expired. Checking the levels of all our cleaning products and toiletries, to see if anything should be added to the shopping list. I cross each one off as it's completed. I dedicate my day to being unobtrusive and productive.

One by one throughout the day, Brooke finds us and prods us into showering. It's easy to forget something like "showering" between chores and missing sisters.

She doesn't forget about me. Mercifully, she also doesn't

question me about the forest or anything else. She just shoves me into the upstairs bathroom with a pair of clean pajamas and closes the door.

I wash my face and brush my teeth, and get into the shower. The moment I feel warm water on my skin I'm transported. I'm somewhere where we're all whole and together. When I'm out, Jane will be in our room. She'll be putting her pillows into the fresh cases I dropped off, and her bed will be made with a freakishly perfect neatness. She'll roll her eyes at how carelessly I make mine, and I'll insist that there's no point in being perfect about it if I'm just going to make the top sheet and blanket into a cocoon anyway.

By the time I turn off the water, it's pooled in the tub up to my ankles. I get out, put my glasses back on, dry off, put on the new pajamas, wrap my hair in a towel. The water hasn't gone down.

*Shit.*

I'm not exactly handy. I'm good at cooking, I'm good at growing us new and interesting produce, I'm good at spelling lessons. I've spent my life at the lake house worming out of fixing anything. It's usually not a big deal. Several of my siblings can do simple things, and Frank fixes basically everything else.

A clog is probably a simple thing.

Winnie can fix it. Even pissed at me, she won't make me ask Frank.

But I open the door, and Frank's passing by in the hallway. He must see panic flit across my face.

"Something wrong?" he asks.

"Oh. Uhm," I say. "I think the tub is clogged? It's not draining."

Frank sighs, and pushes past me into the bathroom. "You can't be doing this, not now." I remain pressed against the door frame and stay quiet. He rummages under the sink and comes out with a couple of tools, and kneels over the tub. "There's too much going on. The least you can do is clean up after yourselves."

My whole body heats with shame. He doesn't say anything else, but I feel like I can't move. Like I have to witness the mess I made—somehow just *my* mess, instead of a fairly natural occurrence, instead of this being a shower used by multiple people. If I walk away, I'm certain Frank wouldn't just shrug and continue the work and never bring it up again. He'd remind me that good girls don't make these kinds of messes.

I stare hard at a corner of the shower over his shoulder. My shame shifts to anger, then back to shame, back to anger, then back to shame again, but this time because I'm too scared to act on my anger. My arms start to ache from being crossed tightly over my chest, but I don't move. I try not to breathe too loudly. I can't leave, and he can't be too aware that I'm here.

*It could make a person think that you're broken.*

In the end, he retrieves a decent glob of hair out of the drain. It *plops* into the trash. Frank washes his hands, and leaves without a word.

I look into the trash, at the tangle of wet hair, and wonder how that little thing could lead to me feeling like my whole body would explode from shame and fear and anger and guilt.

I shouldn't go back to the forest. With my siblings watching and Frank already pissed at me, I should toe the line for a few days.

*She's waiting.*

I pretend I'm invisible when I sneak out of the house after dark. If I believe it enough, it might just come true. I imagine that my feet are made of clouds, and I hold my breath when I open the wall. On the other side of the tunnel, I look back at the house only once. All the lights are off. It doesn't mean there isn't someone watching.

I go to the forest anyway. Lightning bugs greet me, swarming me with their warmth and light. They're pleased I've returned.

Jane isn't waiting for me past the tree line. The girl is.

## 10

THE GIRL WATCHES me approach. Lightning bugs dance in the air around her, welcoming me. The girl's expression is unreadable.

For a moment, all we do is stare at each other. That rising tide of horror is back, threatening to overtake me. I dig the nails on my right hand into my left wrist. The pain clears my head a little.

"So," I say. My voice shakes even as I adopt a casual tone. "I take it you know Frank." Then I laugh, because this whole thing is too absurd not to.

"Know Frank," she repeats. She shakes her head, hard, and clears her throat. Her mouth moves, but nothing comes out. She realizes it quickly and stops trying, her face contorted in frustration. "Sorry," she says. "I'm still . . ." She takes a deep breath. Each word seems to take tremendous effort. "Learning."

"To speak?"

"Speak," she whispers, again as if she can't help it. I'm pretty sure at this point that she isn't the wendigo Winnie's parents warned her about, but her repetition does remind me of it.

After her reaction to Frank, I'm also pretty sure that my theory about her being a stray alchemist in need of a home isn't right. So . . . who is she?

*What* is she?

Her brow is furrowed in concentration, seeking her own words. I don't speak—I don't want to interrupt her and send her off repeating again.

"My name," she says, "is Claire."

"Claire," I say. What a normal name. She could be one of my siblings. "I'm Derry."

"Der—" She stops herself. "It's nice to meet you. You— you—you." She's got her own voice, but now it's skipping like one of Frank's old CDs.

"Nice to meet you," I say. I bite the inside of my cheek to quell—*good word*—another burst of laughter.

Claire smiles. She makes it look difficult. She doesn't speak again, so after a minute I say, "I also take it you don't really like Frank."

She opens her mouth. Closes it. Settles on a nod.

I nod too. "I don't know *how* you know him, but . . . I get it. He's not an easy person to be around." She raises an eyebrow, and I laugh. "Understatement. Living with him is having your entire day centered around *his* moods and only his, but you never know what the mood is going to be." I don't need to be telling her all this, but similar to how she couldn't stop compulsively repeating, now I can't stop talking. "One moment, you're his favorite. He makes you feel like you're special, and he *sees* you, and you're a team. You and him against the world." Me and Frank, searching for Jane. "But make one little mistake, and you become . . . nothing." I spread out my fingers in an explosion effect. "Poof. He gave you a chance, you failed, you don't exist anymore until he decides you do."

I stop. That makes him sound terrible. And it *feels* terrible, but—I'm explaining it all wrong. Of course it feels bad to know I disappointed him. All the rules, annoying or strict as they may be, are there to protect us.

Jane and I broke one of the biggest rules, and now she's gone. He just wants to keep us safe.

Claire's hard to read. I don't look in her eyes. I'm scared they'll be distant, like Dr. Sam's. I want to believe she understands what I'm saying.

"I don't know why you hate him so much that you went all . . . vengeful spirit at the sight of him," I continue. "I don't know what he did. He's complicated, I guess. He's family and all, but sometimes it sucks that he's the only one who can help us."

"He can't help a—a—anyone." Claire's voice is still skipping. "He hurts. He only hurts—hurts—hurts—hurts—hurts—" She's stuck. Her head jerks and she repeats *hurts, hurts, hurts.* I reach out, but I don't touch her. Her head stills and she presses her hands against her eyes. "—hurts—hurts—hurts—"

Maybe Frank's right. Maybe I am broken. If I am, I'm in good company.

It's unfair of me, but I still think: seems like there's a lot of broken things that pile up around Frank.

I stay with Claire. That skipping repetition takes a few moments to stop, but it does, and then she doesn't talk again. After an hour or so, she disappears. I go home. Tomorrow's Friday, which is our free day, so I'm hoping to sleep in.

No such luck. Elle shakes me awake bright and early. Her face is blurry without my glasses, but I can still make out her huge, annoying smile.

"You went to bed pretty early last night," she says. "So I figure you got plenty of sleep and you'd be able to join me for morning yoga!"

I glare at her. Her smile doesn't waver. Maybe she doesn't *know* that I went out to the forest last night, but she suspects it.

"Great," I say, forcing my own smile. "Love morning yoga."

On a normal day, my actual feeling on morning yoga is ambivalence. It's like Jane's candles—not exactly my thing, but nice, and I participate occasionally. Today, my feeling is much closer to *hate.*

Violet, Olivia, and Brooke all join in morning yoga with me and Elle. Irene is up, too, but she's sitting on the sidelines, nursing a mug of coffee. Elle guides us through a routine that seems both excessively long and excessively intense. I didn't even know yoga could *be* intense, but I'm left sore and sweating.

The others seem fine, especially Olivia and Brooke, so maybe it's just that I never made much effort at morning yoga before. I didn't used to have Elle watching me like a hawk and correcting every single pose I attempted.

I escape to shower before breakfast, which gives me some relief. Breakfast itself gives me very little. Elle asks a lot of passive-aggressive questions—"How *did* you sleep last night, Derry?"—and Frank doesn't look at me at all. He reads his newspaper and talks pleasantly with the others, but I'm invisible. I barely eat.

Everyone falls into their free day patterns easily enough. Frank returns to his rooms. Olivia grabs colored pencils and the princess coloring book she got for her birthday last year. She settles at the coffee table and peruses the pages, selecting one carefully. She's been rationing because she's unlikely to get another until her next birthday. Brooke sits on the couch behind Olivia, reading a thick book about the history of space travel.

One corner of the room transforms into the knitting area. A couple months ago, Violet started teaching Winnie and London to knit. Violet learned from their grandmother. They have almost boundless crafting energy, but at the lake house it became a little stifled. Most of it was focused into puzzles that, once complete, were saved and hung on the wall, and then on origami. The wall was full and a thousand paper cranes made within Violet's first year. They were starting to lose their mind before Frank finally agreed they could be trusted with knitting needles.

Winnie's little pet poltergeist is particularly active when she knits. She's not very good at it. She's too impatient to do each row neatly, the way Violet and London do. She's determined, though — more than once I've found her alone in the living room at odd hours, muttering curses as she knits and purls. Violet's offered to take Winnie's clumsy scarves and glamour them into order, but Winnie never accepts.

London is more focused. Each stitch is precise. She graduated from scarves and hats to a sweater that's too small for any of us to wear. She's said her next attempt will be a sweater big enough for Olivia, while the small one can make a nice bed for Gabriel, if beetles need beds.

My usual spot is in our biggest comfy chair with my legs over one arm and a book in my hands. I'm in position, and I've got the book open in my lap, but I didn't even glance at what I picked up. I'm staring through the window that faces out to the forest.

I'm pretending I don't notice Brooke watching me, or that I haven't noticed Irene and Elle are off . . . who knows where.

It's barely half an hour before a groan and a clatter of knitting needles signals the usual end of Winnie's knitting endeavors. "I'm going to work on the garden," she says. She can't storm off dramatically right away, since she has to ask Frank for permission, but moments after she disappears down the hall, she comes back through the living room. Storming.

The back door slams. No one breaks a stride in their activities. Getting frustrated with one project and stomping off to do another is Winnie's main hobby.

Irene and Elle return to the living room shortly after Winnie leaves. Elle takes up a spot next to Brooke, signing something to her I can't see from this angle. Not that I should be trying, but they're probably going to talk about me, and that's rude, too.

I don't see Brooke's reply because Irene appears in front of me, smiling.

"Hey," she says.

"Hey," I say, a little suspicious. "Elle send you?"

Irene's smile drops, and she sighs. She drapes herself across the ottoman next to my chair. "I told her you'd know."

"She could just talk to me herself."

Irene laughs. "Yeah? Because you've been so open with her so far?"

"There's nothing to be open *about*," I grumble, turning a page I definitely didn't read. "She saw me go into the forest once. So what? I was looking for Jane."

"Twice," Irene says softly. "She saw you last night. She went to check on you and you weren't in your bedroom. She saw you through the living room window."

I don't respond to that. Of course she checked on me. Of course she saw me.

"What are you doing, hon?" Irene asks. "I know you're worried about Jane, but going into the forest at night, alone . . . it's dangerous."

"I can take care of myself." I proved that well enough in the clearing.

"That's not the point. We stick together." I can feel Irene watching me, but I don't look at her. I stare at the book until my vision blurs.

No one but Jane knows what happened. None of my siblings know there's this gap that's been growing between me and the rest of them for over two weeks. They don't know how Jane's disappearance pushed it a little further.

Claire knows what I did. She must. The way she finished my sentence yesterday. She knows, but she's always in the forest when I come back. She's not scared of me.

My siblings would be.

"Right," I say to Irene. "Together. That's why Jane's still here."

Before Irene can respond, I'm on my feet. Winnie might be mad at me too, but at least she won't talk to me while she's mad. I don't bother asking Frank for permission. Winnie's already in the backyard, so it's not like I'll be alone.

When I step outside, I notice the silence right away. Winnie doesn't *do* quiet. Winnie talks to herself, sings to herself, drums on any surface that can be drummed upon. It's quiet in the backyard, and she's nowhere in sight.

"Winnie?" I call. It's a big backyard, but not get-lost-in-it big. It's just big enough for all the garden plots and a fire pit. There's not a lot of places she could hide. I look anyway, of course. I search behind our largest plants, behind the little tool shed, in that one little corner between the fence and the house.

It takes me an absurdly long time to notice that the back gate is unlatched and oh-so-slightly open. Or to notice that one of the watering cans is on the other side of the gate, between us and the forest, unceremoniously tilted onto its side and leaking water.

"WINNIE!" I scream, even though it's too late. Shadows are shifting between the trees, and the forest has stolen another of my sisters.

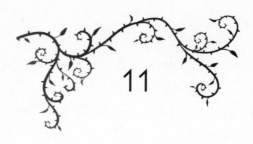

# 11

FRANK'S FACE IS the closest thing to real panic I've ever seen on him when I tell him Winnie's gone. It's still only a widening of the eyes and a small drop of the jaw, but for Frank, that's significant. That little bit of real panic is probably the only reason he doesn't stop the rest of us from joining in the search for Winnie. Elle gets the little twins to patrol the tree line with her instead of actually going in, but the rest of us run right into the trees with Frank, shouting Winnie's name.

We already know that we're not going to find her. Her amaryllis, like Jane's camellia, is drained of its color.

I don't think she's dead, just like I don't think Jane is dead. It's the same feeling. Winnie's here, but she's not. She's alive, but she's lost, so lost that no one can reach her.

*Isn't that kind of what dying is? Being so lost that you can't be found?* I think as I walk deeper into the forest. I cup my hands around my mouth and yell for my sister, knowing she won't respond.

I see Claire only once. She speaks, but she's too far away to hear, even if there's actual sound coming out this time. I still know what she says.

*Tonight.*

I nod, and she's gone.

We search until dusk. At some point in the afternoon, Brooke comes around and shoves sandwiches into everyone's hands so that we eat something. As it gets close to dinner, Frank calls the search off. We file back inside, careful to make sure we have everyone.

Frank's last inside. He locks the door, enters the code into the alarm, takes a deep breath, and punches the wall.

We stumble back as one. Trembling arms wrap tight around me — London. I pull her close. Violet joins in, then Olivia, and soon we're all one huddle shielding each other.

I've never seen Frank be physically violent, ever. He doesn't even slam doors. Now his fist is nestled into a dent he punched in the wall. He's frozen there, the only movement a small tremor through his body. Like he's restraining himself.

When he lowers the fist, there's little spots of red left behind.

Elle's going to have to heal that. She doesn't step forward to volunteer. None of us move at all. One of the twenty-seven DVDs is *Jurassic Park,* and right now, we act as if Frank is the T-Rex. Don't move and he won't see us.

"I apologize," he says, his voice rough and ragged. He doesn't offer an explanation. He just turns and walks past us.

It breaks the spell. Elle trails after him, her hands outstretched to heal the broken skin on his knuckles. Brooke ushers Violet and the little twins away. If there's another outburst, they don't have to be here for it.

Irene and I stay. Irene can't leave Elle. I can't leave either of them. If it does escalate, I can protect them. I did it before, didn't I? I protected Jane in that clearing.

Frank lets Elle heal him without a word. He even graces her with a smile.

"I'm going to head out immediately," he says. "My friends—the ones I told you about, Derry. They couldn't find Jane, but maybe now that two are missing . . . maybe I can motivate them to try a little harder."

He straightens his spine, smooths back his ruffled hair. He smiles at all of us. "Take care of your siblings while I'm gone. No one leaves the house. I'll try to be back by morning, but it depends on how many I have to see before I get answers."

Elle nods, with Irene and me lagging a few seconds behind.

"You'll find them," Elle says confidently. "I know you will."

I might be imagining that Frank's smile wavers when she says that. It comes back so quickly, I can't be sure.

Frank stays only long enough to get his bag and to pull out the TV for us. Any movie we want, he says, as many as we want. As soon as he pulls out of the drive and heads off down the road, Elle turns on me.

"You won't leave this house tonight," she says. "You have to promise me that." When I don't answer, she says, "If you can't manage a promise, that's fine. I'll sleep in your room tonight. Irene will sleep in the little twins' room, right in front of the wall."

"You can't just come sleep in my room," I protest. "I'm not a child."

"You're acting like one! And we're older than you—"

"By like *four months*—"

"So we're above you in the chain of command, and I don't think you're going to get Brooke to side with you, do you?"

My right hand twitches and for a horrible moment, I think I'm going to slap Elle. I'm not sure I'll be able to control it. Elle's eyes widen just a fraction, as if she sees it in me.

As if she knows what I'm capable of.

I stuff my hands in the pockets of my shorts. "Fine," I say. "We'll all have a nice night inside."

Elle's plan is a good one, and if I had more time, I would stay in tonight and tomorrow night and however many nights I had to until she trusted me enough to leave me alone. I don't have time. Jane is still missing and now we've lost Winnie and Claire said *tonight*.

After dinner, I volunteer to make hot chocolate for everyone. As an apology. They accept that reason. They all know by now that I've been leaving at night and thus have something to apologize for. It makes sense that I'm ready to get back in their good graces. *No, no—I don't need help. I can make it.*

While the kettle's on the stove, I take a handful of dirt from one of the kitchen plants, and use it to grow something new. I'm careful. I focus. I know *exactly* what I want. The flowers of the plant are small and white, but I'm after the roots. They writhe over the counter as they grow. When I'm satisfied with the amount, I separate stem and flowers from root, and rinse it off. I chop the root, put it in a tea infuser, and let the water for the hot chocolate soak it up.

I turn toward the living room and lean casually against the counter. When Brooke looks my way, I wave. She smiles, waves, turns back to the movie. *Anastasia.* It's one of our favorites. A girl with little to no memory of her past, raised in an orphanage, finds out she's a long-lost princess.

The lake house is better than Anya's orphanage, and it's not the princess part that we gravitate toward. It's her grandmother. Anya's surviving family has spent years longing for her to return home.

The kettle whistles. I quickly toss the remaining root down the garbage disposal and wash the infuser, putting it back in the drawer wet just as Violet walks up. "Can I help?" they ask.

"Sure. Will you grab the mix and a spoon while I pour water?"

The water that comes out is faintly yellow. The black interior of the mugs hides the color, but it's obviously yellow as it pours. I move fast to finish pouring water in all seven mugs before Violet sees.

"Okay, time to scoop," I say. I lean in and whisper, "Make them extra chocolatey. I think we could use it tonight."

Violet nods, scooping the powder in generously. I follow behind with a splash of milk and a spoon for each mug.

If any of my siblings think the hot chocolate tastes strange, they don't say so. They don't seem to notice that my mug stays full.

The valerian root I put in the water won't hurt my siblings. I wouldn't do this if I thought it would hurt them. I don't know if it will do *anything*. I've never tried to grow something with intent before, not like this. I may have read every book Frank owns on plants and herbology, but I like to grow imaginary plants, and I grow them usually for aesthetic, not purpose.

I've never asked a plant to grow with instructions like, *Not too much taste. Just a little sedative. Just a deep sleep.*

Whether or not it works, I'm a monster for trying. I know that. I'm drugging my siblings.

It's only to make them sleep through the night, without noticing me coming or going. They don't understand that I *have* to go out to the forest tonight, to save our sisters. I don't blame them or anything. They're scared. We all are.

But if I can't make them understand, they'll try to stop me. That can't happen.

By the time Anya and Dimitri are fighting Rasputin on the bridge, the little twins are out and everyone else is yawning. Once the movie's over and everyone's shuffling off, I help Irene carry the little twins to bed.

"Sorry about this," she says. She spreads a blanket on the floor in front of the tunnel wall, yawning. "I think it's a little extreme, but . . ."

"But Elle's worried," I say distractedly. Irene's lying down right against the wall. If I open it, she'll fall backwards. Not sure she'd sleep through that. "I get it. Please, don't worry about it."

Elle's already asleep when I get to my room. She hasn't taken Jane's bed, as if it's off-limits. Instead, she's built a nest of her own blankets on the floor, like Irene did. I sit on the edge of my bed for a moment and watch her. Her breathing is slow and even. Paranoid, I go room to room, checking *everyone's* breathing—they're all fine.

Now I just have to navigate getting out of the house if I

can't use the tunnel or the doors. The windows on the first floor are all alarmed, too.

Not the second floor, though. Those windows are too high to jump from and have nothing nearby to climb on. We can open and close them as we please, for the most part.

I trace the dried candle wax on the windowsill in my bedroom like a prayer before I open the window. I glance at Elle, but she hasn't stirred.

I ask the vine to grow thick and sturdy up the side of the house, with handholds like a ladder. Like the beanstalk that took Jack up into the clouds, my vine provides me safe passage to the ground.

"I won't be gone long," I whisper to my vine. "And I'll need to get back up."

Claire's waiting for me in the forest, like I knew she would be.

"Do you know where Winnie is?"

"No," she says. For the first time, her voice sounds completely normal. No lag, no skipping. "But I know how you can find her and Jane. I'm sorry I couldn't tell you before now, it's been . . . difficult."

"Who *are* you?" I ask. "How can I trust anything you tell me if I don't know who you are? Or *what* you are?"

"I'm just like you," Claire says, stepping toward me with that little crooked smile on her face. "A lost little alchemist who was seen by a man, and then by a forest. The forest sees you, Derry. It saw what you did." She raises her hand to my cheek, a breath away from making contact. "You impressed it."

"Impressed it?" I draw back. "But—I—I didn't do something *good,* it's not something to be *proud* of—"

"Isn't it? You protected your sister and yourself at all costs. You proved there's no length to which you wouldn't go. Admittedly, your technique and control could use a little work. But that's why the forest wants you here. We can teach you."

I shake my head, reeling. "Teach me? To, what, hurt people better?"

"No, no," Claire says. "Of course not." She *hmm*s. "Well, unless you want to. Unless it's needed." She takes my hands, and it's like an electric shock. She's never touched me before. I wouldn't have been surprised to learn she's incorporeal, but she's not. I can feel her. Her hands are a little cold, her skin a little dry.

"The forest sees potential in you, Derry," Claire says. She laces her fingers through mine. I can't breathe. A small part of me still itches, hearing her voice. It still yells that she's a hole in the universe.

She's a hole in the universe I increasingly think I'm willing to fall into.

"And it wants you to see potential in yourself," Claire continues. "Frank's methods build your power little by little, and never enough. We can teach you to build your dreams. And an alchemist who's powerful enough to build dreams . . ."

She steps in closer. I realize I'm trembling. Her breath ruffles my hair when she whispers in my ear. "She'd be powerful enough to find her sisters."

I pull away just enough to look her in the eye. "Teach me."

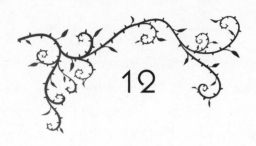

## 12

THUNDER BOOMS SO loud overhead that my
bedroom window shakes. A worksheet on permutations
sits in front of me on my desk. I've done all but three out
of fifteen problems, and spent the last ten minutes staring
at the rain, doodling idly on scrap paper. The window is
cracked just enough for me to smell the storm.

"Tell me something you failed to grow," Claire said to
me after I asked her to teach me.

"Well . . . I failed to grow accurate snowdrops in my
test this week. Real plants are harder, especially out of season."

"Your *test*." She sighed. "Frank still thinks that's how
you nurture an alchemist? Doesn't he *want* better results?"
Claire knelt, and patted the ground next to her until I knelt
as well. "Magic shouldn't feel like a test. It creates a barrier.
When you aren't being tested, what does it feel like?"

"A conversation," I said immediately.

"Good. That's a good answer. Now that you're out
from under Frank's watchful eye, try the snowdrops again.
And don't worry—there's no grade here."

It wasn't easy to drop that stress. Frank wasn't there,

but a teacher was watching, and she *said* there wasn't a grade, but my anxiety said there *was* a grade, a secret one. I tried square breathing for nearly half an hour, even though in my gut I knew that no matter what Frank said, it wasn't the right way.

Claire was patient. She didn't prod me like Frank would, or sigh and get bored. She sat with me, and an hour later, I grew a blanket of anatomically perfect snowdrops. The magic made my blood feel like it was sparkling.

Claire beamed with pride. "Now that you've passed that mental hurdle, we'll really be able to get started."

Everyone was still asleep when I got home, and in the morning, no one seemed suspicious of why they'd all slept so deeply. *Maybe I got away with it.* My stomach twists at the thought. I shouldn't get away with it. I don't want to get away with it. If I did, it means I could get away with it again, and that would just be too tempting.

I don't want to be the person who drugs her siblings every night.

I also don't want to be the person whose siblings won't trust any drink or food she hands them.

Can't admit guilt, can't stand getting away with it.

Lightning flashes. Eyes closed, I whisper, "One Mississippi, two Mississippi, three Mississipp—" and the thunder claps.

When I open my eyes, maybe I'll be home. I'll be nine

years old and standing on the porch with my dad while the tornado sirens rise and fall. I knew by then that sirens didn't always mean you'd get hit with anything. The sirens aren't saying *A TORNADO IS HERE,* they're saying *pay attention, please, it could get bad in a hurry.* My mom will be inside pacing in front of the TV, tuned to her favorite news channel for severe weather, the multipurpose lantern-slash-weather-radio clutched in her hands. Every couple of minutes she'll call out to us, and Dad will say, "We're fine, we haven't seen anything."

I'll hear this, distantly, but all of my focus will be on the huge tree in our front yard. The leaves are so dense that when the wind blows strong enough, they look like green ocean waves. The limbs creak.

I want it to fall.

I know that if it falls, it could hit our house or the car or destroy the garden. I know the tree is big enough that it would be bad, so I don't *really* want it to fall, but I *do.* I imagine how my bones would tremble when it hit the ground with a mighty crash. Mom would scream, Dad would swear. When the storm finally passed I'd go outside in rain boots and pick my way through fallen branches. I want the tree to fall, and I want to climb up onto the thick trunk like it's my own fresh kill.

It was still standing the last time I saw it.

I return my attention to the worksheet. *#3: How many*

*unique ways are there to arrange the letters in the word ORANGE? Your answer should be an integer . . .*

I have the formula scribbled at the top of the worksheet. On scrap paper, I find space around the doodle—another two-legged being with impossible antlers, but this time their entire body is tree branches and flowers—to plug numbers into the formula. I don't get past the first couple of numbers before lightning flashes.

*One Mississippi, two Mississippi . . .*

I give up on permutations. Frank's not back yet, anyway. I just used worksheets as an excuse to be alone. Every time one of my siblings looked at me, I thought, *They know, they know.* It was suffocating. All I want is to be back in the forest.

I wonder if Claire can teach me to grow a tree as big as the one in my old front yard. I wonder if she can teach me to bring it down.

Brooke knocks on my door. When I look up, she signs, 'We're going to watch another movie during dinner. Do you want to choose?'

'No, I'm fine. Let one of the little twins pick.'

She nods, but doesn't leave. She's tugging at the sleeves of her cardigan, biting her lip.

'Is there something else?' I ask.

'How did you sleep last night?'

My stomach twists again. 'I passed out,' I sign. 'Don't

know what it was. I was out like a light and slept right until morning.'

For a moment, all we do is stare at each other. She searches my face for answers, because . . . she doesn't *know*. I don't think she does. She just wonders.

I break eye contact, which is probably all the confirmation she needs. I should meet her eyes again. I should smile. I should do anything but keep my eyes glued on her shoulder, broadcasting my guilt, risking missing anything she might sign.

'How about you?' I ask. My hands stumble over themselves on even this simple question. I train my eyes on her hands.

'Same,' she signs. 'Come to dinner soon?'

After dinner and the movie, Elle announces that she and Irene will be sleeping in their own beds tonight. It's not that she completely trusts me yet, she warns—it's that sleeping on the floor sucked and she's not going to do it again, so I better not make her. Jane's bed isn't even mentioned as an option. I suppose that whether Jane is missing or dead, it still feels wrong to sleep in her bed.

I swear I won't, and I hide my smile. Just to prove how entirely trustworthy I am, I even stay in the living room and play a few rounds of Uno. The little twins go to bed after one round. I spend the entire game fighting not to look out the window, scared someone would notice.

When I finally escape Uno, London and Olivia are in my room. They've got Jane's candles on the sill and Olivia's trying to light a match.

"What are you doing?" I ask. It comes out harsher than I mean to. Olivia drops the unlit match and they both snap their heads toward me with wide eyes.

"We wanted to do the candles," Olivia says. "To wish for Jane and Winnie to come back."

It's harmless, and I should let them do it. There's no reason not to, except that every moment in this house is a moment I'm not in the forest.

"No. You're supposed to be in bed." I whisk the candles off the sill into the box, and grab the matches off the floor.

The way Olivia's looking at me should make me stop and think. It should worry me. Instead, I walk briskly to the closet and throw the box onto the highest shelf. "The candles can't bring anyone back." I slam the closet door closed. "Now go to bed."

As soon as they're gone, I hate myself. I should run after them. Apologize. Bring them back, do the candle ritual. Ask London what she thinks of another option I found for what we could call ourselves—*arcanists*. A fine word. A little stuffy, in my opinion, but what does she think?

I should sleep, too. I haven't gotten much lately, and the exhaustion is catching up with me. A more well-rested version of me wouldn't have snapped at two little kids like that.

I shouldn't go to the forest.

I'm going to, but I shouldn't.

I still can't risk the tunnel. I ask my vine to grow again. The rain stopped hours ago, so I land on dry ground.

It's good my feet know the way, because my brain is full of *you really fucked up this time, you have to stop this, it's not worth it if you're going to hurt them, but I have to find Jane and Winnie, but—*

"Penny for your thoughts?"

"Shit!" I gasp, stepping backwards. "You scared the hell out of me."

"You're the one who was lost in a daydream somewhere," Claire says.

"Not as nice as a daydream," I say.

"Do you want to talk about it?"

I shake my head. "No. I came here to learn magic and save my sisters, not complain about my anxiety."

"Are you sure?"

I smile to show how sure and totally fine I am. "Yeah. Actually, I was wondering—could you teach me to grow a giant tree?"

"Growing a giant tree would be nothing for you. I told you, you're going to build dreams. Don't you want to dream a little bigger?"

"Bigger than 'giant tree'?"

Claire laughs, and it feels like a brush of starlight. I want to make her laugh again. "Bigger doesn't have to mean *bigger.*" She spreads out her arms. "But . . . sure, we can start with a giant tree."

The forest already being full of trees and not having much room for a giant new one, I don't actually grow a giant tree. Instead, I grow more and more trees inside a cluster of trees, until they've wrapped around each other, merged, turned into something like a giant tree.

Close enough.

Maybe next time I can work on bringing it down.

"Are you happy here?" Claire asks as we sit beneath the canopy of my tree(s). "In the house, I mean. With Frank."

"I was happier before my sisters disappeared, of course."

"And how happy was that?"

I shrug, pulling up a few blades of grass. "Frank takes care of us. Teaches us. Keeps us safe."

"We've established he isn't very good at teaching you," Claire says. "He couldn't even get you to grow some snowdrops, could he?"

"Yeah, yeah, I get it, you're a better teacher," I say, laughing.

Claire doesn't laugh. She's looking at me gravely. "What I mean is—he's not very good at teaching you. Maybe you should think about how good he is at keeping you safe."

After she says it, it's hard to think about anything else. On the walk home—which is way too late, it's almost dawn—the same images flash through my mind. The last time I saw Jane. The last time I saw Winnie. Maybe he's *not* keeping us safe right now. But he's not actively hurting us. The memory of Frank punching the wall joins the images of Jane and Winnie. I shake it away. That's not the same as hurting us.

It's not.

For all my belief that Frank wouldn't purposely and physically hurt us, I still freeze on the spot when I see his pickup truck. He's back. And, naturally, upon noticing the large vine outside my bedroom window that wasn't there when he left, he had to go investigate.

I consider running. I could do that. He hasn't seen me yet. I could run back to the forest and hide until . . .

Until when? I'm not going to disappear, give my siblings another sister they think is gone forever. I'm still not brave enough to make the first move. I wait until he sees me.

His face is . . . blank. No anger. No nothing.

Maybe I should run.

Frank doesn't say anything. He goes inside, I follow. I already know where this is going.

I don't look at Frank as I walk past him into the time-out room. I don't want to see that blank mask again. I'd rather he yell. I'd rather he be disappointed.

He doesn't say how long the time-out is going to be. He

doesn't say anything, or even wait for me to sit before he slams the door.

I shut my eyes tight and cover my ears with my hands, but it doesn't matter. Light still pierces my eyelids. The layered, discordant humming still suffocates me.

I still cry.

I still stand there, a turn of a doorknob away from relief, and I don't even try to get out. I just sob and wait for it to end.

I don't know how long that takes. Time gets too distorted. When Frank finally, *finally* opens the door, he's holding his morning newspaper, like he's just on his way to breakfast.

"So," he says. "I think you know that you have some explaining to do."

"I'm sorry," I whisper. "I . . ."

One of the more insidious parts of the time-out room is that it's impossible to use your stay in it to come up with a believable lie. You can't string enough coherent thoughts together for that. You usually start to forget why you're in there in the first place. It takes several moments to pull my thoughts together.

"I was looking for them," I say. "Jane. And Winnie. I couldn't sleep, thinking about them being out in the forest alone and lost, so I went looking. I know—I know I

shouldn't have, I know you were looking for them, but . . .
I couldn't sleep."

Frank nods thoughtfully. "Well. Okay."

". . . Okay?"

"Okay. Let's have breakfast." He nods again and walks
away, leaving the door open.

It has to be a test. But I don't know what the test is,
much less the answer. I also know that I'm not staying in
this room and waiting for him to change his mind.

I didn't think my day could get much worse until I'm
in the kitchen, with Frank and all of my siblings, and none
of them are looking at me. The closest I get to acknowl-
edgement at breakfast—and *all day*—is a little smile from
Violet.

I spend that entire day alone. I try to talk to Brooke,
our peacekeeper, but she glares at me and shakes her head.
I back off.

I can't blame them. I deserve at least some shunning,
don't I? For the drugging, if nothing else—and they don't
even know about that. On the bright side, it's another day
of chores. Those can distract me from the silent treatment
I'm getting from my siblings.

The silent treatment from Frank might be worse. Time-
out doesn't seem like enough punishment for being found
outside. There should be a lecture, an interrogation. Waiting to see what he'll do next is killing me, but I also don't

want to remind him. I'm not eager for whatever he's cooking up.

After dinner, Frank retreats to his rooms. My siblings stay in the living room to knit and read and put on a movie. I sit in my big chair and stare out to the forest. Maybe now's when I run. Maybe I belong there more than I belong here. Claire would welcome me, wouldn't she? Maybe . . .

"I found another word," London says. I whip my head around, startled. She's standing beside my chair, holding the dictionary open. Everyone's watching us.

"Yeah?" I say. My voice cracks. "A magic one?"

London nods. "I found it looking for a word of the day." She peeks at the page she has it open to. *"Druid?"*

"I think druids are more nature-based," I say. "So I could be one. But I want a word that fits all of us."

London nods solemnly. "Me too."

There's no discussion about it. We all have the same idea. We get ready for bed—change into PJs, brush our teeth—and convene in my room. I get the candle box down from the high shelf in the closet. Brooke puts the candles on the sill, and Olivia lights them.

We sit there together, looking out to the stars in silence, for a long time.

I don't know if I'm forgiven. I don't know if I deserve forgiveness, not yet. I know I want to earn it. I know that I'm not going to the forest tonight.

One by one, everyone falls asleep. Elle, Irene, and Olivia take over my bed. Brooke falls asleep leaning against the wall. London curls up in my desk chair. Violet falls asleep with their head in my lap.

Jane's bed goes untouched, and I stay awake, gazing out that window.

"You want to go," Violet whispers, surprising me. I thought they were asleep. "Don't you?"

"Yeah," I whisper. No reason to lie about that anymore. "Really badly."

"I wouldn't tell anyone if you did," they offer.

I run my fingers across their hair, smiling. "Thanks. But you should never lie for me, not to our sisters, okay?"

". . . So I could lie to Frank?"

I snort. "Yeah. Lie to him, if you can get away with it." My smile falls. "If you think he already knows, though, don't. That's a test and you can't fail it, not even for me."

Violet considers that, then shakes their head. "That's not fair."

"What?"

"You can't say I'm not allowed to protect you. You'd do it for me. I'd do it for you."

"Of course I would. I'm your big sister."

"And I'm your little sibling. Still family. So you don't get to tell me I'm not allowed to protect you." Violet shifts their head off my lap and lies down. They tug on my arm until I lie with them. "Get some sleep," they say. "It'll be better in the morning."

I do try to sleep. I get comfortable, I close my eyes. It even works for a little while. I would have gotten something close to a full night's sleep if the nightmare hadn't come back.

It's the version where my parents are in the front seat, unconscious. No matter how I shake them and cry, they don't wake up. The car is sinking and the doors won't open and they won't wake up. Their heads are bloody, like they were hit. Something antlered swims past. The water rises, rises, rises, and I scream.

When I wake up, I'm shaking. Disoriented.

Somewhere outside, a voice that's Jane and Winnie and Claire all at once calls my name.

# 13

IT'S MONDAY. DESPITE everything, that means it's test day. It's raining again, so we can't go outside. Frank has us all in the living room instead. He nodded at me pleasantly this morning, so I guess that's a step in the right direction. There's still a pit of foreboding in my stomach, though, because there's just no way he's letting me off that easy.

Violet's up now. They stand in the middle of the living room with Elle acting as their model. With each wave of Violet's hand, Elle's clothes shift in style and color, and she twirls, showing off Violet's creation.

I love watching Violet work. When I came to the lake house, I hated clothes. Even at nine, I was aware of how my fatness limited my clothing. Girls' clothes didn't fit me right. Neither did the adult clothes—and they didn't really look right on a preteen, anyway. I wore T-shirts and sweatpants and a couple pairs of adult jeans that my mother hemmed, and that was it.

Then I met Violet.

They arrived at the lake house shy and uncertain, but given the freedom and encouragement to glamour themselves into anything they wanted, they *flourished*. They experiment the most with clothes, favoring anything with huge sleeves they can flap like wings. They don't often glamour their face other than hiding blemishes or, when they're in an especially good mood, dusting glitter across their cheeks like freckles.

As Violet flourished, they brought the rest of us with them. They glamoured our clothes, seeking whatever made us feel the most like ourselves. They don't shy away from our fatness—not their own, mine, Winnie's, Brooke's. It's not an obstacle or even a challenge, it's just another canvas, and it's one they often love to put on display. Through Violet, I learned to love the way a tank top showed off my upper arms or revealed the full shape of my stomach.

"Wonderful, as always," Frank says. "Show me something with her face."

Violet hesitates. Theoretically, their glamours should allow them to make anything look like—well, anything—but they've always had an affinity for cloth. They're great at glamouring their own body, but attempts to alter someone else's have never worked right. It's like the glamour struggles to keep up with the movements of the subject. If they stay perfectly still, you won't notice, but even a turn of the head can send a new nose sliding out of place. Makeup is easier, but we all know that's not exactly what Frank is asking for.

Violet tries it anyway. They pass a hand over Elle's face. I've been the model enough times that I know exactly what it feels like. The cool mist of Violet's magic is a comforting chill, like running through a sprinkler in summer.

I gasp, and so do several others. Olivia claps her little hands in wonder.

Elle's freckles now glow like little stars. Her blond hair is shot through with silver, not like natural gray hair, but like tinsel from a Christmas tree. Her eyes have gone blacker than black, blacker than coal. She pulls aside the collar of her shirt and we see the little pearls studding her collarbone.

She looks like a girl someone dreamed up out of the mist, like if I blink, she'll disappear. It's a more fantastic look than Violet often goes for, and it's stunning. We all rush in to compliment the work, leaving Violet blushing.

Frank frowns.

"I was hoping for something more transformative. Haven't we been talking about elevating your glamours into disguising the very shape of someone, not just surface details?"

Violet's face falls. "We have. I've been practicing, but it's not—I'm not *ready*."

"How long until you are? You've been here for almost three years. You've advanced, certainly. Your eye for detail has improved, and your glamours last longer than ever." Frank flashes them that father-smile. "Do you remember when you first got here, for a glamour to hold, you had to concentrate on it the entire time? Now you're able to make changes that are seemingly permanent. But why only to clothes? When will you outgrow fashion and be able to dedicate yourself to something truly challenging?"

My palms tingle and anxiety whispers through my arms and throat as if I'm the one being scolded. I avert my eyes from Violet. They wouldn't want any of us to see if they cry.

*Magic shouldn't feel like a test.*

"By our next test in two weeks, I need to see real progress. I don't just want pretty colors and distracting lights. I want shapeshifting. Can you do that?"

"Yes," Violet whispers.

"Good." Frank leans back in his chair and takes notes on his tablet while Violet scurries away, hiding in the back.

Next is Irene. Along with training to use her magic to track people, Frank has also had her practicing direct telepathic communication. She still can't do full sentences, but she can get across words and pictures. In today's test she successfully transmits pictures of pandas to Olivia while they're both in the living room, and again of giraffes when Olivia's by the stairs. But when Frank sends Olivia to the basement, nothing comes through at all.

It's a pretty good showing, but Frank still isn't satisfied. He sighs, tapping a *lot* of notes into his iPad, and moves on.

"Last but not least, we have Elle."

Elle skips obediently to the center of the room. "Ready!" she chirps.

"And for your volunteer . . ." Frank scans our group.

That foreboding pit in my stomach deepens into pure dread when his eyes land on me.

"Derry," he says. "Would you assist?"

This isn't the first time he's used a test as a punishment. Knowing I don't have a choice, I stand next to Elle. She's picking at her nails. I hear desperate whispering, and glance over to see Irene comforting London.

"It's okay," Irene whispers. "You know how Elle's test works."

But London looks at me with wide, worried eyes, as if she can sense this one is different. I smile and waggle my fingers at her in a wave. It does little to comfort her.

Frank brings Elle the knife.

Technically, Elle could choose to cut herself. Frank has told her as much. But she's too scared of the pain. She's told us, and I'm sure told herself, that cutting us barely counts anyway. Frank provides a sharp knife. Elle's a fast healer. The pain is so short that we probably don't *actually* feel that much of it. Elle's certain that the majority of the pain is a psychological response, not a physiological one, and so it's not her fault if we can't control it.

She only tried to volunteer herself once. It was the only

time I can remember Frank being truly angry at her. She'd wandered off during one of our rare trips outside. We were all in the backyard, meant to stay together, but Frank found Elle in the lake.

On her next test, he called Irene's name. The more Elle protested and said she'd cut herself, the greater his anger. Irene had to make her do it. Elle cut her sister, crying the whole time.

She's never argued with his choice since. Every once in a while, he'll remind her that she can cut herself. She never does.

Elle takes the knife from Frank and takes a deep breath. The smile she aims my way is strained. "Ready?"

I hold out my arm and, because I know she hates it, I don't break eye contact. It makes her falter. She has to steel herself before the slice.

It *is* a sharp knife, and it *does* cut cleanly, but I don't care what Elle says. It hurts. I shudder, waiting for the itch of her magic.

"One moment." Frank approaches and looms over us, examining my arm. Blood is dripping, warm across my skin. "Heal it, but then cut again. Deeper. It might be easier if you stab, actually. We know you can heal these little surface wounds, but what about something that truly requires you to stitch the flesh back together?" He gestures to the widest part of my forearm. "Maybe through there—nothing too major to hit. And stab to the side, we don't want you hitting bone."

Elle and I both gape at him in horror. Of course Frank has had Elle cut deeper, although usually when he wants to challenge her, he has her heal a multitude of smaller cuts. I've wondered what his limits would be. The most natural progression, to me, would lead to things like breaking bones to see if she can mend them, or cutting off a finger to see if she can stitch it back on, or, well, true stab wounds. What can Elle do with a punctured organ or slashed vein?

Those ideas always seemed too ridiculous. He would never put us at that much risk.

"Frank," Elle says carefully. "I'm not sure I'm ready for that. I think it's a good next step, but a stab like you're talking about—it's many more layers than I'm used to. Skin, fat, flesh, and what if I hit a vein or a tendon? I'd feel more confident if I had a chance to work on my speed first. Look."

Elle holds my wrist in one hand, hovering the other over the still-bleeding cut in my arm. She counts out the seconds under her breath, and I count out the time between lightning and thunder.

When it's done, she says, "Thirteen seconds." She looks up at Frank, but doesn't quite meet his eyes. She's good at submission. "Pretty fast, if you ask me, but a deeper injury would take longer, and every second would count. If you think it makes sense, I'd like to wait on attempting stab wounds until I'm under ten seconds for this type of cut."

Frank takes a long time to answer, long enough that Elle's hand on my wrist starts to tremble.

"It does make sense," he says. "But you won't get better if you don't push yourself." He walks to the kitchen island. "Derry, put your arm down here. That'll make it easier."

"No," I say automatically.

His expression turns dark. "Yes. Don't you want your sister to become a better, stronger alchemist? Put. Your arm. Here."

It's absolutely silent in the room. On shaking legs, I cross to the kitchen island. I lay my arm across the wooden surface.

"Elle?" Frank calls. She's frozen in the middle of the living room. "Come here, please."

"Y-yes. Of course." She scurries to join us. The knife trembles in her hands. "Uhm—where, again—I don't . . ." She takes a deep breath, steadies herself. "I don't want to hit anything vital until I know I can handle a deep wound."

"Naturally," Frank says. He laughs. "We aren't trying to *kill* Derry or anything. Just a little stab, right about here," he says, pointing again to the thickest part of my forearm. "To the side. Not too close to the wrist."

I make eye contact with Elle again. Tears are streaming down her cheeks.

"It's okay," I whisper.

I'm not brave enough to watch. I squeeze my eyes shut.

Elle's training has always been barreling down this path. One day, someone was going to get stabbed or have a bone broken. If I take the injury, that means someone else doesn't have to. That makes it easier to bear, doesn't it?

Not really. I scream when the stab comes.

"I'm sorry, I'm sorry, I'm sorry," she whispers. The knife clatters to the island. Blood is everywhere and it's not stopping. "Oh, god—I'm sorry—" She grabs my arm, squeezes, putting pressure on the wound. I cry out and Elle keeps whispering *I'm sorry I'm sorry I'm sorry.* At least it doesn't itch so much this time. Can't feel it over the pain.

The pain lessens. The wound stitches back together. I wipe at the blood, making sure it's completely closed. Elle's hands are covered in red.

"Wonderful," Frank breathes. "Absolutely wonderful. Let's take a quick break before the flowers, shall we?"

As Frank leaves, Irene rushes to Elle, who leans into her. Elle's arms are wrapped protectively around her stomach. That test had to have hurt her, too. She still won't tell Frank, of course. If he knew that excessive healing can bring out deep, gnawing pains in her stomach, he might see her as defective.

I'd forgotten that Frank made this into a show for all of our siblings. Brooke is holding the little twins, rocking them, while Violet trembles next to her.

"I'm sorry," Elle says again. She turns her head toward me, still leaning into Irene. "I shouldn't have . . ."

"No," I say. "Nothing to apologize for. You didn't have a choice."

"I did," she whispers. She returns to pressing her forehead against Irene's shoulder. Her voice is muffled when she says, "I just didn't make the right one." Footsteps mark Frank's return, and Elle sits up, smiling as if she's in no pain at all.

He frowns. "You two should get cleaned up. Irene, take care of . . ." He waves a hand over the blood-drenched kitchen island. ". . . that, will you?"

Blood loss and trauma or not, I still have to do my test. It's . . . fine. Mediocre. I'd wanted to show off what I could do with Claire, but with Frank watching, I can't. My flowers wilt as soon as they bloom.

So it's a surprise to all of us when my flower flashes so bright during the evaluation that I have to close my eyes against it. I feel a surge of pride, followed quickly by fear. What will Frank think? What possible reason could there be in his mind for my magic to grow so much, so fast?

He doesn't say anything. His brow furrows as he taps on his iPad, and he moves on.

That night, I return to the forest. I wait until I'm sure everyone's asleep. They're all in their own rooms now, and I guess no one's thinking about my transgressions anymore. No one guards the tunnel—I go right through. Not risking the vine again.

"Claire?" I call as I enter the forest. "Are you here?"

"Derry." She appears out of nowhere, as usual. "You came back." She says it like she knew I would. She says it like it was a done deal before I even decided to return.

"I'm sorry I wasn't here yesterday," I say. "It's been . . . hard at home."

She looks me over, head to toe. "Something happened."

"Yeah, but I don't want to talk about it." She sounds so concerned, and it makes me . . . angry. "I need to find Jane and Winnie."

"I know. But you aren't ready yet."

I laugh. "Are you serious?"

"I'm not sure why you think I wouldn't be."

"By what standards are you measuring my *readiness*, exactly? Yours? Because you told me magic isn't a test. Frank makes it a test because he's trying to teach me, and that's apparently bad, but it gets to be a test when my sisters are *missing?*" I'm shouting, but I lower my voice, letting my next words come out sharp and cruel. "I don't come out here so another Frank can manipulate me with some bullshit tests."

Claire regards me coolly, unimpressed with my anger. "I said, you aren't ready yet. I'll thank you not to argue with me when you have no idea what you're talking about."

Temper flaring, I step up close to her, getting in her face. "What I know is that you're keeping my sisters from me and I've had enough. You're going to take me to them, *now*—"

I don't see Claire move. I feel the push, and I go flying backwards. I land hard on the ground. The wind is knocked out of me. As I struggle to sit up, Claire smooths her hands down her dress.

"I'm not saying this because your magic isn't up to *my* standards," she says in a clipped voice. "It's fact. Your sisters are lost in this forest, and only power can bring them back." She looks me in the eye. "You don't have enough."

We stare at each other in tense silence. Claire sighs, walks over to me, and holds out a hand. "If you're done throwing a tantrum, I had a challenge for you tonight that I thought you'd enjoy."

"It wasn't a tantrum," I mutter. I ignore her hand and stand up on my own. The pressure of her hands on my chest as she pushed me feels too recent. It was a glimpse of a Claire that used to send me running. "What's the test?" I ask. My anger is dying out and I sound petulant.

She purses her lips disapprovingly, but if she has another reprimand in mind, she doesn't voice it. "Is there something you thought about growing, but you didn't believe it was possible, so you never thought to try?" she asks. "Maybe never even thought to *hope*. Just a little daydream. Nothing that could be real, of course."

I go still in the act of brushing myself off. I have the answer immediately, but is it really something I want to grow? Sure, I keep sketching it, and it shows up in my dreams, but . . .

"Maybe," I say carefully. "I might have something like that."

Claire's crooked smile makes its first appearance of the night. She never smiles with teeth. I hadn't really registered that before, but tonight it makes me shudder. It makes me wonder what she's hiding.

"Then grow it," she says. I look at her doubtfully. She only continues to smile.

I get down on my knees. I press my hands into the ground, dig my fingers in. Claire kneels beside me, so close that I would feel the heat of her if there was heat to feel. Her proximity feels dangerous now, but I don't want her to move.

"Ask the earth for a dream," she whispers.

I don't have the words to send into the ground. Only images. The curve of a tree limb, the flare of glowing flowers. Even the inspiration for this dream wasn't something

I *saw*. I was able to draw it before I ever encountered it, before I felt its breath on my neck. Some primal part of my brain knew it, latched on, wound itself around those antlers as they reached into the forest canopy.

The lightning bugs descend around me, circling my head like a crown as I feed the earth my dreams. I close my eyes tight. All I can hear is my own breath, my own heartbeat.

And then a step.

Tears I didn't realize I'd even cried blur my vision for a moment, until I rub them away and lift my gaze upward to the creature stepping toward us.

It's vaguely human shaped, and made of intertwined branches. The roses woven among those branches glow like the lightning bugs. It has no mouth and no eyes and no anything except for that basic form—two legs, two feet, two arms, two hands, a torso, a head, and those *antlers*. Massive, magnificent antlers ringed in glowing roses.

"Beautiful," Claire breathes.

"Did I . . ." I swallow, hard. "Did I make that?"

"Didn't you intend to?"

"Yes, but . . ." Everything I'm feeling is too big. Emotion after emotion swelling up in my chest until I can hardly breathe. Pride. Anxiety. Fear. *Love*. There's a living thing walking the earth that exists because of *me*. I made that. It's not the creature I felt in the forest days ago. That was something else, something old, something I may never truly see with my own eyes. Something I don't *want* to see, when just thinking of it fills me with dread.

But this? This is *mine*.

Slowly, I rise to my feet. There are no eyes, but I feel my creation watch me as I approach. After a long moment, it bows. I laugh breathlessly, and bow in return.

My creation doesn't stay for long. Its head cocks to the side, as if it hears something, and it wanders off into the forest.

"Wait—" I reach out an arm, but Claire pushes it down.

"Let it go. You made it, but it belongs to itself. You'll see it again."

My heart aches with it out of my sight. Something I made out of a dream lives in this forest now. I can't begin to guess the implications of that. What impact could it have on the ecosystem? What does it eat, if anything? This isn't like growing a flower. This is my magic being *real* and leaving footprints in the earth.

"Can I ask you something?" I say. "Something I've been wondering."

"Of course."

I turn to her and look her in the eye. "Are you Claire, or are you the forest?"

She does that curious owl-tilt of her head. "I don't see why you have to make the distinction."

It's not a satisfactory answer, but I suspect it's all I'll get for now. Instead of pushing, I say, "Frank did something today. Something that makes me worried about what else he could do."

"Anything," Claire says. "Never underestimate him. Whenever you think *Surely he wouldn't,* know that he would."

I laugh, and she doesn't. She's not kidding. It has to be hyperbole, though.

"I can think of plenty of things he'd never do," I say. It's not like he would have stabbed me himself. He's never asked Irene to invade our privacy by learning to read minds, even though she thinks she could. He's never made London do anything too terrible with her magic, and she can do terrible things. She told me about a nightmare she had once. In it, she used her magic to pull at a person's torso until the skin and flesh parted and their intestines came into view. It didn't bleed like a wound. Just a window. But the person screamed and screamed.

I told her it was just a nightmare, but she shook her head and whispered, "I could do it, though. If I tried. Don't tell Frank, please?"

Claire heaves a huge sigh. "You really don't know anything."

"Excuse me?"

"You don't. You're standing there completely unable to

see past his pathetic facade, and it's going to get you and your siblings killed."

I rear back at *killed*. "Okay, seriously, that's enough. I know he's done some shitty things, but—"

Now Claire laughs, but it's like mine was earlier—humorless. Like she's echoing me again. "I thought you were smarter than this. You need to stop being so obtuse if you ever want to be powerful enough to find your sisters."

"Not powerful enough? After I made *that?*" I gesture emphatically in the direction my creature went.

"You made yourself a little friend. Impressive, but no, you still aren't there yet. Power is more than what you can make."

"What does that even *mean?*" I shout. "If you know all the goddamn answers, why won't you just tell me?"

"Maybe because you keep proving you aren't ready for them," Claire sneers.

Anger blurs my vision. I lash out. Thick, sharp vines shoot out of the ground, rocket toward Claire. I scream, trying to take it back. It's too late. It's too late—

The vines go right through her.

I stumble back, gasping for air. Claire didn't even flinch, but my heart is pounding painfully and I'm shaking so hard I can barely brush the small purple leaves off my arms as they grow.

I can't lose control like that. I thought the first . . .

incident was also the last. Just a one-time unfortunate event, something I'll agonize about for the rest of my life, but nothing I'd ever do again. Does it matter that Claire is all fog and mist and magic, not flesh and blood and bone? Does it matter that I didn't—maybe couldn't—hurt her?

Or does it only matter that I wanted to, and that I *tried?*

Claire doesn't call after me as I run off. I guess she knows I'll always come back.

I descend into the tunnel, lighting the way. I'm so absorbed in my thoughts that I don't notice I'm not alone until I nearly stumble into them.

Brooke and Elle are waiting for me at the end of the tunnel.

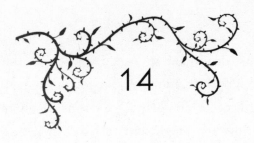

14

'YOU'RE TELLING US everything,' Brooke signs angrily. Elle stands next to her, arms crossed tightly, glaring at me. Her anger doesn't seem to include much of the concern I see in Brooke.

Any other night, I would have argued. But tonight, in the aftermath of Elle's test and what I tried to do to Claire, with the weight of what happened in the clearing fresh in my mind, with my sisters looking at me like that, I burst into tears.

I hate crying in front of people, even my siblings. At least we're still on the other side of the wall, so no one can hear me. Brooke and Elle let me cry—they don't try to interrupt, don't try to comfort me. When I finally calm down enough to swipe at my eyes and nose, square my shoulders, and face them, they act as if nothing happened. They spare me the embarrassment of being seen, or the new wave of tears that would surely start if they asked how I am.

'I don't know where to start,' I sign.

'Why do you keep going back to the forest?' Brooke asks.

How do I word this? 'The forest is magic.' Understate-

ment. 'And I think it can help me find Jane and Winnie.'
True, but . . .

Elle drags her hands down her face, then signs, 'They're dead. We have to accept it.'

I recoil as if slapped. 'How can you say that?'

'Where are they, then?' Elle demands.

Brooke holds up her hands, interrupting. 'That's not what we're here to talk about. Derry, the bigger issue is that you've been lying to us. You've been sneaking out, putting yourself in danger. I know you made the little twins cry the other night, and you've been putting us' — Brooke gestures to herself and Elle — 'through absolute hell trying to get you to just *talk to us*.'

I stomp my foot, like a child on the verge of a tantrum. 'You don't understand.'

'What's to understand?' Elle asks. 'You're being shitty to everyone, and it's all for a bunch of stupid trees!'

'It's not just trees!' It's magic. It's power. It's the being I created that's walking in that forest right now, alive, because of *me*. 'I'm looking for Jane and Winnie —'

'Who are dead.' She fingerspells *dead,* putting emphasis on each letter. 'D-E-A-D. Maybe you should pay attention to the siblings you still have.'

'Just because you don't care enough to look for them —'

Elle gasps. "How *dare* you," she hisses. "I'd be out there with you if there was a chance they were still alive."

"You goddamn *bi*—"

Brooke inserts herself physically between us. She looks at us both reprovingly, like we're children and she can't believe our behavior. 'Enough is enough. Elle—this isn't how we're going to solve anything. Derry—that forest . . . it's like . . .' One hand waves about as she searches for the words. 'A virus. It's infected you, and you aren't acting like yourself.'

She spares us each one more glance. 'If neither of you are going to take action to actually *end* this, then I will.' Brooke pushes past us in the tunnel, stomping outside. She leaves me and Elle stunned in her wake, trying to parse what she means.

"What is she . . ." I trail off.

Elle's confusion is slowly replaced by realization, then by a small smile. "My guess? She's burning down your forest. And I'm going to go watch." She turns, jogging after Brooke. My heart has dropped all the way into my stomach.

She can't. Brooke's powerful, but that doesn't mean she could destroy a whole forest. She wouldn't, even if she could.

. . . Or would she, if she thought it had infected me like a virus? If she believes, like Elle, that Jane and Winnie are dead? If I were her, and I believed those things, and I'd just seen the fight Elle and I had, I'd probably see burning the forest as the right move. She's already lost two sisters, and she thinks she's losing me.

So she's going to protect me, at any cost.

If anyone can understand that, it's me.

But what Brooke and Elle don't understand is that our sisters are *still alive* and the forest is our only shot at getting them back. I stumble into a sprint, racing after them. I didn't think fast enough, I'm going to be too late, the forest will already be burning.

I emerge into the night. Brooke has planted herself at the edge of the trees, feet digging into the mud. Elle stands back from the coming flames. I shout for her. She turns, looks me up and down, and does nothing to stop Brooke. I feel the magic before she releases it.

I've always known that Brooke is the most powerful alchemist in the house. Even if she never says it, the blinding glow of her flower gives it away. I never understood exactly what that meant until the wall of flames towers over us. It roars loud enough for me to worry that Frank will hear it from way across the lake. The flames climb high, reaching for the stars, and then, with a push, Brooke sends them cascading over the forest.

I scream. Fire plummets between the trees and swirls through their leaves like a living thing. It's too easy to imagine it overtaking the lightning bugs and catching my creature by surprise. Burning up my only lead on Jane and Winnie. I don't know if fire can hurt Claire, but I scream my throat raw for her, too.

For a moment, the world stands still.

Brooke's fire hangs in the air, shimmering, and then dissipates until it's nothing but sparks rising to the sky and a thick cloud of smoke. Confused, Brooke brings her hands back up and conjures a breeze to banish the smoke.

The forest is untouched. A bright full moon shows the trees unscathed, uncharred.

"What the fuck," Elle whispers.

Brooke's signs come out in pieces. She's unsteady on her feet. 'How—the rain—if it were drier . . .'

I don't respond. We all know it has nothing to do with wet wood. Her fire should have taken hold and spread. Even if it couldn't become a wildfire that took down every acre, a few trees should have been destroyed.

Instead, impossibly, there are several *new* trees. They're all babies, barely to my hip, but they're real and new and they shouldn't have been able to grow that fast. It's like the forest took Brooke's magic and turned it into new growth.

We stare at the impossible trees for a long time before Brooke, without a word, walks back to the tunnel. Elle and I don't look at each other, don't talk—we just follow her. Nothing is said or signed between the three of us all the way back to the house. Brooke puts a hand on my arm before I can climb the stairs up to our rooms. Elle stops too, until Brooke nods at her. Elle hesitates, looks at me in a way I can't translate, then hurries upstairs.

'Don't go back,' Brooke signs. 'Promise me. It's too dangerous.'

My hands come up, ready to argue. Brooke stops me with a shake of her head. 'Please. Promise me.'

I don't want to. I'm too scared it'll be a lie. The way the forest killed that fire should be enough to warn me off. It's a blazing neon sign saying SOMETHING IS WRONG HERE.

It's had the opposite effect. I want to go back and learn how it did that. That's where the power is. That's where I learn to find Jane and Winnie.

But Brooke's lip is quivering even though she's trying hard to conceal it, and her hands shake when she signs.

I bring my index finger to my lips, and spread my hand flat as it lowers to meet the closed fist I've made of my other hand. 'Promise.'

Brooke smiles weakly. 'Thank you.'

I follow her upstairs, each step taking me farther from the forest. Taking my breath away. I close my bedroom door and lean into it, trying to breathe slowly. My brain is a mess, all *she doesn't have to know if you go back* and *you can't break a promise* and *you have to break it* and—

I can't go back, not tonight. Even if I hadn't been

caught . . . I rub at my eyes. I'll have to break my promise to Brooke, because the promise to find Jane and Winnie overrides it, but I can at least keep it for one night.

I lay in bed, trying to sleep. I manage a fitful doze, waking almost every ten minutes for an hour. The third or fourth time I wake up, my throat is dry. I try to get back to sleep, but that dry throat is all I can focus on. Frustrated, I sneak downstairs in search of water. I'm on my way back with glass in hand, nearly to the stairs, when the sound snags me. At first, I think I imagine it. It's distant and quiet. It comes again.

I walk tentatively down the hall, toward where I think it's coming from. There—a weird, high moaning sound. It almost sounds like someone in pain.

It's coming from the basement.

I never go down to the basement unless I'm on laundry duty or there's a tornado warning, and for the laundry, I won't go at night. The stairs are the wooden kind with empty space behind each step, begging to either trip you or let a hand sneak in and grab your ankle. The basement itself is unfinished stone, and always cold, even if you sit with your back against the dryer. The lights don't reach the corners and there's too much space behind the water heater and furnace for something to hide.

The last thing I want is to walk down those stairs in the

middle of the night, and for the life of me, I can't fathom who it would be. I press my ear to the door. Maybe Frank is running a late load of laundry? Sometimes the dryer squeals, the pitch rising and falling in a way that could sound like an anguished moan, I guess. That could be what I'm hearing.

I touch the doorknob.

Nearby, a door shuts, and then loud, boot-laden footsteps. Frank's awake and he's walking around his rooms. I run, holding tight on to my glass of water. I'm five steps up and out of sight when I hear his door open into the hallway, right by where I was standing seconds before. Another few seconds later and I'm burrowed into bed, water shoved onto the nightstand with haphazardly tossed glasses.

I hold my breath even as my lungs burn from the sprint. I have to listen. If he heard me, if he's coming up the stairs, I need to be ready.

Several moments pass. I let out a slow breath. A minute goes by, and another, until I'm able to breathe normally. My eyelids slip closed as my adrenaline crashes. Distantly, I think I hear the front door open and close. I wonder why Frank would be going out so late at night, but sleep claims me and I forget I heard anything at all.

The first thing I feel when I wake up hours later is Irene. Her panic radiates through me, which is enough to raise my own panic. Irene is usually careful about letting anyone feel her thoughts and emotions. If she's lost control of that, something is very, very wrong.

Footsteps come up the stairs, down the hall. Irene skids to a stop in my doorway. I sit up and when I put my glasses on, the wild, scared look on her eyes becomes clear.

"Have you seen Elle?" she asks.

"No, I just woke up. Why?"

"Because she's gone!" Irene says, voice raising into a shout, then coming back down into something fast and frantic. "When I woke up, she wasn't in our room, and I thought she'd just gone down to start breakfast, but she wasn't in the kitchen and Brooke hasn't seen her and no one has seen her, and I can't . . . I can't *hear* her. I keep trying to talk to her." She presses her fingers to her temple, the skin dimpling from the pressure. "I can't hear her."

The pain on her face is real and raw, and I know we're thinking the same thing.

The last time we couldn't find someone, we never got them back. Even if Jane and Winnie aren't dead, they're not *here*.

"We'll find her," I say. I swing my legs out of bed and stand up, grabbing a hair tie off the nightstand so I can pull my hair back into a more efficient ponytail. Now that I'm more awake and focused, I can hear the commotion downstairs as others search for Elle. "Is Frank looking for her?"

Irene shakes her head. "I couldn't find him. He doesn't know she's gone yet."

"Have you checked the tunnel?"

"No. I should have. Right? I should." There's a plea in her voice, asking me to tell her what to do. With her emotions so unguarded, I can feel them almost as if they're my own. She's lost sight of which way is up.

"Yes. Hurry. Check the whole tunnel, but don't go outside. There's no time. You need to be back before Frank comes asking for you."

Except it's already too late. The lower register of Frank's voice cuts through my siblings calling for Elle.

Something snaps in Irene. She runs downstairs, with me following as close as I can. Frank is in the living room with the rest of our siblings. I guess I was the last to know.

"Where have you been?" Irene demands. I wince. Hopefully, Frank gives Irene a pass on that kind of tone, given the circumstances. "Elle's gone! Where were you?"

"I was just getting caught up on the situation," he says calmly. It doesn't escape my notice that he didn't really answer the question. "Have you searched everywhere?"

"Yes!" Irene says, too close to a shout for anyone's comfort. "And I can't hear her."

"Your range isn't that wide," Violet offers. "Maybe she's just outside of it."

Irene shakes her head. "I can't hear her," she says again.

"We'll find her," Frank says. I search his face for any hint of if Irene will be forgiven, or if he's just tallying up every mark against her for later, after Elle is found. "Everyone—split up, search the whole house again. I'll look outside."

"Let me come with you," Irene says. "If she's out there, if I'm closer—"

"Absolutely not. This is the third one of you who's gone missing. No one leaves this house until I have answers."

Irene clearly wants to argue, but I bump her hand with mine. It's enough to deflate her. She buries her face in her hands until Frank leaves.

'We'll start the search,' Brooke signs to me. 'Look after Irene.' She gathers the others up with her, leaving me with Irene.

"I'm scared," Irene whispers. "I was just talking to Elle about—" She rubs her face. "I was wondering if Frank did something to Jane and Winnie. She called me crazy."

"Frank wouldn't do anything to Elle," I whisper to her, too scared to speak at a normal volume.

The situation is already volatile, and it would be worse if Frank came back in and caught us signing without Brooke around. It's a weird sore spot for him, a paranoia that comes from us communicating in a way he can't. We asked once for books on Spanish, because Violet had been teaching us what little they remembered from their Mexi-

192

can grandparents. We all wanted to know more, and Frank had given us the books for ASL, so why not Spanish?

But he refused. He didn't give us a reason—Frank never has to explain his decisions—but Winnie, Irene, and I had all quietly theorized that languages are hard for him to learn. He hadn't wanted to learn as much ASL as he'd had to learn to spy on us, and he didn't want to learn Spanish, too. Us being able to speak it and him not being able to was out of the question. Brooke tried to supplement Violet's remembered Spanish with what she'd learned to read and write as a child, but none of us were going to achieve any kind of fluency.

"She's his favorite," I continue. "She always does what he wants."

"She's just trying to survive this place," Irene snaps.

"I'm not criticizing her." Of course, I have criticized Elle for just that, but quietly to Winnie when we were alone, usually after one of us had gone under her knife. "I love her," I say. I do. *I do.* "But I'm telling you, if he was going to hurt one of us, it wouldn't be Elle."

I don't know about him hurting Jane or Winnie. It hadn't occurred to me. I saw Jane go into the forest when Frank was nowhere around. He was in his rooms when Winnie disappeared. I don't *think* he could have been involved with either.

"I kept pressing it," Irene whispers. "I kept saying *what if he did something, what if he killed them,* and . . ." She looks around. Frank is nowhere in sight, but still, she steps closer. Lowers her voice still more. "What if this is to punish *me?*"

I search desperately for words to comfort her, but I can't find anything except pretty lies. It wouldn't be the first time Frank had hurt someone to punish another. We were all close, but he knew who was closest to who. I'd been put in time-out when he was actually mad at Jane more than once.

"No," I say. "He'd just put her in time-out. He wouldn't . . ." Wouldn't what? This lack of imagination is exactly what had Claire sneering at me, and I still can't break through it.

"I can't hear her," Irene says. Her voice cracks. She presses her hands over her ears, as if blocking out the world will make Elle loud enough to hear.

I touch her shoulder. Her eyes shine with tears when she looks at me. "We'll find her."

I join our siblings in the search. Violet and Brooke are walking the length of the tunnel, the little twins are checking every closet and under every bed.

I go to the basement.

Ever since Irene said that Elle was missing, there's been a sick feeling in my stomach. I've done the mental math, tallying up the crying I heard with Frank's mysterious departure in the middle of the night, adding Elle's disappearance . . .

All Irene did was call down into the basement, so I'm

the first to really get a good look. I shake the way I do in a particularly bad winter, when the cold gets so deep that the chattering of your teeth travels through your whole body, just under the skin.

I don't want to think that Frank would kill one of us.

But then, I know from experience that people are capable of all sorts of things you wouldn't expect. I've crossed lines that seemed impossibly far away. Frank could have, too.

So I'm half-scared that I'll find a body in the basement. It wouldn't be the worst place to hide one, with how rarely any of us come down here. I'm scared that I'll look into one of the shadowed corners and find Elle slumped, not breathing, already cold.

I look into every corner, and she's not there. There's no evidence that she ever was. The only new thing in the basement is a pile of Frank's dirty laundry heaped near the washer. I glance into the dryer, and sure enough, there's some of his laundry in there, too. Frank doesn't like us to touch any of his property, so he always does his own laundry, minus sheets and pillowcases. It definitely could have been the dryer that I heard last night.

Someone touches my shoulder and I nearly jump out of my skin.

'I'm sorry!' Brooke signs emphatically. I shake my head, steadying myself.

'You're fine,' I sign, heart rate slowly returning to normal. Is there news?'

'No. Have you found anything?' she asks.

'Nothing.'

Brooke nods absentmindedly. She peers into the same corners I already checked, not getting close, just craning her neck to look. Her bottom lip is chapped from anxious nibbling.

'Are you okay?' I ask, even though none of us are okay.

At first, she nods. But that quickly changes, and tears start to fall. She turns away from me. Her shoulders shake. I wonder if I should reach out and hold her the same way she did for me last night, or if that would make it worse. Brooke turns back before I have to make the choice.

'Is this my fault?'

I blink, confused. That's definitely not what I expected.

'What?'

'Is this my fault?' she asks again. 'Last night . . .'

Maybe I'm being obtuse, but I still don't understand. I shake my head and lower my eyebrows the way Brooke taught us to when we ask a question in ASL, though I don't have a specific question to accompany it.

'The forest took Jane and Winnie,' she signs. 'Right?' From what Claire said, it's more that they got lost instead of taken, but my answer doesn't matter. Brooke plows onward. 'Last night, I tried to burn the forest, and today, Elle's gone. She's gone and she was right next to me when I tried to burn it. That can't be a coincidence.'

'I think it is,' I sign. 'Jane went into the forest willingly.' Well. Maybe. 'Winnie may have, too. They just got lost. Elle would never go out alone, and certainly not to the forest.'

'Not if she was in her right mind, but what if she wasn't?'

I'm really struggling to follow her train of thought. 'What do you mean?'

'She was worried about you. She even asked if we should tell Frank.' Brooke signs that part close to her body, almost like she's scared I'll see it. 'I don't think she would have, but — maybe I was right when I called the forest a virus. It's certainly been changing you.' She shoots me a glare before I can argue, so I don't, even though I want to. 'You saw all those new trees last night. The forest is closing in. What if it's already started to infect the rest of us?'

I try to assure Brooke again that it can't be her fault, that the forest isn't "changing" anyone, but nothing soothes her. Upstairs, everyone else is in similar distress. There's no sign of Elle or where she went. Our only hope is that her snapdragon still shines pink on the shelf.

Feeling lost, we huddle together in the living room. Irene refuses to leave the flower. She occasionally glances at us to keep up with the signed conversation, but otherwise stares at the flower, willing it to stay bright. Olivia and London stick close to her. They can probably guess at her pain in a way the rest of us will never be able to.

'Someone had to have done this to her,' Violet signs. 'Elle wouldn't leave.'

'Not without Irene,' Brooke signs.

'Then . . . what?' Violet asks.

No one says Frank's name. Maybe no one but me and Irene have even thought it. I've made *Elle is his favorite* into a chant. *Elle is his favorite. He wouldn't hurt Elle.* That has to matter, or else why did Elle spend her years here sacrificing us and herself to make him happy? Or else what *does* matter? If Frank did hurt Elle, then what does that mean for the rest of us?

The front door opening signals Frank's return.

"Anything?" Irene asks when he enters the living room. She doesn't look at him. She only has eyes for that flower.

"No," Frank says. "I searched the grounds, I walked through the forest. There's nothing. You're sure none of you saw anything?"

"You think we'd hide it if we did?" I ask. "We want to find her."

"Or you're protecting her."

"Elle wouldn't run away," Irene snaps. She tenses, closes her eyes, and I know she's swearing to herself and thinking *stupid stupid stupid.*

But Frank just nods. "You're right." We all glance at each other, eyes wide. Frank doesn't tend to admit he's wrong, ever. He runs a hand through his golden hair. "I just don't know what's happening in this house, and it . . . frustrates me. Worries me." He smiles at us, a sad, fatherly smile, and sighs. "We're going on total lockdown. No more going outside, not even to the garden. Understood?"

He looks at all of us, but at me hardest of all. I nod.

"We should all have breakfast," he continues. "We need our strength up. Afterwards, I'll do another sweep of the forest. I'll make sure you all get set up with distractions—"

"Distractions?" Irene interrupts. Frank's eye twitches. Irene's running out of my-twin-is-missing goodwill, and fast. "We're supposed to just distract ourselves while she's somewhere out there? Why won't you let us help you? Maybe, with all of us, we'd really find her and Jane and Winnie."

"I told you, we can't risk it," Frank scolds her. "It's bad enough that I'm down to six out of nine. I can't protect you out there if I don't know what I'm protecting you from, and I'm not losing another. Until further notice, other than any searches I have to do, we are all staying in this house. We are keeping windows closed and curtains drawn." His annoyance shifts into a smile, but not a nice one. "I don't want anyone getting cabin fever, so yes, Irene. I'm going to be sure you have all the distractions you need."

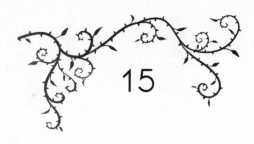

# 15

ELLE AND IRENE'S birthday is May 17th. Two months ago, they turned sixteen.

They'd been with their families longer than any of us, coming here when they were twelve, so of course they had better memories of what family birthdays had been like. A sleepover with their closest friends. Two ice cream cakes, decorated for each twin. Any dinner they wanted. Any movie (within reason—for their eleventh birthday, Elle had begged for a horror movie, and their mother had insisted they were too young, so instead it was Irene's superhero movie choice).

Elle and Irene don't miss their family like some of us do. Their single mother did her best, they say. She worked two jobs to support their little family. She didn't blink at finding out she had a trans daughter. She fought for both of them—right up until their magic came out. Then she panicked. Then she shut down.

Frank found her through one of his friends, or maybe their mother found him in a whisper network. Elle and Irene don't know for sure. What they know is that when they were twelve, they held hands and watched their mother drive away and never saw her again. She'd done her best, and they appreciated that, but they refused to miss a mother who abandoned them.

I don't remember watching my parents drive away. I don't think I realized they were leaving. I was distracted with Jane and Winnie and Brooke, girls I didn't know would become my sisters.

Elle and Irene don't miss their mother, but they love their birthday. At the lake house, we can't get ice cream cakes, but Frank will provide ingredients for regular cakes. Elle and Irene can't have their pick of *any* movie, but Frank will roll out the TV and the big twins can choose from any of the twenty-seven DVDs. Birthdays are also our best chance for sleepovers. Frank will let us make the living room into a huge blanket fort on a birthday, so long as it's all cleaned up by noon the next day.

For their sixteenth birthday, an unexpected treat changed all the usual plans.

Frank was gone. He left for an extended trip of nearly three days, and we were right in the middle, so we all felt confident enough to haul the cake and blankets and a picnic out to the lake in bright sunlight. Elle and Irene swam in their underwear, moving through the water like fish. They coaxed Violet and Jane in, but the rest of us were content to sit at the edge and let the water lap at our feet. The air rang with shrieks.

Later, we gathered around the towel-wrapped Elle and Irene and sang "Happy Birthday" over the three-layer cake Brooke had made. When we returned through the tunnel, arms entwined, we swayed as if drunk. Our laughter echoed all around us. There was no movie without Frank there to roll out the TV, but we made the biggest blanket fort yet.

It's easily one of the happiest memories I have of the lake house. It might be the happiest any of us have.

Remembering it makes it all the more painful to watch Irene, who's abandoned the flower to pull up a chair to the living room window and keep an eye out for any sign of Elle returning.

Frank, true to his word, gave us things to distract us while he's out searching. He gave us extra assignments. For my part, that means another twenty problems on permutations. He rolled out the TV and Violet and the little twins have set up camp with *Anastasia*. Again.

Everyone feels a little differently about their parents, but I'm in the same camp as Winnie and Violet: we miss them. When it's dark and we're alone and the house is quiet, we hope for the impossible.

We hope they'll come back for us.

When I watch *Anastasia,* usually it makes that hope a little brighter. If she could wait for that long and still find her grandmother, maybe we can get our families back, too.

Right now all I can see is everything I can't have, and

everything I'm losing. So I return to working permutations instead.

Irene only glances away from the window to check the flower. *Anastasia* turns into *The Princess Bride* turns into *Mamma Mia*. I find myself wishing, not for the first time, that there was more variety in our movie collections. Twenty-seven DVDs, and not one horror movie, or drama, or tragedy. It's virtually all princesses and happy endings and *The Fast and the Furious*. *Jurassic Park* is the scariest one of the bunch. It's not that the movies are bad. It's just the sameness. It's the repetition of twenty-seven movies that are all striving to make us feel the same positive emotions.

Today, it feels like an especially stark representation of the repetition of our very lives. The chore lists, the tests every Monday, getting up in the morning and seeing only the same nine faces, only the same book collection, only the same twenty-seven DVDs.

Frank specifically tried to prevent cabin fever, and it sure shouldn't be setting in this soon, but I can *feel* it. Between Frank's decree and my promise to Brooke, I have no escape. I'm ready to climb the walls or jump out a window.

The urge to do just that is actually so powerful—I recognize it, it's what Irene and Elle call *intrusive thoughts*—that for several minutes, I have to sit perfectly still. I know that if I move, the momentum will send me crashing through glass and running, bloody and scratched, out into the forest, never to be seen again.

But if I can get through thirty seconds, I can get through one minute, and if I can get through one minute, I can get through five, and then I can breathe again. I can stare at the permutations worksheet for at least fifteen minutes — maybe twenty! — before the intrusive thoughts barge back in.

It's heading into late afternoon when a low moan from Irene transforms quickly into an anguished wail that brings all of our attention to her. Even Brooke turns when she sees the rest of us doing it. Irene doesn't seem to notice us at all. She's just staring at the shelf of flowers. The back of my neck tingles with dread as I turn to look at what I already know I'll see.

Elle's snapdragon is drained of its color, and is clear glass.

"Shit," I whisper, which is maybe the most unhelpful response I could have had.

Irene doesn't say anything. Even her wailing has trailed off. She's so quiet that it's scary. I can't feel anything out of her — not anger, not grief, not anything. She isn't trying to reach out to us with her magic at all. She's gone into total radio silence.

It's nearly another hour before Frank returns. Brooke has pulled the little twins into helping her make dinner, hopeful that doing something with their hands will be a better distraction than yet another movie. Violet sits with Irene, neither of them speaking.

My post is near the window, standing very still, trying to get through one minute at a time. Every minute I don't dive out is a victory.

It's behind a wall and down the hall a little, and my back is to it, but the basement door seems to burn into me nonetheless.

It was only the dryer. It had to have been only the dryer.

Frank's return doesn't change much. Violet sits a little straighter, and Brooke stops chopping, but no one else moves. He looks at each of us, then the flower.

He deflates.

He looks disappointed, but . . . I wouldn't say he looks *surprised*.

Unless I'm imagining that, or projecting. Yes — that's it. I'm projecting my fear and paranoia onto him. Seeing what they want me to see.

"What a horrible week," he says. "We'll just have to stick even closer together, won't we?"

I'm suddenly furious that he includes himself in that *we*. *We* is me and my siblings. *We* is my family, the only family I have left. *We* doesn't include the man who lost my sisters, who I could rip to shreds right now —

Frank rubs a hand over his face and sighs again. My

anger shifts, and my heart breaks. Elle said that he probably felt guilty over failing Jane, and then Winnie. How much worse must that failure feel with Elle—his favorite? Isn't he my family, too? He's the one who gave me a home when my parents left.

It's a blessing when he walks away without a word, retreating to his rooms. If I don't have to look at him, I don't have to try to sort through what he is to me. Not right now.

He doesn't come back out for dinner, and we all go to bed early. Whatever fight we had is drained of its potential. Tomorrow, I think. Tomorrow, the motivation and energy—*vivacity? Verve? What's the best word for this?*—will return. In that distant, magic tomorrow, we are driven and powerful and we will find our sisters.

That's not the tomorrow I wake up in.

When I wake up, it's dark. I'm trembling and breathing fast from a nightmare. It was the same as always—a car, water, screams—but different, too. This time, I'm in the lake. *Our* lake. As water rose over the windows, I looked through them and saw Elle floating outside the car. Her arms are outstretched, beckoning me, welcoming me into the water. She smiles and the last thing I see is all of her too-many teeth.

*Find me.*

I detangle my spine and limbs and crawl out of bed. I put on my glasses. My steps are careful. I skip every creaky

206

floorboard and stair. Only the shadows watch me slip silently into the little twins' room.

The wall opens as easily as a promise is broken.

I walk down, down, down, fingertips running through the grooves Jane left in the wall. Elle had to have left something behind, too. We just haven't found it yet.

I am a shadow.

I am a spirit.

I emerge into a moonless world, but not a dark one.

The forest is *alight*.

Lightning bugs fill it by the dozens, by the hundreds. They beckon me, and I answer.

The forest floor is damp. It must have rained in the night, just a little. The air is filled with the smell of—what was that word? A really good word, one of Jane's favorites.

*Petrichor.*

The lightning bugs gather around me. Their light tingles a little, like the sun on a very bright day telling you it's time to put on more sunscreen. I smile, thinking of how Winnie always ignored that warning and inevitably ended up red, peeling, and whining about it. The tingle should worry me, but it doesn't. The prospect of a lightning bug burn almost excites me.

They pull me. Not physically, but by drawing their light away.

I follow the lightning bugs, eyes in the sky, in the leaves.

"Derry?"

I whip around. That was Elle's voice! I know my siblings' voices like I know my heartbeat, and that was Elle.

"Elle?" I call back.

She says my name again—"Derry"—but it's soft and scattered and for a moment I think it comes from the lightning bugs. They're blinking at me.

"Do you know where she is?" I ask them. I wonder, briefly, where Claire is. Does she exist when I'm not here? Does she have to load up, spinning, like a DVD that wasn't prepared for you to hit the menu button during the previews?

The lightning bugs twinkle on deeper into the forest, faster than before. I have to run to keep up. I keep my eyes on the cloud of stars, afraid to lose them. All around me I hear Elle calling my name.

"Derry!"

"Derry?"

"Derry . . ."

I don't look down until my feet hit something new. Not dirt. Not sticks or rocks or grass.

The lightning bugs draw my gaze downward.

I see Elle. Her arm, the skin so pale and cold it's nearly blue. Her glassy eyes.

I stumble backwards. My vision goes hazy for a moment, and I'm pulled kicking and screaming back into reality.

# 16

THERE'S SOMETHING RED leaking through her shirt. Elle is in her pajamas.

And there's red.

There's *so much red.*

I crouch and try not to touch her skin—but I feel bad for that. It's *Elle.* I shouldn't be scared of my own sister. Still, I shudder when my fingertips make contact with cold skin as I pull up her shirt just enough to reveal the wound.

Something sharp dug into her abdomen. Something sharp dug in and in and in and bled her out.

I stumble away, but I shouldn't be scared, she's my sister, but there's *so much*—

I fall, hitting the ground hard. I notice for the first time that it's muddy. It must have rained sometime in the night. It's taking so long for me to understand everything I'm seeing and feeling. Only now, with mud on my hands and knees and clothes, do I realize that Elle's shirt was damp when I touched it.

How long has she been lying out here in the rain?

I rub my hands across my face, not caring about the mud. I don't know what I'm supposed to do. I can't tell

Frank. He won't accept another instance of me being outside like this. I don't think I can even tell my siblings. Frank would notice something was wrong, and we'd be back at the original problem: I can't tell Frank I found Elle without telling him I was in the forest.

If I can't tell anyone, then I have to leave her here, but I can't imagine that either. She'd be alone and unprotected. But this isn't like before, not like that day in the forest with Jane, not like the man we buried.

Elle deserves more than to be dumped in a messy grave and left behind like a dirty secret.

"Claire?" The name comes out hoarse and broken. Claire appears all at once, as if she'd always been standing in front of me. She doesn't say anything, or seem surprised to see Elle. She just waits. "What happened? Did you see?"

She doesn't answer. If she saw anything, she's not going to tell me yet.

"Figures," I mutter. There's a spark of anger at her silence, but it's muted, dulled by grief like everything else. I can't yell and scream. I'm not even sure yet if I can stand. "Will you . . . stay with her? Just until I can come back."

Claire nods, and says, "I'm sorry." I don't look back when I leave. I trust that she'll stay.

The flower-lights I bring up on the tunnel walls are dimmer than usual, just enough to see by, and they shrivel as I pass. When I look back, I can only see half a dozen of my muddy footprints before the darkness takes them.

My feet are dry enough to not leave such obvious tracks by the time I reach the little twins' room. Just spots of dirt flaking off.

Each step up the stairs is numb and laborious. I know I *should* hurry. I need to change, bury these muddy clothes deep in the hamper, get the drying mud off my legs and hands.

Frank could wake up, could be awake for all I know, and I can't be found like this.

Elle is dead.

The bathroom doors, like every other door, have locks but no keys. Not even Frank's doors are kept locked. It's all about knowing which unlocked doors you can go through, and which are tests.

I strip. There's a full-length mirror on the back of the door. I stare at myself, head cocking slowly to the side, a little too far. Like an owl. My feet and legs are filthy. I don't think the dirt that came off as I walked was enough to leave a trail unless you know what you're looking for, and one of my chores for tomorrow is the sweeping. That will be okay.

My knees are a little scratched up from scraping against whatever rocks and debris hid in the ground. The cut on my shin isn't deep, but it is bleeding and I'll have to bandage it. I'll want to wear pants and longer skirts until it's all healed, and that will be hell, warm as it's been. We have air-conditioning but Frank won't turn it cool enough and I run hot.

Vast and pale, my stomach hangs gently over my upper thighs. Short dark hairs circle my navel. I put a muddy hand right where Elle's wound was. My breath is coming and going too fast. I'm hyperventilating. Mud is drying into dirt under my fingernails so thick that I can feel it. My skin is cool, but warming up.

I'm thinking *Elle will never touch anyone or feel anything ever again.*

It takes two washcloths and multiple passes to get all the mud and dirt off me, and then another to swipe it up off the floor. I bury them and my clothes under the laundry from the rest of this week. That's Violet's job this week, and they aren't going to tell on anyone when they find the dirt.

I'm not exactly competent in first aid. I never had to be. *Better than Band-Aids.*

We have bandages somewhere. I dig around under the sink and come up with a box of plain beige Band-Aids. My mom used to buy the ones with princesses and kittens.

It takes five to cover up the cut. There was probably a better way to do it, but I don't know it and this will have to do.

I grab one of the really big towels out of the bathroom

closet and wrap it around myself for the walk back to my room.

I don't make it two steps down the hall before I'm snagged—not by Frank, but by thoughts. Irene's thoughts. They pull me toward her bedroom, and with one glance inside I know she doesn't realize she's projecting them. She's asleep. Her dreams radiate off her in such dark waves that I can actually *see* the magic. They wash over me and leave my heart both wrenched and pounding with grief and fear.

Violet appears in the doorway, and holds a finger to their lips. I nod in understanding.

'Can't sleep?' they sign.

'No.' That's the simplest answer right now. I have to do an awkward arrangement of arms and terrycloth and squeezing to keep the towel up while I sign, but I manage it. 'Is Irene okay?'

'She'll be okay when she's awake,' Violet signs. 'Her body needs the sleep, so it took her down, but her mind . . .' They glance back at her, then to me. 'She'll be okay when she's awake.'

'Are *you* okay?' I ask. The momentary exposure to Irene's nightmares has left me shaken, and Violet's sharing a room with them.

They nod. 'I'm used to it. Her dreams are like this. They're not usually this bad, but they tend to be noisy.' They see the confusion on my face, the question—*how did*

*I not know?* 'They don't usually make it outside the room. It's really shortwave stuff.'

'Can we help her?'

'Elle could. Elle always knew what to do when Irene had nightmares, but it was some twin thing. Twin magic. Nothing I know.'

We both look at our sister helplessly.

'You should get some rest,' Violet signs finally. They close the door, and Irene's nightmares cut off for me.

I walk away, my brain muddled and confused. When I get snagged again, it's by crying. Brooke and Winnie's room is across from mine and Jane's. I didn't even notice their door was partially open when I came up. I was too in my own world.

Brooke doesn't see me, but I see her. Her hand is over her mouth in an attempt at silencing herself, or at least making those great, racking sobs a little quieter. The room looks so empty, as if Winnie's absence is visible. Why didn't I ever talk to Brooke about that? I know what it feels like to go from sharing a room to suddenly being alone. I know the void it creates. We should have been leaning on each other.

I almost walk in. Take a seat on the bed next to her. Hold her while she cries. We could talk about it.

I pull back. No. I can't put that on her, or anyone. I can't tell any of them what I know. Or maybe it's the other way around—I can't *not* tell them. I can't add to their grief by telling them Elle is dead. I can't prolong their grief by letting them live in uncertainty longer than they have to.

I get dressed again in my room, then stand there, unable to make a decision. I stare at Jane's bed. The thrown-back covers. It should still be warm from where she just left it, but I know it would be cold to the touch.

Out the window, out in the forest, a swarm of lightning bugs flash their glowing abdomens and wait.

I'm trying not to think about the thing that must be thought about. I'm pushing it aside with cleaning and first aid and memories of anything except *what must be thought about.*

Maybe I should go back out the tunnel and—what, escape? *Abscond.* Good word. But you can't just abscond, can you? You abscond *with* things. I could abscond with my *heart.* My *hope.*

My life.

I can't sleep, so I pace. But then I have to stop pacing, because the adrenaline is gone and my legs are making it clear they're sore. I try to sit at my desk, but I can't stop bouncing my leg, and the chair is creaky, and what if one of my siblings hears?

I can't think about it.

I grab my math workbook and get in bed with my book light. I try to concentrate on permutations, but it doesn't make much sense to me even when Elle explains it, and now I'm thinking about Elle again, and—

There's nothing to stop it anymore. I lie in bed, hands folded tight over my stomach where Elle's wound was.

Where the blood was, clotted, congealing.

Old.

Too old for Elle to have been calling my name.

But if it wasn't Elle in the forest, then what was using her voice?

If it was whatever magic I've been communing with in the forest, if it can mimic voices in that way, then it makes the question even worse. It forces me to ask if I really heard Jane in the forest begging me to find her, or if that was a trick.

And if the forest can mimic voices—the more I think about it, the more I'm certain it can, even if I don't want to believe it—then can it make a person feel things? The kind of thing that draws them out of their homes in the middle of the night?

The kind of thing that makes them feel so, so certain that their missing sisters aren't *dead,* just *lost.*

I should have already been questioning everything I saw in the forest, with Claire being . . . whatever she is. She said I don't need to make the distinction between a real girl named Claire and the forest, but it has to be made, doesn't it? If I'm ever going to know what's real.

I swallow down bile and close my eyes tight against the epiphany—*good word, light on the tongue, nothing like the weight it's placed on me*—that reality is . . . what's another good word?

*Malleable.*

I sleep fitfully. I dream the same dream over and over. I walk into the time-out room, and one of my siblings is there, crying. I hug them. I rip out their throat with my teeth. I wake up—or, I think I do. But I'm not really awake, because when I manage to get out of bed, I'm back at the door of the time-out room, and the next sibling is there, and I rip out their throat. Blood sprays and I spit flesh onto the floor.

It takes me a long time after waking to detach from the dream. I'm certain that in a moment I'll be tasting blood again. I work my consciousness through each limb and breathe into my stomach.

I'm awake.

The sun is rising. My alarm clock reads 6:47. Elle had the earliest alarm, at seven. In thirteen minutes, it'll wake Irene up, reminding her all over again that her twin is missing.

I stay in bed for as long as I can. I want to cling to each minute I have left before I see Irene and have to look her in the face, and not tell her what I know. I wait until Violet comes in, hair ruffled from sleep, grumbling that Brooke said to call me down for breakfast.

The day feels like a blur. It's like I'm not even the one living it. My limbs move and I talk, but it's all on autopilot.

Frank's patience is short, more than usual. Everyone's quiet while we eat, which makes Frank ask what's wrong with us, but when we try to talk to each other, he turns the page of his newspaper with a snap that sounds like a whip. We can't do anything right today. Violet gets time-out when they trip at breakfast and break a plate. I end up in time-out right after them, because Frank thought I was ignoring him when I was zoning out.

That grief-fueled autopilot mode becomes a temporary blessing. I still close my eyes against the lights and cover my ears, but I can leave my body and suffer a little less.

I remember my first time-out. Frank got a quick handle on what would screw with me. Most of us, when we get here, raid his selection of night-lights and white noise machines and music boxes. Most of my siblings need gentle noise and light to get to sleep.

Not me. I cut a big strip off an old T-shirt and wrapped it around my eyes at night. For sound, I'm fine. I like the ambient noise of the house and of the forest beyond it. If there was more, I might run into issues, but the house at night is often the perfect level of quiet I need to sleep.

My first big offense was questioning Frank too much. I'd been there a couple of weeks, and wanted to know where my parents were, and why they left me here, and why couldn't I ever leave? Couldn't I go outside? What about the rest of my family? I had aunts and uncles—none that I knew very well, but maybe they missed me, even if my parents didn't.

I never got in much trouble at home. Even when I did, my parents weren't big on punishments. They'd lecture and help me understand why what I'd done was wrong, but otherwise believed that the guilt I felt was often punishment enough. They were right.

When Frank walked me down the hall to the time-out room for the first time, I was crying before I even understood what was happening. The lights and humming changed until I was all-out sobbing, and then he left me there. For fifteen minutes, he left me.

My legs shook when I came out of the time-out room. Frank was there, smiling at me. That night, he presented me with a sleep mask that would block out all the light.

There's no reward waiting for me at the end of this time-out. Just Frank, still scowling, still unsatisfied. I wonder if this is just what he's like when his golden girl isn't around to placate him, but I don't think so. I was in this house three years before the big twins arrived. Frank had bad days, but he was mostly just Frank.

Today, it's something else.

I float on through the rest of the day. I know that I make conversation, but I can't remember any of it. I don't know what we have for dinner. I don't fully register anything I do until I'm back in the forest.

The ground is dry now. The slightly cooler temperatures brought by the rain are long gone. It's a muggy summer night.

Elle is where I left her. Claire, too. She's kneeling next to my dead sister, gazing at her face. Claire's expression is as inscrutable as ever.

I'm scared, at first, to get too close. Thanks to—well, Elle—I know about decomposition. I know that a body left to the elements doesn't necessarily last long. I know what animals do to bodies. There's a good word for it, something Elle taught me. I can't remember what it is.

For all that I have gruesome, bloody dreams and urges, I don't want to see my sister with the soft tissues of her face nibbled away by scavengers. I don't want to see her skin mottled with decay.

I wish I still had that detachment from the rest of the day. It would make it so, so much easier to just *look*. The more I don't look and know for sure, the worse my imagination gets.

It's when I start worrying about what could have gotten into her wound that I finally step forward, determined to banish those images with certainty.

She looks ... the same. I kneel across from Claire and

examine Elle. Her eyes are still open and glassy, but they're also still *there*. Same for her lips and her cheeks. If Elle's books were right, they should have been among the first to go. Her skin still has that blueish cast, but there's none of the bruising and mottling from settled blood that Elle described.

She's still undeniably dead, but another day in the forest hasn't changed her.

That doesn't seem right.

Claire offers no answers, and I don't ask for any. I just cry. Every time I try to look at Claire, I remember Elle's voice calling to me when Elle was already dead. I don't know who or what Claire really is. I'm not ready to find out.

I'm not ready the next night, either. Another day passes in that same blur. I think I did chores? If I concentrate, I remember doing dishes, and I remember navigating around the pile of Frank's dirty clothes still sitting in the basement while I helped the little twins with laundry. There's a memory of a flavor on my tongue. I think dinner was something with lemon.

But none of that feels entirely real. It was time I had to navigate to reach the place that actually matters. I only came alive when I reached the forest.

It's been another twenty-four hours, and Elle is still the

same. She's the same the night after that, too. I know by then that it's not normal. *Something* should be happening to her body.

"Are you keeping her like this?" I ask. It feels like sacrilege to speak after so many nights of silence. Claire and I make eye contact, briefly, just long enough for her to shrug. "I appreciate it, if you are." I don't know if I'm talking to Claire or the forest.

I still don't know if *Claire* and *the forest* are the same thing.

Some nights, my creature joins us. I kneel with Claire and it stands behind us. It rests a wooden hand on my head. I think it's trying to comfort me. I don't know if it understands why I need comforting, but the action still brings tears to my eyes.

Every night, my walk out of the forest is half a second longer, because every night, there are new young trees.

Then the fifth night.

## 17

"I LIVED IN that house," Claire says. We've been quiet for so long that it startles me.

"What?"

"Before you. Before the alchemists, before that. Before those alchemists, and before *those* alchemists, on and on, I lived there, with my sisters." Her voice hitches and she clears her throat. Some kind of reflexive movement, an echo of a living body. The difference in her speech is startling. She talks like a completely normal living human. "And Frank."

"I don't understand. There were alchemists before us?"

"Quite a few. You've been a long cycle, though. Ten years since Jane came, wasn't it?" Claire sighs, almost dreamily. "My sisters and I lasted for six. I was only here for four of those years, though."

Nothing she's saying is making any sense. "But how long ago was that? You can't have lived with Frank. He's not that old." When I met him for the first time, I remember thinking it made sense he was friends with my parents, because he seemed to be around their age. They were around thirty, I think, and it's been seven years, so he's probably not more than forty. I could buy him raising one group of alchemists before us, but Claire was making it sound like there had been . . . a lot.

"It would be more accurate to say he doesn't *seem* that old," Claire says. "I think you already know that not everything is as it seems." Her gaze drifts to Elle. "Not everything is as it should be."

"I don't understand," I say again, but this time it's half a whisper, mostly to myself.

"Once upon a time, there was a quiet lake ringed by a magic forest," Claire says. "And then a man came, and he built a house."

Frank built the lake house? It seems ludicrous. There's something about buildings—houses especially—that makes it seem like they've always been there, or like they've been grown. Architecture springing up from the ground.

"When the house was done, he brought two girls to live with him. They were magic, too. They called themselves witches, but the man said that was a bad word. A silly word. Hardly worthy of the science they were going to do here. He called them *alchemists*. He found a way to tie their magic to glass tethers. The first ones lived for . . . three years, I think. He harvested what he could, reset, and brought more. Five that time, and for five years. Again, the harvest. Again, the resetting."

"What do you mean, *harvest?*"

Claire doesn't seem to hear me. Or if she does, she ignores me. "It continued like that for five more cycles. Then a princess arrived." She glances my way, winks at me, and whispers, "I'm the princess in this one."

She clears her throat and continues. "The princess, like all the other girls in the house, had magic powers. Almost anything she could imagine, she could create out of thin air. It wasn't always permanent, or solid, especially not when she first arrived. But the man trained her and trained her, until she could have conjured up a—a whale, or her own castle." Claire pauses. Then, softer: "Or an escape from the house that the man would never know was there."

She reaches out and passes her hand across Elle's face as if she's brushing hair away. Elle's hair doesn't move at all. Claire's hand might as well have been nothing.

"But the princess couldn't leave without her sisters, and by the time preparations were complete, it was too late. The man used the glass tethers attached to the alchemists to take their magic. It flowed into him like lifeblood. Which means, of course, that it flowed *out* of the alchemists just the same. He took, and he took, and he took, until there was nothing left and the princess's sisters were all dead. She ran into the forest but she couldn't run far enough. He caught her." Claire moves a hand to her throat. "He wasn't able to take the princess's magic, but he took her life all the same."

"Frank killed you," I say in a horrified whisper.

Claire smiles.

The *ghost* of Claire smiles.

The world feels both too big and too small all at once. My vision narrows into a pinprick, but all around me is a wide world of shadows, and they all have Frank's face. Frank, who protects us, who raised us when our families abandoned us like trash. Frank, who makes us hurt each other in the name of tests we'll never truly pass. Frank, who knows we'll never step too far out of line. Who *needs* us to stay in line for . . . for *harvesting*.

"He killed you," I say again. "He killed more than just you. Do you"—I swallow, and make myself look at my dead sister's face—"Do you know what happened to Elle?"

Now, finally, Claire gives me the answers I wasn't yet ready to hear.

"I only saw the end. I saw Frank place her right here. She wasn't quite gone yet. She held on for a long time. She kept trying to heal herself, but she was weak from blood loss." I press my hand to my stomach, to the spot matching Elle's wound, and swallow hot bile. I picture Elle, pale, bleeding out into the forest, crying, needing someone to save her. "He had to smother her eventually. He must have thought she'd bleed out on her own, and she would have, given even a couple more hours. I suppose he got impatient."

"And you didn't do anything?" I demand.

Claire casts me a scornful look.

"You could have come to get me—"

"I can't leave the forest. It's grown—I'm sure you've noticed—but it hasn't grown far enough for me to come to you. Only Frank knew she was here." She returns her gaze to Elle's body. "He came back. He spent a long time out here, pacing and pacing." She laughs. "I think he almost felt guilty! He kept asking her, *Why did you make me do that?* It was more anger than guilt, of course. Anger that he'd already lost two from this batch in a manner completely beyond his control or knowledge, and then anger that he had to dispose of another too early and so unceremoniously."

It's too much. I turn away from her, from Elle, onto my hands and knees. I throw up. I'm left gasping for air, with a sour taste in my mouth. Eventually I'm able to roll back into a seated position next to Claire.

"Did he . . . did he say *why?*"

Claire shakes her head. "I think she discovered something she shouldn't have. I can only think of a few things that he'd kill her to keep secret, but I can't imagine how she would have learned them. He still doesn't allow anyone in his rooms, does he?"

"No, but . . . Elle was his favorite." Claire raises her eyebrows, alarmed. "No, no. Not like that. I just mean—if he would trust anyone to come into his rooms, it would be her."

"If he did let her in, she could have seen something."

"What could be worth killing her over?"

Claire's crooked smile. "The same thing he killed all of us for. *Immortality.*"

"Immortality," I echo. "You're telling me that we're just trapped here? He can kill us, but we can't do anything to him."

"I didn't say that. Immortality isn't the same as invincibility. He's spent a century stealing lives out of alchemists, but he can be hurt. He can bleed. He can die."

There's something wild and altogether too intoxicating in Claire's voice. I remember the dream I had where I tore out the throats of my siblings, and imagine that Frank is in their place instead. For a fleeting moment I almost taste copper.

*I taste blood because it got on my hands when we shoved him into the ground, and I wiped my face without thinking—*

I pull myself away from the memory, heart racing. No. I'm not back there. I'm here, with Elle, and with Claire— maybe. I look at her and she's still wearing that crooked smile, almost like someone hit pause on her remote.

"What are you?" I ask. "Tell me the truth, please, for once. Are you Claire, or are you the forest?"

"Does it matter?"

"It makes a difference!"

"Why? Either I'm the ghost of a girl who died in this forest, or I'm the projection of the ghost of a girl who died in this forest. I'd still be the same dead girl."

"But if you're a projection, then you could be anything. Maybe a girl named Claire really died here, and the forest took her face and made you. And if you're just something the forest made, then everything you said about Frank could have been made up."

"It's not. And you don't believe it is, either. There's probably evidence floating around in your brain—something you saw. Something you heard. You just won't let yourself put the pieces together because it's easier to believe he's innocent."

I push myself onto my feet. "I don't know anything. And neither do you."

She doesn't try to stop me from leaving. I breathe hard the whole walk back, clenching and unclenching my fists, nails digging into my palms. Red flowers are left in my wake, bursting out of my footprints.

In the tunnel, I take the time I need to get a hold of myself. Can't be trailing flowers everywhere. Can't let Frank know I've been up. Can't, can't, can't—so many *goddamn* rules to remember.

I don't know how I sleep, but I do, at least for a few hours.

The next morning, Frank is gone. He's never left without giving us specific instructions before, but this time, there's just a note on the fridge.

*Searching. Back soon.*

While my siblings puzzle over the note, I go to the basement.

I push aside the pile of Frank's laundry that's been sitting on the floor for days now, unmoved because we've all learned so well not to touch his things, even if we think we're being helpful.

The floor is stained a dark reddish brown underneath the clothes.

"Okay," I whisper to myself. "Okay."

I return to the kitchen. The decision to tell the others about Elle is no longer about what it will do to their grief. It's about keeping them safe. It's about keeping them *alive*. If I could keep them safe while also shielding them from what I know, I would, but they can't continue obliviously living with a murderer.

When I get to the kitchen, I don't draw attention to myself. I beg time to move just a little slower. I look at each of my siblings, wanting to remember their faces from before I became the bearer of such horrific news.

I've been in my own little world, somewhere outside my body, so I haven't noticed the changes to the others in the days since Elle went missing. Brooke's face has settled into a frown, when usually smiles come so easily to her that they're part of her resting face. The little twins cling to each other, one never even standing up from the couch without the other following her, unwilling to lose a twin the way they keep losing sisters. Violet listlessly sorts through a new jigsaw puzzle on the floor.

Irene is a deflated, washed-out version of herself. She's back at the window, staring, on the watch for Elle, but it's clear in the slump of her shoulders that it's more of an obligation. It's the thing that keeps her from acknowledging what she must already know is true.

Here I am to confirm all her worst fears.

"Hey," I say. The little twins and Violet look up. Violet taps Brooke's shoulder and she turns her attention to me, too. "I, uhm. I have something I need to tell all of you."

Only Irene is left, and if I'm honest, I don't *want* her to look at me when I say this. But I need her to, because I need to sign for Brooke, and I'm not good enough to sign and speak at the same time. "It's about Elle," I say, because I know that will get Irene's attention, and it does.

All of my remaining siblings stare at me, and wait.

'I don't know how to say this,' I admit. 'Elle is dead. I found her in the forest. She was murdered, and Frank did it.'

This is the third time I've had to tell my siblings bad news about one of our sisters, and it's not easier. It's worse, because three times feels like a pattern. It feels like it's my fault now. I didn't kidnap Jane or Winnie or kill Elle, but still, my fingers curl into fists, my nails dig into my palms, and I think I deserve the pain. I must have caused it, because why else do I keep being forced to bear witness?

The room is very quiet while they process what I've said. It's quiet just long enough for that antsy, jump-out-a-window feeling to form in my veins.

'Are you sure?' Irene asks, her signing eerily slow, almost serene in its movements.

'I saw her body,' I sign. 'I'm sure.'

Irene nods but otherwise remains still. London's the first to start crying, with Violet close behind. Olivia grabs their hands and even without being able to see it or feel it, I know she's shielding them with her magic.

London takes a deep, hitching breath and pulls her hand away.

"Don't do so much," she whispers to her twin. Olivia looks woozy. She was drawing on her own energy to power the shields.

Brooke laughs, an uncomfortable, disbelieving sound. 'What do you—' Her signs falter, and she laughs again, covering her mouth for a moment to muffle it. She shakes her head. 'How do you even know she was murdered?'

'The . . . condition of the body,' I sign reluctantly. 'And there's blood in the basement. And . . .' How much do I want to tell them? If I reveal Claire's existence, will that just make them think I'm crazy and making it all up?

But I'm hiding so much. It's ruining me.

Brooke nods, like my explanation makes sense. She's not laughing anymore, but she's smiling, as if I'm playing a strange and cruel prank.

'I'm pretty sure you all know at this point that I've been going to the forest at night. I haven't really told you . . . why. There's someone out there, in the forest, who's been helping me.'

Brooke's eyebrows shoot up. 'You didn't tell me that. Someone *lives* out there?'

'Not lives, exactly.' This is the moment where they'll definitely think I'm crazy, but, well, I've gone too far. 'She's a ghost. Or something like that.'

'A ghost,' Irene signs. Her lips curve up into a smile, as if I've told a joke.

'She saw Frank bring Elle into the forest. She saw him—' My hands trip over each other as I hesitate, unsure of how much they actually need to know. 'She saw him,' I sign again. They don't need to know how long Elle was alive in the forest, alone, bleeding out. They'll figure it out eventually from the timeline—how long between her disappearance and her flower's color draining?

There are a million questions on the faces of my siblings,

but they don't get to ask any because there's a pounding knock low on the front door. More like kicking, actually, louder than it should be. When Frank yells, "Open the door!" I know it's because of his steel-toe boots.

I can't think of why he wouldn't open the door himself, and a creeping dread falls over me. 'Stay here,' I sign to my siblings. I get up and go to the door, but it feels like I'm fighting my way through mud. I'm not just opening the door for Frank now. I'm opening the door for a killer.

There's proof of it as soon as I open the door. Elle, who's been dead-but-not-decaying in the same forest he's supposedly searched for days, is in his arms.

Frank pushes past me, and I stay rooted where I am at the open door.

A warm summer breeze comes in off the lake and I close my eyes. I try to believe that I'm lakeside with my siblings, that everyone is alive, everyone is here. We're lying in the grass and squinting up at the clouds.

Distantly, I hear screaming. It's one thing for me to say Elle's dead, and a whole other thing to see her body. I hope Brooke is taking the little twins away before they see too much. I don't want them to be dreaming red.

I could run. With a dead girl in his arms and several on-edge, grieving alchemists to deal with, Frank wouldn't be able to stop me before I got to the forest. Before I disappeared into the trees and scattered into a million million lightning bugs.

I open my eyes. The lake sparkles under the sun. Behind it, the forest is more shadow than light. Something moves in the trees.

*Run, wild girl.*

I close the door.

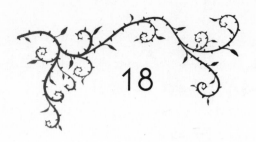

# 18

I REMEMBER THE drive to the lake house. I was nine years old and wearing a purple shirt with unicorns on it that my mom found at some store in the mall. It was an adult size, and slightly big on me.

I didn't know where we were going. They just said it was *someone who could help.* The drive took hours and hours. I didn't mind that. I loved long car rides. I'd put on cheap pink plastic headphones and listen to music on the old iPod my mom passed down to me while I stared out the window and imagined a dancer running alongside our car. Her footfalls matched the beat of the song, her jumps perfectly timed.

We only have CDs at the lake house, and not an impressive collection. Not that I'm not grateful for what we have, but it's all to Frank's tastes, not ours. You can only listen to the discographies of Elvis Presley and The Smashing Pumpkins so many times before you're ready to lie down and die. I miss being able to bring up any song with a few button presses. At nine, I was mostly listening to the music my mom had left on the iPod. I wanted grown-ups to be impressed with my taste. My favorites—other than Veggie Tales—were Sheryl Crow and No Doubt.

When I think about the drive, I hear "My Favorite Mistake" on a glitchy loop in my brain. I watch rolling hills turn into flat land turn into corn turn into trees turn into the lake.

I wish I was still *her*. I wish I was still a little girl on a road trip with parents she thinks will be with her forever. I want to be the girl with music-filled ears who sat warm and safe in the backseat of the car.

But I'm not. I'm something different, something grown, something with two sisters missing and another sister dead.

Frank has placed Elle on the couch. She looks comfortable, at least, nestled into the corner of the couch as if she's going to take a nap. Frank must have closed her eyes, so that she seems more asleep than dead.

Irene sits on the floor in front of her, rocking, rocking, her strange calm broken. The crying and screaming come freely now. Brooke, Violet, and the little twins are all absent. Good.

"Where did you find her?" Irene asks, not looking away from her twin's body. She hiccups her way through it, but it still comes out like an accusation. "Where was she?"

"Far into the forest. I thought I'd already searched there, but—I know this is crude, but she isn't very far gone.

I'm not sure she's been dead long. She may have been alive, and then dumped in the forest."

Neither of us challenge him. Maybe we should. Maybe if we all stood up and said *No, you're lying, Derry saw the blood, you killed Elle,* we'd win. Six alchemists all against one man? We could take him. We could do it.

"I think . . ." He clears his throat. His voice even wavers, like he's truly broken up, like he's even scared.

I hate that I can't tell if it's real or an act.

"I haven't wanted to scare you," he continues. "But I've been wondering if we're being hunted. I found little things in the forest that give me reason to suspect people have been through there, and we don't live too far from a town. You know it's been dangerous just for me sometimes, and—if they did follow me back . . ."

It doesn't make sense, and I know that, because if it was some vague mystery hunter, there wouldn't be blood in the basement. I also know Elle's body has been in the forest for a lot longer than Frank's claiming, though it's smart of him to take advantage of how well-preserved she is.

But the idea of people from the outside creeping through the forest, hunting us, still brings such an intense rush of fear that I almost believe it.

"How could they have gotten her?" Irene asks. "Elle wouldn't leave the house on her own, and wouldn't we know if they came in?"

"I wish I knew," Frank says. "It's one of the parts of this that has been so frustrating. How did they lure Jane and Winnie away? And how did they get to Elle when she was on high alert?" He shakes his head. "I don't know, but I'm going to find out. After I'm done here, I'll be going out. Our home has been attacked and I don't know the best means of defending it. I'm not even sure of who the enemy is. I need to see those friends again."

"The ones who couldn't find Jane or Winnie?" I ask.

"Yes, them," he snaps. "Do you have a better idea?"

I don't. I don't want him to stay, anyway, so I don't fight it.

Frank nods, satisfied with my silence, and picks Elle up again. Irene stands as the body rises. "What are you doing with her?"

"She has to be buried," Frank says gently. "I can't leave her here. It won't be good for any of you — psychologically, or frankly, physically. Derry?" He turns his head, sees me. "Good. I'll need you outside. Come with me."

"What?"

The gentleness disappears instantly. His words are practically a snarl. "Stop asking questions and do as I say."

I almost don't. I almost stand my ground, almost argue —

But I don't. He looks at me, and everything is fucked, but he's Frank and he raised me and I'm supposed to be good.

I follow him to the back door. I open it for him, since his arms are full. He walks to a spot away from the house, and he places Elle on the ground.

"How can I help?" I ask. I'm still not sure why he wanted me with him.

"I have a use for your magic right now. I know we've mostly focused on your plant-growing abilities, but I have a theory that it's connected to another ability to manipulate the earth. Not just plants. The dirt as well. And if it doesn't work, well, I'm sure you can imagine some plants to do the digging for us."

I swallow down bile.

Oh.

He wants me to dig Elle's grave.

Does he know I've done something like this before?

"Here," he says. "I think this is a good spot. It should be deep, and she's a tall girl, so take that into account as well."

"Doesn't she get a coffin or something?" I ask. "We're just going to throw her in the ground?"

Frank does his best comforting fatherly smile. "It's all very natural, Derry. She'll feed the earth. She'll feed the plants. Her life will nurture other lives. Don't you think that's fitting?"

I do, actually, but I don't believe for a moment it's why Frank is doing it this way. He wants whatever's easy and fast.

I sit down where he's indicated the grave should be. He crouches beside me.

"Now. You know how you've said that your magic is just a push and pull?"

"Yes."

"This is no different. But instead of giving magic into the earth to make it grow something, you're using that magic to do a literal push. To push the dirt up and out. Do you think you can do that?"

"I can try," I say. I know it's not the right answer. Frank doesn't like *trying*. But if I say *I can do it*, it's too close to saying *I've done it before*.

I dig my hands into the ground. It won't be as simple as a *push*, like Frank says. I need to get my hands dirty. Feel the soil, let it under my fingernails, breathe in the minerals. Frank just wants it to be *push* and here's a grave, *toss*, now he's rid of an inconvenient dead girl.

He takes everything for granted.

"Square breathing," he says encouragingly. I ignore him. My magic whispers to the earth, *Please. Help me.*

At first, nothing happens. It's so much easier in the forest, with Claire. I'm not sure if it's because I'm doing something wrong, or if the earth just doesn't want to listen, or if it's because this feels like a test. I keep feeding my magic and pleas into the ground and I ignore Frank, who has stood up and started pacing.

The earth between my fingers *moves*.

Not much, but it does move, like trickles of sand. I pour my whole being into the magic, because Elle deserves so much better than being unceremoniously thrown into the ground but right now this is all I can give her.

The dirt on the surface shakes. I've stopped breathing. I know Frank has stopped pacing because I can feel his feet on the ground, like they're on me. It's different than the first time. Then, in the clearing with Jane, the earth felt my desperation and it ran from me. Now it's answering a call, and the difference in the power is indescribable. My eyes roll back into my head—

—and I fall. Deep, deep, deep into the earth, through rock and sediment and past fossils and veins of precious metals, into the core, which isn't molten, but is made of blinding-white stars—

I come to, and blink into the clear blue sky. I'm not in the core of the earth. I'm lying on the ground, which is solid as ever. When I breathe, it's in gasps.

"Good, you're awake," Frank says. I sit up, with some effort, because tendrils of flowering vines connect me to the earth and I have to detach them from along my arms like dozens of the IVs Dr. Sam had to put in Winnie during a serious illness years back.

"What happened?" I ask. "I . . ."

"You did a good job, is what," he says. "Look."

I didn't exactly dig a grave so much as part the earth. Waves of dirt are piled on either side of the hole, which is deep and wide, if not the perfect rectangle I think of graves as being. It's rough. But it'll work.

"I did that?" I whisper. I stand up on shaky legs.

"Yes. It took something out of you, though. Why don't you go inside, get some water, clean up?" He stands by my sister's corpse and grins at me. "I can take care of the rest."

On the way inside, I risk only one glance back, and wish I hadn't. I'll be replaying the moment when Frank rolled Elle's body into the ground over and over for the rest of the day—maybe the rest of my life.

I wash my hands in the kitchen sink. I scrub and scrub, under my fingernails, checking the fine lines of my palm. I don't want my siblings to see Elle's grave dirt on me. *I* don't want to see Elle's grave dirt on me. My breathing is coming in too-fast, too-short gasps. The corners of my vision are tunneling. With a low moan I bury my face in my wet hands.

All I can think about is every mean thing I said about her. Every time I rolled my eyes when she performed for Frank like a prize dog. Every time I was annoyed with her for being selfish, for whining, for being overdramatic.

She was my sister. Whatever she turned into in order to survive Frank, she was my *sister*.

Piece by piece, I pull myself back together. I splash cool water on my face and dry it. I breathe normally.

I can't keep doing this. *We* can't keep doing this.

As soon as Frank leaves, before the sounds of his car have even fully faded, I'm in the tunnel. I don't tell the others where I'm going. They'd want to come with me, and I don't have the strength to look after anyone right now.

Claire is easy to find. She's always waiting for me.

"I believe you," I say. "But what do I do about it?"

Claire walks up to me. "I'm sorry," she says, before placing a hand on my cheek.

All at once I'm underwater, flailing, screaming out bubbles. It's only gradually that I realize water isn't filling my lungs. I'm not drowning. I'm probably not even really *here,* though I know exactly where I am. I'm in the lake.

And before me is a vast graveyard of cars.

My veins *buzz buzz buzz.* There are dozens of cars in front of me. I squint and still I can't see them all. It's like an underwater parking lot. Some appear to be rotted through, others are hanging on. That means something, I know it means something, but I can't put it together.

My stomach is rolling and my veins are full of bees and I *don't understand.* And yet, if I thought I had more than a few moments left in this vision, I'd go digging among the cars, looking for what I'm missing.

It clicks. I see what it means that the cars are in different states of ruin. They went under the water at different times. Years apart. Decades apart.

*No.*

I'm flashing back to years of nightmares, of a car crashing into water, of screaming.

Did my parents leave me, like I always believed?

Or are they buried in the lakebed?

I'm back in the forest, gasping for air, even though I'm sure I never left dry ground.

"Did you see?" Claire asks.

"What was that?"

"The truth."

"That wasn't real," I say shakily. "That was—an illusion, or—"

"You know it wasn't."

I clench my hands in and out of fists, trying to deny what I know, horribly, to be true. It wasn't an illusion. Claire showed me what's really under the lake.

"Do you understand?" Claire asks. "This is important, Derry. You're learning a lot at once and you need to understand all of it."

"He doesn't just kill alchemists," I say. "He . . . he does whatever is necessary to make sure he can have us."

"And you understand why he thinks you're worth killing for?"

I furrow my brow. "You said he's immortal, and he takes it from us."

"Yes. He takes what isn't his. He grabs on to beings that

should thrive for centuries, and he cuts their lives short. He's been doing it for a very, very long time, Derry."

Claire cups my face in her icy hands. I shiver. I can't break away from her gaze, from those dark eyes. If I look deeply enough I think I'll see stars. She leans in close and whispers, "Don't you think it's time someone did something about that?"

## 19

'WE NEED TO search his rooms.'

I can't believe I'm suggesting it. My siblings stare at me in shock, and I nod, signing again, 'We need to search his rooms. We need to know what we're up against.'

"We're not allowed in Frank's rooms!" Olivia squeaks.

'No, we're not,' Irene signs. She's not crying, but the tear tracks still stain her face. 'But she's right. There's too much we don't know.'

'We shouldn't all go,' I sign. 'Someone needs to keep watch.'

'I don't want to go,' Violet signs.

'I'll stay with you,' Brooke signs. 'London, Olivia, you too. Don't argue.'

They do argue, of course, but not that hard. They're curious and want to be included, but they're scared of the punishment if Frank catches us. I'm not sure they really understand that this is life or death, not something that would just land us in time-out. I don't know if they even understand what it means for Elle to be dead. They're eight and overwhelmed and they cling to Brooke as they watch us go, eyes wide and watery.

It breaks my heart.

The door to Frank's rooms is just beyond the time-out room. He doesn't lock it. Like the time-out room, it's a test.

And here I am, standing with my hand on the doorknob, preparing to willfully fail that test. I feel sick. I want to run.

From the look on Irene's face, I'm not alone in that.

*Don't you think it's time someone did something about that?*

I open the door.

"It's like his own apartment," Irene says as we wander in. She whispers, like we're in a library or museum. I feel the same.

She's right, too. Frank has his own bathroom, a little kitchenette, a bedroom, even a study. He's obsessively neat. The kitchen is spotless, the bed is made. The study is full of books, and—

"A computer," Irene whispers in awe. "Do you remember the last time you saw a computer?"

"Barely," I say. "I don't even know if I'd know how to use it anymore."

"I do," she says. "And if there's going to be anything anywhere, it's gonna be on here. Or his iPad, but he'll have that with him."

Irene slides into Frank's desk chair and wiggles the mouse. The double monitors come to life.

"No password protection?" I ask.

"Makes sense," Irene mutters. "He's *that* certain we'd never disobey him."

"Until now, he was right," I say. "What does that say about us?"

Irene looks up at me. "Nothing. It says something about how he's treated us." She turns back to the monitors as her words settle on me. "Let's see what he's got on here."

I hope she's right. I'm just not sure it's in my heart to believe it. Not yet.

There are about half a dozen folders in the upper corner of the righthand monitor, and a desktop background of sand dunes at night. Strangely peaceful.

"What's that one?" I point to the folder labeled *Surveillance*.

Irene gives me an impatient look. "Pretty sure it's self-explanatory," she says. She opens the folder and the screen displays a list of subfolders labeled *Gen 13, Gen 14,* and on and on. Irene sorts by most recent, and we get Gen 19. She opens it. Ten folders: *Basement. Bedroom #1. Bedroom #2. Bedroom #3. Bedroom #4. Hallways. Kitchen. Laundry room. Living room. Time-out.*

"He's been recording us," I whisper.

Irene opens *Living room*. It's full of more folders, labeled by month and year. Irene, again, opens the most recent—and now we finally hit files, labeled by the full date.

"Video files," Irene says. "He's recording us." She opens one at random from a few months ago.

"Fuck, does that mean he could see our ASL conversations this whole time?"

"Probably some," Irene says grimly. "But depending on where we were sitting in relation to the camera, and also how good his fluency actually is, maybe not that much."

It makes me dizzy to think about all the things he could have eavesdropped on—all the complaints, all the more seditious talk—so instead I concentrate on the screen.

It's security footage. The camera is up in a corner, I think near the kitchen. A tiny me is on the screen, working a puzzle with the little twins. A tiny Violet demonstrates glamours for Frank.

Jane is on the couch, drinking tea, watching. My heart squeezes.

Irene opens a dozen files, and they're all the same angle. The videos aren't a full twenty-four hours. It looks like Frank examines and edits the footage to just the times when one of us is in the living room. Or maybe it's motion activated? I can't imagine him having the patience to do all that editing.

"The little twins' room," I say suddenly. "Check it for last night or the night before, I went out both."

Irene looks up at me in horror. "The tunnel. He can't know. If he knew—"

*"Check."*

She does, and it's the strangest thing. At the time marker when I *know* we should have been opening the wall, the camera glitches out. It's just static, for minutes at a time. Irene checks several other times when we were going out, and it's the same thing.

I sigh in relief. Whatever magic built the tunnels and protects it from sight extends to cameras. I also have to wonder exactly how much of these videos he watches. Wouldn't it be suspicious enough if he saw me sneaking into the little twins' room every night, disappearing after the static, reappearing, walking back up to my room? Maybe the same arrogance that keeps him from locking his door or putting a password on his computer also makes him dismiss the idea of any nighttime shenanigans.

"What about the other folders?" I ask. I'm pretty sure I know what at least one of them is, but I'd like to be wrong.

Irene has backtracked and opened Gen 18. The same labeled folders for different parts of the house, and then the dated folders.

"These are from a little over ten years ago," Irene says. "Jane only got here nine years ago." She opens a video from the living room folder.

More security footage. The same living room.

Different girls.

Different magic tests.

Frank holds up cards where a redheaded girl can't see them, but she appears to correctly identify them every time. Irene skips ahead in the video, and we find an Asian girl hovering several feet off the ground. She soars up to the ceiling, laughing. When she touches the floor again, Frank is smiling, but there's a familiar hard look in his eyes.

"Who are they?" Irene whispers.

"They're wearing our clothes," I say. I feel like I'm going to throw up.

Claire was telling the truth.

Irene covers her face for a moment. Her breathing is fast and shallow, too close to hyperventilation. I touch her shoulder, and she shrugs me off. "I'm fine," she says into her hands. "I just—" She shakes her head, dropping her hands. "I'm *fine*."

She opens another video, and now we see those girls being examined by Dr. Sam. I recognize all the equipment.

"He *knew?*" I hiss.

"Gen 19. Generation 19. Is every generation a new set of alchemists? How long has he been doing this?" Irene asks.

"A long time," I say. I'd never thought too much about how Claire is dressed, but isn't it kind of old-fashioned?

Irene goes back to the desktop and opens a folder called *Profiles*. That one has folders going back to Gen 1, and Irene opens it.

There are only two files, alphabetical. *Bertha* and *Josephine*.

Irene opens *Bertha.*

There's a photo of a girl. A really old photo, like *back toward the beginning of photography* photos, with that weird sepia quality they always seem to have. Her clothes are old-fashioned. She's pale all over—her skin, her hair, her eyes.

Along with the photo, there's information. Bertha Smalls. Adopted when her parents abandoned her at twelve. She was a powerful pyrokinetic.

"Amaryllis," I say. I point at a line in the profile. *Connected to the amaryllis.* "They used the flowers, too. She had the amaryllis, like Winnie."

"Born *1877*," Irene says in a shaky voice. "Died 1891 when the generation was . . . terminated."

Without warning, Irene launches out of the chair and to a nearby trash can. I look away as she throws up into it. While she stays hunched for a minute over the trash, breathing hard, I grab the mouse.

I try to remember what Claire said. She talked about the first two, then I think she said it continued for five more cycles before she arrived. I open the folder for *Gen 8*.

There are seven files, all alphabetical. *Ada. Audrey. Claire.*

I open that folder, and there she is. The picture is in black and white, but I know her dark eyes, and that unreadable expression she apparently had even in life.

"Who's that?" Irene asks. She's still on the floor, face gone pale, but she's turned so she can see the computer.

"That's the girl I've been talking to in the forest," I say. Irene crawls back into the chair. "Claire Whittaker," she reads aloud. "Born 1921. Parents sought help—resisted and were terminated. Died 1939 when the generation was terminated." She closes her eyes. Swallows hard. Shakes her head, then keeps reading. "Ability to manifest physical objects." She looks up at me. "You had the same flower. The poppy."

I reach out, touching a finger to the black and white girl's cheek.

"This can't have all been Frank," Irene says. "He's not old enough."

"Claire said that he takes our magic to become immortal," I say. "But I guess it doesn't stick—he has to keep refreshing it. Why else would he have taken on so many generations?"

"So what you're saying is . . . he's going to kill us," Irene says. "When he's done with us, he's going to terminate our generation. Is that why Elle's dead? Because he started the process?"

Irene sits up straight, steeling herself. "Let's find out."

She navigates back to our generation's surveillance folder, then to the night Elle disappeared.

"Irene," I say. "Are you sure you want to . . ."

"Of course I don't *want* to," she says. She's already pulled up the videos for each part of the house, dragging them into different parts of the two screens. "I have to." She takes a moment to inhale once, deeply, and exhale, before playing the videos side by side.

The first we see of Elle is her slipping out of her room. We track her to the downstairs hallway. She goes to Frank's rooms, and paces. She keeps looking at his door, pacing back and forth, chewing her nails.

"What is she doing?" I whisper. But I think I know. This wasn't long after our fight, and Brooke trying to burn down the forest. "Fuck. She's trying to decide if she should tell Frank about me going to the forest."

"She can't have actually told him," Irene says. She's defensive, but she's also right. If Frank knew what I'd been doing, I'd be dead.

*Would* she have told him, though, if she hadn't died first? Would she have betrayed me that badly?

My heart sinks. Yeah. She would have. She was convinced the forest was hurting me, convinced it had killed Jane and Winnie, and she'd just seen that not even Brooke could destroy it. She would absolutely have told Frank . . . if she thought it was the only way to protect her siblings.

Elle finally stops pacing, and knocks on Frank's door. Moments later, he opens it. They talk briefly before Frank steps aside and lets her in.

I look up. From where we sit at the computer, we have a line of sight to his front door. Elle had stood right there.

There's no surveillance in Frank's rooms. We don't know what happened in there. We can't know what led from Frank willingly inviting Elle into his rooms, and the moment when his door opened again, to when he walked out with Elle in his arms.

Irene whimpers, hands over her mouth.

"She saw something she shouldn't," I whisper. "She came to confess, and Frank trusts her so he let her in, but she saw something she shouldn't—"

We watch as Frank carries her down to the basement. The basement camera shows him setting her on the floor, right where his laundry would sit for days after. I don't understand why he'd take her to the basement when he could have hidden her in his rooms for as long as he wanted, but . . . maybe he panicked? He doesn't look like calm, collected Frank on the basement surveillance video. He paces. At one point he punches the washer. Does he feel guilty for killing Elle? Or just upset that it wasn't according to his master plan?

Eventually, he returns to his rooms. Just as his door closes, I walk out of my room. I get a glass of water. Before I go upstairs, I pause. I walk right up to the basement door.

I make myself watch. On one screen, Elle writhes in the basement. On another screen, I press an ear to the basement door. I remember the sound of her moaning.

I was *right there.*

Then I run, and seconds later, Frank's door opens. Another few minutes pass and he carries Elle upstairs, out the front door.

I know how the rest of it went. He put her in the forest. He pretended to search while he figured out his next move and waited for her to die, but she kept *not dying,* so eventually he smothered her and we all watched the light in her flower go out.

Irene closes all the surveillance videos. We're silent except for her hitching breath. Her fingers curl against the desktop, into fists, and out, spreading over the wood. Her anger spreads out of her like a toxic cloud, and I welcome it. It'll have plenty of company with my anger.

"I can't . . ." she says. She groans, slams a hand on the desk. Her anger withdraws as she gets control of her magic again. "Not now." She's talking more to herself than to me. "I want to know everything this fucker has been doing."

She navigates back to Frank's desktop. I don't know what she's searching for, or if she's even looking for anything specific. She double-clicks a file. The map it opens covers an entire monitor. It's centered on Indiana—where we are—and stretches out east to Pennsylvania, up north into Canada, west to Nebraska, south into Alabama. Across the map are a few dozen scattered, glowing dots.

Irene clicks one. It brings up a profile, like the ones on the alchemists in each generation, but this is a girl who's still safe in her home.

"Alexandria Mason," I read. "Fourteen years old. Edinburgh, Indiana. Talks to animals."

Irene clicks a dot farther west. "Tara Brody," she reads. "Eight years old. Des Moines, Iowa. Can breathe underwater." One to the north. "Ashleigh Reese. Three years old. Toronto. Specific power not yet manifested."

"He must have gotten this all from his psychic friends, right?" I ask. "He's tracking potential alchemists to bring into the house."

"But *why?*" Irene asks. "He doesn't—I mean, he doesn't just take us from our homes. Elle and I were brought here by our mother."

"And mine brought me," I say. "But . . ." It's right there in Claire's file. *Parents sought help—resisted and were terminated.* "Claire showed me something. It's, uhm. It's not good."

"Tell me," Irene demands. "And don't look at me like that. Like I'm about to break. It's too late to worry about that, so just tell me. I want to know."

Hesitantly, I tell her what Claire showed me at the bottom of the lake. "It was a vision, but it was real. I'd swear it on my life that it was real."

Irene stares at me in horror. "He kills the parents, too?"

"Not all of them," I say. "Bertha's file said her parents abandoned her. Some of us really were abandoned."

"We watched our mother drive off," Irene says. "So unless she came back . . ."

"I'm guessing it'll say in our profiles," I say. "If we want to know what happened to our parents, it's all in his notes."

Our gazes turn as one to the computer. The answers we've longed for are all stored away digitally right here. Either our parents really abandoned us, or they're dead.

I don't know which answer is worse.

"What are you doing in here?"

We freeze. Dr. Sam is standing in Frank's front room, watching us. Violet is right behind him, face twisted in apology. They must have tried to stop him.

"Uhm," I say intelligently.

"What are *you* doing here?" Irene asks. "We just had our exams."

"Frank's been worried about your mental states. He called last week about doing some counseling."

He must have called before Elle's death, and he must have forgotten about it because I don't think he'd have left otherwise.

"And I think he was right to do so," Dr. Sam continues, "if you've decided breaking into someone's private quarters is a good course of action. I'll have to tell him, of course. Where is he?"

"Out," I say. "It was an emergency."

Dr. Sam sighs, and does a maneuver with his arm to make his sleeve shift enough to reveal a watch. "If he isn't back soon, I'll have to call him, I suppose." He returns his attention to us. "Well, come on. That's enough snooping for you."

With a few quick, nearly imperceptible movements, Irene closes every window we had open. Then we all follow Dr. Sam out into the living room. Brooke must still be taking care of the little twins elsewhere, and I'm not about to mention that to Dr. Sam.

"Do you have to tell him?" I ask. "Couldn't it just be between us?"

Dr. Sam looks at me sternly over the top of his glasses. "I think you know we can't, Derry. But don't worry. Frank will understand, I'm sure of it. You've been through quite a bit recently. It can make people act irrationally. I probably should have suggested the counseling sooner."

I lower my head contritely. I don't feel contrite, but I know how to look it. "I'm sorry," I say. "I just don't want to get in trouble."

"Of course not. But there are consequences to your actions, girls, and you have to face them." Dr. Sam takes a seat on the couch. "Would you be so kind as to get me a cup of tea?"

At that, I brighten. "Yes!" Irene and Winnie look at me strangely for my cheery tone, but I'm too pleased with my idea. I spin on my heel and go into the kitchen.

I grow the valerian root I used to make my siblings sleep, but I make it more potent. I use it to brew his tea. It comes out bright yellow—that's unfortunate. It makes the tea look herbal, and I know Dr. Sam hates herbal tea.

I call for Violet in the most casual voice I can. They come jogging into the kitchen, clearly happy to be out of the awkward living room atmosphere. "Yeah?"

'Glamour this tea brown.'

They look down into it. Then up at me. Back down at the tea. They touch the cup, and inside, the yellow tea turns brown. It looks just like decent, normal black tea with a little bit of cream.

I touch my fingers to my chin and move my hand down toward Violet in thanks.

I stir in a generous amount of honey to mask the taste, then take the tea out to Dr. Sam. Irene is sitting next to him on the couch, her leg shaking. She hops up when I come into the room.

I keep my smile pasted on. I keep my voice calm.

"Would you like anything to eat? We have some strawberries, I think. Or toast?"

"No, thank you, Derry," he says. He holds out his hands to accept the tea, but before I give it to him, I want to know something.

"Did Frank tell you that Elle is dead?" I ask.

Dr. Sam looks startled. Believable enough. "No, no he didn't. What on earth happened?"

I shrug. "Maybe it's just bad luck. Elle. Jane. Winnie. And the girls who lived here before us. Didn't they die, too?"

He tries to keep his expression neutral, which is proof enough of his involvement for me to hold out the tea. He accepts it, and takes a sip. "I don't know what girls you're talking about." He doesn't remark on the tea, so it must taste normal. Good, even, because he sips it again, and again.

I don't know exactly what it's going to do to him. Yeah, the valerian root I gave my siblings worked exactly as intended. But when I grew *these* my brain was a storm of urgency and *we have to stop him.*

As he sips again, I nearly smack it out of his hands.

Can I trust my magic not to have grown something lethal?

But maybe I really am the monster I worry I am because

I don't say anything. I watch him drink. I listen to his breath catch. I don't move when his body starts to slump, except to tilt my head, curious. His gaze meets mine before his eyes close and I don't feel guilty.

I feel *proud*.

"Derry," Irene says carefully, like I'm a wild animal to placate.

"He's not dead," I say. "I think. Probably." I think I'd feel it if my tea had killed him. "Help me."

I slip my arm between him and the chair, and put his arm over my shoulder. Irene does the same on the other side. It's good he's not a large man. It means we can, together, hoist him up and carry him.

"Upstairs," I say.

My idea for now is to hide him in a closet. *For now* because I don't know where my plan goes after this. But I know we have a couple of closets not currently in use, and I know Jane's is not only the bigger of the two, but cleaner. She hated clutter. Elle, on the other hand, could never get rid of anything. It all went in her closet.

Irene and I haul Dr. Sam's dead weight clumsily toward the stairs. Violet comes out of the kitchen, probably drawn by our labored grunts.

"Uhm," they say. I guess no one has words for what I've done. That's okay. They don't need to.

"I'll explain in a moment!" I say. Irene and I get up the

stairs and into my bedroom. We try to set him gently on the closet floor but he slips and lands with a *thump*. I pull him up and lean him against a wall. I don't want him to be *too* uncomfortable.

"Sorry," I whisper, and press my hands to the floor. Vines grow out of the wood. They wind around Dr. Sam's wrists and ankles and stay rooted into the house. I grow another to gag him with.

I shake my head, and tiny blue flowers fall from my hair and onto the floor.

"What did you drug him with?" Irene asks. She's crying again, but I don't think she's noticed, and I don't point it out.

"If I did it right, it *should* be a really potent valerian root," I say, brushing hair off my sweaty face. "Normal valerian root tea wouldn't do this, but it was the only plant with sedative properties I could think of in the moment, so . . . I tried to make it stronger. I think it should keep him down for a while."

Brooke appears in the doorway. I haven't closed the closet yet, so she sees Dr. Sam, and she sighs heavily.

'Violet said you drugged him.'

'He'll be fine,' I sign.

She narrows her eyes at me. Is she putting it all together? This, with the night they all slept like the dead? 'Why?'

'We can't let him talk to Frank. We don't want to end up like Elle.'

Brooke, who doesn't know yet what we saw on Frank's computer, glances at Irene.

'She's right,' Irene says. 'Going against Frank right now would be . . . dangerous.' She launches into an explanation of what we found. I cut in occasionally.

With each passing moment, Brooke grows more and more grim. She sits heavily on my bed.

'I never thought he was *that* bad,' she signs slowly. 'I knew he could be manipulative and emotionally abusive, but I thought we were all at least physically safe.'

'We are until we're ready for the harvest,' I sign. 'Or until we become a liability.'

'Elle and who knows how many others. We're generation *nineteen*. Even if the other generations didn't have as many alchemists as we do, we're still talking a death toll in the dozens—and that's before we get to the parents.'

Brooke doesn't seem to know how to respond to that, and she doesn't have time to find a way. Loud, running footsteps come up the stairs and Violet careens into the room. They pant. Their face is tear-streaked.

'Come quick,' they sign. 'The little twins are gone.'

'What do you mean *gone?*' Brooke demands. 'I told you to look after them!'

'They said they were going to the bathroom,' Violet signs. 'I sat in the living room and waited, and waited, and waited, and when I went to check on them—they weren't there. So I checked their room, and . . .'

She hands the note over to Brooke. Irene and I crowd around to look over her shoulder. It's in London's precise handwriting.

*We've gone to find Jane and Winnie.*

"They went to the forest," I breathe. I'm running down the stairs before anyone else can react, though no one is far behind. We gather in the little twins' bedroom, and for a moment, stare at the wall that leads to the tunnel.

'I'm going,' I sign. 'I don't know if it's safe for anyone in the forest, so no one has to come with me, but I could use the help.'

'Don't be ridiculous,' Irene signs. 'I'm obviously coming.'

'So am I,' Brooke signs. 'No point arguing.'

We all look to Violet, who shakes their head. 'I'm staying.'

'I don't know if you should stay alone—' I start, but Violet shakes their head, casting me a withering glance that, for a moment, reminds me of Elle.

'You all need to find the little twins. Someone needs to stay here and start packing. Because I don't know about all of you, but I think it's time we run.'

'I should stay with you,' Brooke signs.

'No—three already isn't enough to search the forest. But one person can pack essentials, and I happen to be the one who can glamour them in case Frank comes back.'

Everything they're saying makes sense. We still hesitate. Violet's years older than the little twins, but I've never been able to stop thinking of them as one of the children. It feels wrong to leave a child behind.

But they're only two years younger than me, and they're right.

'If you're sure,' I sign. Violet nods. 'Okay. Then let's go.'

Brooke takes their hand, squeezes it. Violet smiles reassuringly, and because we have no more time to spare, the three of us dash down the tunnel, leaving Violet behind.

"Will your ghost know where they are?" Irene asks.

"Hope so," is all I can manage to say.

We reach the forest, and immediately I start calling for Claire. When several minutes pass and she still hasn't shown up, Irene and Brooke start to look nervous.

'Don't do that,' I snap. 'Don't start thinking I've made her up.' *If you do, I might start believing it, too.*

'Derry . . .' Brooke signs.

'She probably just doesn't know what to do about other people being here. It's always just us.' I turn in a slow circle and yell, "Claire! Please! I need your help!"

My sisters gasp. I complete my circle, and there's Claire,

as if she had always been standing right in that spot. I'd be angry she made me wait if I wasn't so relieved that she is, in fact, real.

"Have you seen two little girls?" I ask Claire. "Twins. Black, both with short hair, one with glasses."

"I have. They're looking for Jane and Winnie, and if you're not quick, the forest will let them find its hiding spot."

"Hiding spot?" Irene asks.

"Sometimes the magic here is unpredictable," Claire says. She only has eyes for me, as if my siblings don't exist. "It can do strange things. It can, for example, take a girl out of time and space and tuck her away somewhere safe until her sister's strong enough to find her."

"Am I?" I ask.

"That's up to you to answer," Claire says. Then she smiles. "But I think so. I think you've proven your potential to the forest. For you, it'll let them out."

Claire turns and walks deeper into the forest. I look back at Irene and Brooke.

'Ready?' I ask.

'No,' Brooke signs. 'Let's go.' Together, we follow Claire.

It's easy to recognize the path we're on. Claire glances over her shoulder, and I know she knows, too. She's giving me a chance to stop her, like I did the last time she tried to show me where the forest put Jane.

I don't stop her. I have to do this.

We emerge into a clearing. It's normal enough. A pleasant, sunny little clearing, perfect for a picnic. If you knew where to look, you'd find a slight rise in the earth and an unusually high concentration of wildflowers.

I know where to look. Not only did I dig the grave the flowers hide, I killed the man inside it.

# 20

WE WERE NEVER supposed to be in the forest, but sometimes Jane broke that rule, and sometimes I broke it with her. There was a little forest near the farm where she grew up, and she missed the trees. She found a small clearing where there was room to spread out a blanket, but when we lay on it, we could still only see a little section of sky between the branches.

I remember how doing magic here seemed to feel just an inch more powerful, have a little more sparkle, but I thought it was just side effects from the adrenaline of breaking rules and the joy of being with Jane. I'd grow sunflowers up to the treetops. She'd take sticks and use her magic to form them into animals, into whole dramatic scenes of princesses saving themselves from dragons. We were always trying to make each other smile and laugh a little more than we had the last time.

On that day, Frank was off on one of his trips. We all went outside as a group. While the big twins swam and the others enjoyed the sun, Jane and I snuck off to our clearing.

We weren't planning to be gone long. A few minutes, nothing more. I wanted to show Jane a new trick I'd thought of.

"I haven't tested it very much, so it might not work," I warned. Jane waved it off.

"Show me!"

I knelt, pressing my hands to the ground. I closed my eyes. I knew I'd succeeded when I heard Jane's gasp.

I'd turned a whole circle of the clearing's natural wildflowers shimmeringly iridescent. Jane clapped her hands over her mouth and laughed.

"Oh my god!" she said. "Derry, holy *shit*."

I beamed. I normally can't alter the appearance of an already-existing plant that much. I can grow new plants out of it, but changing the color or shape of the base plant has always been tricky. I'd been practicing just for this moment.

It was just the crack of a branch that alerted us to the hiker's presence. He stood at the edge of the clearing. His eyes were wide, his mouth slack. He'd seen. He'd *seen*.

Every horrible story Frank had told us, every warning about what they did to alchemists outside our little home, every time he'd come home with black eyes and bloody lips just because people suspected he *might* be harboring alchemists — it all flooded into me. I stood up and shoved Jane behind me.

The man advanced.

271

My hands shot out, and with them, vines. They rocketed out of the ground and toward the man. It was just like when I'd lashed out at Claire, except the hiker wasn't a ghost. He was human, and solid, and my vines went right through his chest.

As soon as I realized what I'd done, I withdrew. When my vines whipped back, they splattered his blood everywhere.

I saw the blood that burbled out of his mouth. I saw the confusion in his eyes. Jane gripped my arm tight when he fell.

"He was—I had to—"

"You did," Jane assured me in a shaking voice. "You protected us."

"What do we do?" I asked. "We can't leave him here. What if Frank finds him?"

"We'll figure it out. We'll go get the others—"

"No!" I shouted. "No, no, Jane, please, we can't tell them."

Jane grabbed on to my hands and held them tight. "It'll be okay," she said soothingly. Her hands trembled where they were wrapped around mine and her eyes were shining with the tears she was forcing back. "They'll understand it was self-defense."

"Please," I whispered. I couldn't find the words to explain why I didn't want them to know. We shared everything. We had no one else to share with. Stripped of the families we were born into, we'd made a family out of the one Frank cobbled together.

Jane was right. They would have understood. But all I could think—then and now—is that they'd look at me a little different. The Derry who could murder a man thirty seconds after meeting him wasn't the Derry that London would go to for her word of the day, or that Winnie would curl up in bed with when her own bed was too lonely and full of nightmares. It wasn't the Derry who would be called upon to settle Scrabble disputes.

Murderer-Derry would still be loved and treated mostly normally, except that there would be a hesitation. An uncertainty. Every time she grew a flower, they'd remember what she could do with vines.

I couldn't survive being feared by my own siblings.

"We have to bury him," I said.

"We can't do that on our own—"

"No, no, we can. We can!"

I fell to my knees. That's when I dug my first grave. It wasn't like digging Elle's. It was messy and fast. The jagged, uneven shape of it mirrored my panic.

Jane helped me drag him to the grave, and she watched me cover him with dirt. I wiped my hands over my shoulders and neck, up over my face, because the skin there was covered in quickly blooming purple flowers. I recognized them. The flowers that grow from my magic are usually indistinct little things, but those flowers—I knew those flowers. They were mandrake flowers.

In legend, mandrakes grow where the blood falls under a gallows.

I tasted copper where the hiker's blood had smeared across my mouth.

*How many unique ways are there to arrange the letters in the word KILLER? Your answer should be an arrangement of mandrakes on the sloppy grave of a man who will never go home.*

I swore Jane to secrecy again and again. Two weeks later, she was missing.

"You woke the forest up," Claire tells me as the memory fades around me. "When Frank first arrived and built the house, the forest thought it would finally get its fill. But Frank kept it all for himself—all the magic, all the souls. He burned the bodies instead of burying them beneath the trees. It would occasionally get scraps across the decades, like when a certain princess ran from Frank when she saw him kill her sisters. Oh, how Frank screamed after strangling her in the forest and realizing all her magic had been wasted. None for him." Claire smiles upward at the trees. "All for the forest."

"It feeds on death?" I ask, voice thick with dawning horror.

"Among other things. For the longest time, it never got enough to wake up. Until you and Jane."

"What do you mean? Why us?"

Claire rolls her eyes. "You've really got to snap out of it, Derry. You know so many truths that you're always hiding from yourself. Your visits to the clearing and the magic you both showed off were the tinder." She points at the grave. "The spark. And all of your returns? All the magic you two did here? You revived the forest until it could breathe again. Then Brooke's fiery display, then *Elle* . . ."

The new trees. All of those new, young trees that began to sprout up after Brooke tried to burn it all down. The ones that only multiplied after Elle's life and magic bled out into the forest floor.

"You're connected now," Claire says. "The forest is part of you."

Brooke and Irene aren't with me anymore. How much did they hear? I back away from Claire, whose crooked smile is so much more sinister than it was before, and join my sisters at the edge of the clearing.

They've found the little twins. Both are clinging to Irene and Brooke as if they're life preservers. Olivia clings with just one arm, though. The other is cradling Gabriel's terrarium. The beetle crawls up the inside of his cage, unimpressed with anything that's going on.

"Oh my god," I whisper. 'Where did you find them?'

Brooke disentangles herself enough to sign. 'Here, hiding in the brush.' The little twins don't say anything. They've turned their big, scared eyes on me, but remain eerily silent.

I crouch down. "What did you see?" I ask.

Olivia looks past me to Claire, and neither of them respond. I decide not to press it.

I'm ready to get us all back home when I see it. There's a tree, only feet from where the little twins were hiding. It's nothing impressive — just a standard maple, the ground around it littered with helicopter seeds. It would never catch my eye, except that it's covered in blazing red amaryllis. Next to it, another tree, covered in bright pink camellias.

It could be a trick. The forest can grow whole new trees now. Flowers would be simple.

But this isn't a trick. Or if it *is* a trick, it's the kind that still leads you to what you're seeking, only without telling you the real price.

If I'm right, it doesn't matter. There's no price I wouldn't pay for what's in those trees.

My sisters are confused by my sudden silence, and even more when I walk away. I should explain. Instead I press my hands to the trunk of the camellia tree, finding a place between the flowers to make direct contact with the bark.

This tree is different from anything I've met in the forest so far. It doesn't feel like a tree, exactly. I don't hear that laughter and joy. This tree is something . . . I can't find the words. If Claire is a hole in the universe, then this is a piece of the universe that fell to earth and formed into a tree. It's older and bigger than it looks. It's cosmic.

I press harder. I gasp as my hands sink right through the trunk. Okay, *definitely* not what I was expecting, but . . . it's still exactly what should happen. I sink in up to my wrists, then farther.

"What are you doing?" Irene asks from behind me. I don't answer. Pushing through this tree is like pushing through mud. The deeper I go, the more resistance. Irene says something to the little twins, and I hear the small sounds Brooke often makes while signing, all of them trying to figure out what's going on.

I'm honestly not sure I could explain it if I tried.

The sparkling I've come to associate with forest magic threatens to catch fire inside me. I keep reaching, and reaching, until I'm buried nearly to my shoulders and camellias brush my face. I'm dimly aware that the tree should not be this deep. I stretch out my fingers as far as I can.

Another hand brushes mine. I lose it for half a beat, then it brushes again, and I grab on. I *pull*. I grab the second hand, and I *know* these hands. I pull harder, backing up, heels digging into the earth. My feet slip, pitching me forward, and the hands slip from my grasp, and I don't know what happens if I fall fully into this tree —

Arms wrap around my waist. Brooke shouts for Irene

as she catches me. I'm soon surrounded by my sisters. They steady me. They won't let me fall.

I reach until I find those hands again. This time I hold on so tight that it hurts, but I'm not about to stop. "Pull!" I yell. My sisters help me back up, hauling ourselves away from the tree, fighting against it, until suddenly we're free.

We fall to the ground together in a heap, me and my sisters. The wind is knocked out of me but as I stare in wonder at Jane, there's just enough breath left to whisper, "I found you."

# 21

"WHERE WAS I?" is the first thing Jane says once she sits up. Her eyes are a little wild, a little unfocused.

I laugh, mostly out of sheer relief. Brooke sobs into her hands. The little twins are all over Jane in moments, no matter Irene's admonishments to give her space. Jane smiles at them, clearly dazed. I talk to her over their heads. "I was hoping you'd know. We pulled you out of a tree, but I'm not sure that's where you really were."

Jane's brow furrows. "No. I don't think I was in a tree. I was somewhere else."

"Hold that thought," I say, standing and running to the amaryllis tree. *Please, please, please, if it worked once, it has to work again.* I turn to Brooke and Irene. 'One more go?' I ask.

With Brooke and Irene as my anchors, I reach in and search for another pair of familiar hands. When I first touch them, they're cold and unmoving. "No," I whisper. "No." I grab onto them and pull. It's no easier than it was with Jane. Brooke and Irene have to add their strength to mine. *God, I really fucking hope I'm not pulling out a corpse.*

The fingers twitch. Slowly, the hands return my grasp. I grin. "Okay. Come on, then. No time to be stubborn."

We're better braced this time, but when Winnie pops out of the tree, Brooke and Irene are the only ones who manage to stay standing.

Winnie's eyes are like Jane's—wild, unfocused. Her braids are barely intact. We help each other to our feet, gripping each other's forearms tightly.

"What happened?" she asks. "I was . . ." She looks back at the tree we pulled her from. "I thought I was . . ."

"Hey," I say. I squeeze her arms, bringing her attention to me. "You're here now."

Nearby, Jane is trying to get an explanation about what the hell is going on. I can see her signing to Brooke and Irene, and I can see both of them shrugging.

"I couldn't wake up," Winnie says. "It's like I was dreaming, but I couldn't wake up. I couldn't move and there was something just out of the corner of my eye. Something in the shadows."

A shiver runs up my spine. What was happening to them in those trees? I draw Winnie in for a hug. She tenses and her little pet poltergeist protests with a weak puff of air in my face. For all the affection we've shared, Winnie and I have never been huggers. Not with each other. But right now I need her to know she's not in that tree anymore. *I* need to know it.

"You're here now," I repeat. "You're back with us."

After several long seconds, Winnie sags, relaxing into the hug. Returning it. "I'm awake?" she asks in a whisper.

"Yeah. You're awake."

Winnie pulls away and offers me a big smile meant to distract from the tears gathering in her eyes.

"Great," she says brightly. "So now you can tell me what bullshit trouble you got us all into. I assume this was your fault, Miss 'I Sneak Out Into The Forest At Night'?"

The accusation would hurt more if she knew how true it is, but she doesn't. It's not really aimed at me. It's more deflection.

That's what I tell myself, anyway, as I brush off the deep ache of guilt, roll my eyes, and let the others have their chance at hugging Winnie.

Jane lies back on the forest floor, one arm around each little twin. She gazes up into the forest canopy, squinting, as if the memories are hiding in the leaves.

"I thought I heard my mom," she whispers as Irene translates for Brooke. "I thought I heard her laughing, and I could smell hay and sheep. I felt the scratch of corn stalks on my arms. It was just a dream, I guess, but it felt *real.*" She closes her eyes. "I was at the window. You were asleep. It must have been a trick of moonlight, but it looked like the trees were moving like corn in the wind, and I knew I had to go outside. So I did, and then . . . I don't know. I remember stars. I remember being stars, or maybe fireflies? And then—" She falls silent. Her eyes open, and there's something in them. A haunting, maybe. Did she experience the same thing as Winnie?

Jane shakes her head. "And then . . ." she says again. She pulls her arm out from under Olivia to reach toward the sky. She's thinking of our arms outstretched, seeking each other. She smiles at all of us in turn. "And then my sisters were here."

Winnie kneels next to Jane. 'Yeah, I was in the garden and . . . I heard my mom, too. And my dad. They were calling to me from the forest. I knew that was impossible, but I thought maybe it wasn't. Maybe they came back for me. Maybe they were worried Frank wouldn't just let me go, so they were going to sneak me out. I walked into the forest, and . . .' She trails off.

Claire's nowhere to be found, and that doesn't surprise me. She wouldn't want to be here when I realized the forest *took* my siblings. They didn't just get *lost*. It drew them out here and it hid them from me on purpose. Blood rushes in my ears. I clench my fists. The forest could have led me to them at any time. *Claire* could have. She tricked me, she—

The hand on my shoulder surprises me. I only just remember to keep my magic pulled up inside so that I don't lash out when I whip around to face Irene.

"Are you okay?" she asks. She glances down toward my feet.

I look down, too. "Oh," I say. In a jagged circle around me, the grass in the clearing has withered. "Yeah, I'm . . . I just got upset."

Irene nods, like that makes sense, as if this is something that has ever happened before.

'Where's everyone else?' Jane asks. She and the little twins are sitting up, but the twins still cling to her. 'Irene, Elle really let you go on this adventure without her? Is she back at the house with Violet?'

Of course Jane wouldn't know. There's no way she could. Winnie won't, either. I long to be them in this moment, to be able to picture Elle without picturing her cold on the forest floor or rolled unceremoniously into a grave.

Maybe I'm not alone in that, because no one else says anything immediately. Jane glances between us, a confused half-smile on her face. She settles on me and signs, 'Did I miss something? Are we angry at Elle right now?'

God, it's all so excruciatingly *normal*. This could be any day, any moment when Jane found me sulking and asked, "Who are we mad at?" It was just a way to get me to talk it out, because she knows that nine times out of ten, giving me a chance to talk the problem out will end in me forgiving and forgetting.

'She's gone,' I sign, but the euphemism is more frustrating than the truth. 'She's dead. Frank . . .'

I can't finish the sentence. My vision is tunneling as the grief hits with a fierceness I hadn't yet managed to feel. All I can see is Jane's brown eyes widening, her lips parting as if to say *no,* but no sound comes out. I *think* no sound comes out. Blood is rushing in my ears so loudly that she could be screaming and I wouldn't hear it. She wrenches away from the little twins and doubles over.

And there's nothing to do about it except let her be in pain. All any of us can do about our pain is *feel* it, sharp in our hearts, stiff and grimy under our fingernails like grave dirt.

Winnie makes the first move. She crashes into Jane. She's clumsy as she burrows into Jane's arms, and they hold each other up, crying together. The little twins follow, then Irene, then Brooke. I join last. I hold them, and let myself be held, too.

Our bodies don't fit together cleanly. Shoulders knock together and hands don't know where to land. Our skin is sticky with sweat. Our breath mingles in the center of our huddle, ragged and too hot. It's awkward and uncomfortable and I never want to leave. For this moment, we're joined. Grief travels through us like electricity through a power line—the charge of the pain isn't lessened, but spread across us, it's a little easier to bear.

'What are we supposed to do?' Winnie asks when we finally pull apart. 'We can't just go back there and pretend like everything's normal. Any one of us could be next.'

'Violet's at the house, packing,' Brooke signs.

'So we can run away,' Winnie signs.

I raise my hand, then sign, 'I'm for it.'

'Me too,' Jane agrees. 'But . . . can we really?' She looks exhausted, ready to collapse. I move in and let her lean on me. 'Where would we go?'

If we were a group of normal kids, we could throw ourselves on the mercy of strangers, but we aren't. We're alchemists. If we're going to leave the lake house, we need our own money and transportation to stay hidden from *everyone,* not just Frank.

'We're supposed to talk out our problems,' London signs. 'Use our words.'

Jane smiles down at her, fondly stroking back her curls. She opens her mouth to speak, but doesn't seem to have it in her. She settles for the smile.

I step in. 'You're right, in most situations, we should use our words. It's almost always better to speak honestly about something that's upsetting you so that it can get worked out. But sometimes, it's not a good solution — and this is one of those times.'

London considers that, then shakes her head. 'I don't understand.'

Brooke takes over trying to explain to an eight-year-old why, no, we can't just talk it out with the man who murdered our sister. I can feel the hiker's grave at my back like a bonfire.

We can't run away. We can't talk to him.

I did it once before.

Couldn't I do it again?

'What if we *do* go back and act like everything is normal?' I ask. 'We have to go back anyway for Violet. Maybe he'll let down his guard if he thinks we don't suspect anything. Make him less dangerous.' *Make him less careful,* I think.

'How do we explain Jane and Winnie?' Irene asks. 'We won't just be able to bring them back in and pretend nothing happened.'

I don't have an answer for that, so instead I say, ". . . Shit."

Brooke and the little twins rejoin the conversation, and Irene catches them up on the plan. 'What if the story will be that they just . . . came back?' Brooke asks. 'We're never going to come up with something more elaborate that sounds believable and doesn't get us killed. So we keep it simple.'

'Like we just, what, appeared at the front door?' Jane asks uncertainly. Then her face clears of confusion, and she nods. 'We can say we don't remember anything other than being lured into the forest. Blame it on this place. We can make him believe that, make him . . .' Her hands flutter as she searches for the words, stares off into the distance. A few new tears streak down her cheeks. 'Make him believe we aren't a threat, so he doesn't . . .' She can't finish that sentence, but we all know.

'It'll work,' I sign. 'We can do this. Just have to act oblivious long enough to find a way out for good.' I hold Jane's hand tight all the way back to the lake and our tunnel, even tighter when we pass a copse of new trees, and tighter again when the sweat condensing between our palms makes the grip slick. Maybe I'll just never let her go again.

The forest watches us leave. The pressure of its gaze bears down on me with such force that I nearly stumble, but Jane keeps me upright. I wish I could say that I'll never be going back into the forest, that taking my sisters was the last straw and I'll dedicate my life to destroying it.

I *could* say it. It just wouldn't be true.

I know there's something wrong before we reach the tunnel entrance. My flowers light the walls as usual, but just around the final bend there's a different kind of light.

The wall is open.

My sisters and I exchange uneasy glances. "We closed it, right?" Irene whispers. We never leave the wall just open like that. We know Frank can't see the tunnel from the lake side, but there's no reason to think a missing wall would stay hidden from him.

"It's fine," I say, not because I believe it, but because it has to be. "It's fine."

The wall is open, and nothing is fine, because Frank is waiting on the other side. Violet sits on London's bed, crying.

The gun in Frank's hand is pointed directly at us.

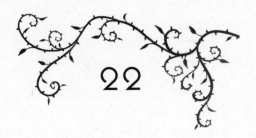

## 22

I DON'T KNOW how to deal with guns. I don't even know what kind of gun he's holding. It's big, but he holds it in one hand. Does that make it a handgun? Which kind is the revolver?

A gun seems . . . indomitable. That's it. Perfect word, on the first try and everything. *Indomitable.* If I see a gun, I'm supposed to *run run run.* That's what I want to do. *Run run run.*

But I can't. I don't have parents or police to run to. I have Frank, who has the gun, and siblings, who I need to save from the man with the gun. I need to *run run run* into the dangerous place.

I'm not prepared.

I step in front of the siblings I can still shield.

"Welcome home," Frank says. His voice is steady but there's something wild in it that I've never heard before. I stand very still, as if that will calm him, because I don't want to know what Frank is like when he loses control. He narrows his eyes at Jane and Winnie. "Look who's back. I don't know where you went or who you saw or who you spoke to, or what you thought you were doing by running away at all, but you aren't leaving again."

He's turned paranoid. Something's broken him, just a little. He had to go outside his plan and kill Elle, and now he knows we had a way out of the house all along. He didn't have as much control as he thought.

"You can't keep us here," I say. My voice shakes. I clear my throat, too aware that I don't make much of an intimidating figure as the fat bespectacled girl with dirty bare feet. "We know that you're a murderer and we know that you were always planning to kill us. It's eight against one, and we have magic. You don't."

"Derry, it's been nine against one for years. Didn't do you much good then, did it?"

"This is different," Winnie snaps. "*We're* different."

"Are you?" Frank grins. He spreads his arms, gun held casually in his right hand. Brooke, eyes sharp on the sweep of his arm, takes the chance and pulls Violet to their feet. Frank lets them join us. "Winnie, your magic is barely worth stealing—though don't worry, I will. But I won't stop you if you want to try. Really. Go for it. I'll give you a head start."

Furious heat radiates off Winnie. She steps forward, nudging past me. Her little pet poltergeist kicks up. Books fly off the shelves. Unswept dust and dirt swirls into a little cyclone at her feet. She reaches out with both hands, trying to guide it. It swerves, and she sidesteps toward the wall, leading it back on to the path she wants. She only has eyes for Frank.

The cyclone moves toward him. London's music box crashes onto the floor next to him. Olivia's terrariums rattle under her bed. Her little pet poltergeist is *actually following her direction*. Disbelief and joy light up her face, and—

Frank shoots a bullet right through her delight, and her face is gone, and I'm screaming, and everyone is screaming, and Winnie is *gone*.

"Looks like I win," Frank says, the grin still stretched out across his face, turning into a distorted maw that threatens to devour us all.

All I can think is this: my glasses have Winnie's blood on them.

Her position kept the rest of us out of his line of fire, but she was close enough for the blood to splatter out of her skull and onto me. Irene, too. She's wiping desperately at the blood on her arms, smearing it.

"Anyone else want to throw a tantrum?" Frank asks. "Or are we going to be good little children?"

I can't look at Winnie.

I can't take my eyes off her.

We just got her back.

Frank strides over to us and nudges the gun against my shoulder. "Should I make you bury her, too?" he asks. "You did such a good job with Elle."

*No no no*

"No," he says, and I'm indescribably angry that he has me so fucked up I want to *thank him* for not making me bury another sister. "I think she's better left here. A nice little warning for all of you. Can't get out unless you want to step through her blood." He laughs. "I just don't think any of you are that brave."

That's when I lunge.

It's stupid. It's beyond stupid. I just watched him kill my sister, I know he killed Elle, I know he's killed countless others.

I don't think about that. I want to see him bleed. I want to dig my teeth into him and I want him to bleed *because of me.*

He steps easily out of the way and grabs my hair. I reach back, scratching at his hand. He pulls my hair hard and my head snaps back.

"Are you volunteering to be next in the ground?" he asks. "I'd hate to do it, Derry, but I will if you don't calm down."

He pushes me back into the group, where Brooke and Jane catch me. Or hold me, so I don't dive back in. Maybe a little of both.

There's blood under my nails. The warmth burns into me like fire. I hold on to it. I relish it.

"How about we all move to the living room in a calm and orderly fashion?" Frank asks.

We let him lead us away from Winnie and our secret passage. Violet and Irene walk ahead of us. Violet is crying. The little twins are shielded in the center of our group, with Brooke and Jane behind them, holding hands as if they're keeping each other tethered to the earth. I follow at the back, hands clenched into fists, all rage and grief with nowhere to go.

Violet and Irene crowd onto the couch with the little twins. I perch precariously on the arm, trying not to remember how Winnie would always sit here. Jane and Brooke stand next to me. Tears stream silently down Jane's face. I reach out, taking the hand not held by Brooke. I squeeze, and she squeezes back.

Frank tucks the gun into his pants and stands in front of the flowers, hands on his hips. Winnie's red amaryllis has turned into clear, colorless glass.

There's still blood on my glasses. Winnie on my glasses. I whip them off and rub furiously with my shirt. They don't get *clean,* but it's good enough. I can see, at least.

Frank looks us over and sighs, like we've been misbehaving. "I'd really hoped for a few more years with you. You all had promise. I'll take what I can get, but . . . it's a shame." Frank frowns at us. He's not *angry* we're forcing him to kill us early; he's *disappointed*.

"What are you going to do to us?" I ask. I don't let my voice shake. If he wants fear from me, he's not going to get it.

"I *could* just drain out all of your magic," he says. He turns to the flowers, and plucks my poppy off the shelf. I feel his grip on it like it's a grip on my heart. "It's not an unpleasant death. It hurts at first—I won't lie to you about that. But from what I've observed, after it passes the halfway mark, the pain lessens, then numbs entirely." He describes it all so casually. "You'll lose consciousness before you actually die, don't worry about that. You won't have to experience the actual moment of death. You'll just . . . go to sleep."

Violet muffles their loud sobs behind their hands. Brooke has her arms wrapped around the shellshocked little twins and each of her hands are over one of their ears, as if it can stop them from hearing it. She can't hear him herself, of course, and Frank's not signing. Brooke squints at his mouth in an attempt to read his lips. I dimly realize one of us should translate for her.

"But." Frank holds up a finger, a little *wait*. "I'm actually hoping we can come to some kind of agreement," he says. "Like I said—I was hoping for a few more years with all of you. I don't want to kill you."

"But you wanted to kill Elle?" Irene asks harshly.

"Elle was . . . regrettable," he admits. "That she had to die so soon, of course, but also the manner of her death. She surprised me, and instead of killing her the way I should have"—he gestures to her clear snapdragon—"I was a little sloppier, and her magic was lost. But it doesn't have to be that way for all of you. You could live out those next few years—longer, even. I'd be willing to let you live indefinitely, fulfilling your true purpose a little bit at a time instead of all at once. It's my preference, actually. In an ideal scenario, I'd take your magic in smaller amounts and allow it to recharge before taking more." He clucks his tongue. "Of course, it does recharge less and less as time goes on, but I suspect I just haven't found the ideal dosage yet. That's not the real problem, though. The *real* problem is . . . insolence."

"What's the point of this?" Violet asks through their sobs. "You don't have magic, you can't use ours!"

"You haven't been paying attention, Violet," Frank snaps. "Of course I can't use your magic like you do, but I'd argue I use it better. It feeds me. It regenerates me."

"It isn't yours to take!" Irene shouts.

"Why not?" Frank snarls. "Why do *you* deserve it? Why do a few silly children get to have inhumanly long lifespans and magic just because of a trick of birth?"

Claire said something about alchemists having long

lifespans, but can they really be *that* long? I guess none of us have had the chance to find out. Maybe we never will.

Frank clears his throat, forcing the rage off his face. "That's not important," he says, brushing the topic away. "What's important is that you don't have to die today. You don't even have to die soon. If you can all manage to just be good children and submit to regular withdrawals, you can live . . . well. Longer. How long depends on you. Do you find that agreeable?"

None of us respond. What are we supposed to say? *Sure, Frank, we'll sacrifice the rest of our lives to feed your artificial immortality. We'll spend the tiny remnants of our childhood and who knows how long after that as your prisoners, existing only for magic transfusions.*

But maybe that *is* what we should say.

"I wish I could give you some time to think about this," he says. "But I'd like to know as soon as possible if you're going to be useful past today."

I look up at Jane, willing her to read the question on my face, willing myself to understand her reply.

It's not a real offer. Surely we all know that much. He'd keep us alive past today, but he wouldn't really keep us alive *indefinitely*, unless *indefinitely* means *until we annoy him*. We'd be on borrowed time.

We could still agree to it, though, because we need all

the time we can get. That morsel of borrowed time might be enough for us to figure out how to escape.

Jane nods. I have to trust that we're thinking the same thing.

"Okay," Jane says. She sounds defeated. "If you'll promise not to hurt us anymore, then I think we can find that . . . *agreeable*."

"I also say okay," I add. I brace for sounds of betrayal from my siblings, terrified that Jane and I have read the room incredibly wrong.

It's hard to say if they have more trust in me than I deserve, or if it's all their trust in Jane, but no one argues. Instead of gasps and protests, they murmur their assent.

"Wasn't terribly excited about living out there anyway," Irene says.

"It's safer here," Violet agrees.

A smile spreads over Frank's face. "Splendid," he says. "I think we can make this all work. But first . . ." He holds up my poppy to the light. "You've grown so much stronger lately, Derry."

He's right. The red is richer, deeper, more vibrant. It's because of the forest, but it's still *mine*. My heart skips a beat as my magic answers with a surge of power. Vines climb up the couch and the walls and the floor rumbles gently with new roots. Flowers blossom up and down my arms.

I tighten a fist, thinking, *I'll get the roots to break through the floor and crush Frank and then this will all be over*—

Something stabs into my heart. I actually look down to see if blood is spilling out of me, if he's killing me like he killed Elle, but there's nothing happening. Then the pain comes again. I double over. I fall off of the couch arm, onto the floor. Multiple voices call my name. Someone screams. Frank's shouting, but I can't make out the words. Through eyes blurred with pain, I look up at him.

The red is seeping out of my poppy and up his arm. His veins glow red, and the redder they are, the paler my poppy is. His eyes flash scarlet, just for half a second, short enough that I think I imagine it.

His other arm is stretched out, gun aimed. My movements are agonizingly slow. I follow the line of his aim. It's pointed at Irene, who's placed herself in front of London. There's a fury on London's face I've never seen, but I recognize it. She wants to hurt Frank. She knows her magic could hurt him, and she's longing to lash out. She strains against the arm holding her back—Violet. Olivia's wrapped her small fingers around Irene's wrist and enveloped her in a magical shield, desperate to protect Irene while she's in Frank's line of fire, even though I don't think her shield can withstand a bullet. Jane is saying something to Frank, trying to calm him. Brooke stands by her side with a small spark of fire in her fingers. A warning.

The red glow of Frank's arm flickers and my pain cuts off all at once. I'm left gasping for air. Sound returns.

"Let's all calm down," Frank says. He turns his gaze to Brooke, who warily lowers her flame. Violet lets London go so that she and Irene can come to my side.

"Are you okay?" London whispers. I want to reach out and smile and comfort her, but I can't seem to make the motions happen. Irene places a hand on my shoulder and tries to project calm. There's nothing for it to take the edge off of. The pain is gone—I'm just empty now.

Frank places my poppy back on the shelf, and straightens it until it's centered to his satisfaction. It's a pale shadow of what it used to be.

I touch my hand to the floor and try again to bring the roots up. But I can't feel them anymore. I can't hear them, and they can't hear me. All I manage is half a dozen weak poppies that wither in seconds.

I curl into myself, whimpering. London kneels over me, her little forehead pressed to the back of my head, and she whispers, "You're okay. You're okay."

Frank crouches next to me. I know it's him because I can feel him—feel *my magic* radiating off of him. His fingers ghost across my hair. "This is why you were born," he whispers. His voice, like everything else, is muffled. I press my ear to the floor and try to hear the roots, but there are only distant, tinny cries that dissipate so fast I'm afraid I imagined them.

"I don't want to do this, you know," he says. "But at this point, it's self-defense. You've been a bit of a ringleader in this rebellion, Derry, and I need to make an example out of you. I need you and all of your siblings to understand what will happen if you don't keep to our deal."

His palpable presence fades as he stands. "And you do all understand now, don't you?" No one says anything, but they must nod, because Frank says, "Wonderful. I've got a few things to work out with this, and unfortunately I'm not prepared to trust you roaming around, so for the time being, you're going to be isolated to your rooms. Let's all make the trip upstairs, shall we?"

Irene and Jane help me stand. My legs wobble, my head buzzes, but I'm able to make it up the stairs on my own.

We walk ahead of Frank. He doesn't point the gun at us, but I feel the phantom presence of it anyway. I imagine the metal against my temple. I imagine my glasses broken and bloody like Winnie's.

I wonder if her blood is still warm. How long does it take for blood to cool and—what's the word? *Coagulate.*

Irene and Violet are sent into their room first. Frank locks them in with a key from his pocket. He's never locked us in before, but it shouldn't surprise me that he has a way to do it. Next, he locks Brooke into her room. He lets the little twins stay with her instead of locking them in their room with Winnie. It's not a kindness. It keeps all of us away from the tunnel.

Now he's left with just me and Jane, but he stops us before we can enter our room.

"Actually, Jane," he says, "you come with me. I have quite a few questions for you, and I think you'll agree that after all of this, you've more than earned a time-out."

I grab her hand. "Can't you just talk to her in here?" I ask. He raises his eyebrows at me. Anxiety vibrates through my whole body, and I still feel so weak from the draining of my magic that I might collapse. I stand strong as I can.

"Derry, I think you're still a little confused," Frank says. "From this point onward, the less cooperative you are, the more disposable you are. Your dictionary taught you *disposable,* right?"

Jane pulls her hand out of mine. Frank stares at me until I back away into the room. He closes the door with him and Jane on the other side. The lock clicks into place.

Every swear I know flashes through my mind. Once their footsteps fade I try the knob. It jiggles but doesn't turn. I lean hard against the door and twist, but nothing budges.

It can't be said that Frank didn't build a quality house.

I try the window next. Sure, going out this way would

301

set off the alarms, but that doesn't mean I wouldn't be able to get to the forest before he caught me. The forest is its own form of danger, but I'm reasonably certain it doesn't want to kill me, so I'll take it over Frank until we can figure something else out.

The window remains firmly shut. That's weird—the second-floor windows have always opened, even if the first-floor ones don't. I run my hands over the frame, looking for a lock. I don't find one. I do find the nails that Frank hammered into it.

Did he do it after he found me returning from the forest? Or while we were gone, rescuing Jane and Winnie? Is it every room, or just mine? I slap my hand against the wall, angry at all these pointless questions that aren't going to get me out of here any sooner—

There's a groaning sound from Jane's closet.

*Dr. Sam.*

With everything going on, I completely forgot that I drugged a man and stuffed him in a closet.

It's been a weird few days.

He's never helped us before, but things are different now. Girls are dead now. Maybe he *didn't* know that Frank was killing all the other alchemists. Maybe he thought they just left. He's a doctor. He took an oath, didn't he? He'll help us when our lives are in danger.

I throw open the closet doors. Dr. Sam looks up at me,

wary at first, and then wide-eyed as he sees Winnie's blood still on my face. I kneel beside him. "Please don't yell," I say. "Things are going really bad."

He doesn't agree, but I remove the vine-gag. When he remains silent, I start working on the vines that bind him. They're too strong for me to tear by hand, and my magic is sluggish. It takes time to release him, but I do.

"I'm sorry," I whisper. "I couldn't let you tell Frank we were in his office."

"You've always been impulsive," Dr. Sam says. His voice cracks. I stand up and grab a glass of water from my nightstand. I come back with it.

"Sorry again," I say, back on my knees. "It's old and I did drink from it a little, but—"

His hands are released and he takes the cup, drinking greedily.

"Please, listen," I say. "You know things have been wrong in this house for a long time, don't you?" His red-rimmed eyes turn to me. He swallows hard. "How long have you worked for him?"

"A little over twenty years," he says.

"So you know. You know about the other girls. Did you help him kill them?"

Dr. Sam coughs, and thumps on his chest. "*Kill?* No, they just left when they were of age." He won't make eye contact with me. "That's what Frank told me, at least."

"But you knew," I say flatly. Why did I get my hopes up for even a second? Of course he knew, just like he knew that Frank was manipulating and emotionally abusing me and my siblings until we were completely dependent on him.

"I . . . wondered, I suppose."

I sigh, and go back to the vines around his ankles. "They're all dead," I say. *And you knew that.* "All the girls from before. And now Elle and Winnie." I pause, swallowing, my fingers moving feather-light to the drying blood on my face. "He killed them both, and now we're all locked in our rooms." The vines finally disintegrate. "For once, please . . . could you try to be *useful?*" Dr. Sam can't be trusted. That's obvious. I don't have a better choice, though. I need his help.

"For once? Derry, come now, I've taken care of you for years—"

"You've turned your back on me for years," I snap. "Don't pretend otherwise. So, yes, for once in your *goddamn life,* be useful to one of Frank's victims instead of to him."

He glares, still defiant. I smile. "That's fine. If you help me or not, I can still tell Frank you did. Imagine it. He comes to check on me. And you're here!" I gasp for dramatic effect. "You're helping one of his precious alchemists escape!"

"He'd never believe that," Dr. Sam scoffs.

"Oh, I think he would. You haven't seen him. All those girls going missing, and then killing Elle—he's unhinged. Paranoid. Now, *I* know that two decades of watching children die wasn't enough for you to grow a spine and stop him, but he doesn't." I lean in too close for comfort, the smile still plastered on my face. "And if he'll kill his most loyal alchemist without even getting to take the magic keeping him immortal, do you think he'll spare you?"

I shouldn't be excited by the fear in his eyes, but I am.

"Fine," he says. "How can I help?"

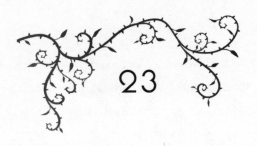

# 23

"WE NEED A distraction," I say. "All I need is enough time to get my siblings out of here. So, here's what you're going to do." I stand up, brushing myself off. "You're going to pound on that door and scream until he gets here."

"...Pardon?"

"Yeah. You're going to tell him some of the truth. That I drugged you and trapped you in my closet, yes, definitely that. You're going to insist on talking to him alone."

"Why?"

"I don't know, you make that part up. Just distract him. Get him away from here. And don't let him lock the door again. Clear?"

"Not really—"

I don't let Dr. Sam argue. I start pounding on the door with my fists, hard and loud as I can. Dr. Sam pulls me away and I scream "NO!" the way I would scream if Dr. Sam were trying to escape and expose me.

When footsteps start pounding up the stairs I retreat back to the window. I mess up my hair a little, like I've been struggling, and school my face to appear shaken and scared.

It's not far from the truth.

The lock clicks and the door flies open.

"What—Sam?" Frank asks. "When did you get here?"

Dr. Sam glances back at me. From behind mussed hair, I give him a hard look.

"I was drugged." He points at me. "I came for the counseling we talked about and found several of the girls in your office. Derry gave me drugged tea. I can't say how long I was in that closet."

Something I can't identify flickers across Frank's face when he looks at me. If I didn't know better, I'd almost call it fear.

Oh, I'd love to see fear on his face like I saw on Dr. Sam's.

"How did you get out?"

"She got desperate when you locked her in. She let me go and tried to convince me to help her escape." Dr. Sam smiles at me, then at Frank. "You'll find this hilarious, Frank. She tried to threaten me." Okay, that's more of the truth than I thought he'd tell him.

"Threaten you?"

"She thought that if you found me here, you'd assume I was trying to help her and kill me." *You can stop telling the truth at any moment now!* "So she tried to threaten me into distracting you so that she could free everyone else."

Frank laughs as my heart sinks. "They always think they can use you." He claps Dr. Sam on the shoulder. "At

307

least I can count on you, Sam. Everything else has been going to shit. Derry!" I jump. "Looks like Jane's time-out is done early and yours is about to begin. Come with me. Sam? Can you see yourself out? I'm afraid I can't play host at the moment."

"No need to explain, Frank. You'll call if you need me?"

"Of course."

Dr. Sam goes down the stairs ahead of us and I can't stop the angry tears from slipping down my cheeks. Frank grips my arm too hard. He turns me down the hallway toward the time-out room. I look back at Dr. Sam, allowing myself one final hope that maybe he *will* grow a conscience.

But he looks at me, and I know that he's not getting the others out. He smiles at me sadly, as if this is something that can be forgiven with a shrug and an apology.

He walks out the front door, closes it, and he's gone.

We are well and truly on our own.

Frank opens the door to the time-out room. It's dark. That's what it is for Jane. Dark, and quiet—but not completely quiet. Little sounds will come through occasionally. She can never fully relax.

The light from the hallway spills in and illuminates her on the stool. She's not crying. She's staring straight at Frank as if she's been waiting for him.

Maybe you can't be intimidated by the dark anymore

once you've experienced whatever she did when the forest took her.

"Good news, Jane, you've earned a reprieve," Frank says.

Jane looks between him and me. "What will you do with her?"

"I don't know," he says. "I need time to decide if she's made herself too disposable, and I think she needs to spend it in here."

She slips off the stool. She stumbles, and catches herself. We pass each other as we trade places in the time-out room. Her hand brushes mine. Briefly, our pinkies entwine.

Then she's in the hallway, and I'm in the room. Frank flips a switch, and the fluorescents come on.

"Well?" Frank asks. "On the stool."

"I did what I had to do," I say. "I'll do anything to protect them." I need another plan, but so far, I'm not having any brilliant epiphanies. I'm lost and scared and stalling.

"And just how long do you think you'll be around to protect them if you keep pulling stunts like that?"

My eyes meet Jane's in panic, and he closes the door, severing our connection.

I'm left in the too-bright. It's not long before the noises come.

I close my eyes tight, trying to block out the light. I have to concentrate. I need a new plan.

I need to keep stalling. I need to keep Frank's attention off my siblings. As long as he's hurting me, he can't hurt them.

So I start pounding on the door. Smaller fists pound inches below mine. I stumble back.

A girl no older than nine, her face streaked with tears under round-rimmed glasses, pounds on the door. Panic-flowers are growing out of the floor around her. *Please let me out!* she cries. *I'll be good!*

She vanishes. Just a memory.

I slam back into the door. "Let me out!" I yell. I don't promise to be good.

There's no answer. Either he's gone, or he's ignoring me.

This is such a delicate balance. I want to be difficult enough that he has to use all of his energy to control me, but not so difficult that he snaps and shoots me. I won't be much use to anyone if I'm dead.

No matter how loud I am, he doesn't open the door. My hand rests on the knob. I know it's unlocked, and yet . . .

I press my forehead to the door. I don't know a lot about praying. Winnie, Brooke, London, and Olivia came from religious families, and all upheld their nightly prayers. Even Winnie, at her angriest, would pray. Sometimes with Jane and her candles, other times alone in their room.

They all tried to teach me, and I listened, but it was like

I couldn't connect to what they were saying. Believing in something bigger sounded *so good*. I wanted to be folded in with them and pray to God. It seemed to give them real peace, and I longed to feel the same way.

But I couldn't. Something blocked me. I wanted to believe so badly, and couldn't.

Brooke is probably praying right now. London and Olivia might be praying. Winnie . . .

I squeeze my eyes shut. I squeeze them so tight I see bright spots and, with the noise, my head starts to hurt. I can't tell how much time is passing. I slap my hand on the door. I whisper, *"Please."*

Something answers.

It's not a word. It's a feeling. An image. I see Violet and Irene, trapped in their room. Irene sits on her bed, concentrating — concentrating on contacting me.

At the last test she couldn't get anything to Olivia from rooms away. Is it because her room is right above the time-out room? It doesn't matter. What matters is that it's working, and we can communicate at least a little.

I picture the things she needs to know. Dr. Sam in my closet. Dr. Sam leaving us. Me, in the time-out room. Jane, in the hallway with Frank. I don't know if the images are going through. I was her guinea pig a few times, but only when we were feet apart.

But she does respond, and when she does, I realize she's communicating with the others, too. She's relaying information between all of us.

She shows me Jane in our room. There's something about the feel and lighting of the image that lets me know this came *from* Jane. I see her watching Frank slam and lock the door, and hear how she heard his muffled steps down the stairs.

He could be back in the hallway, right outside this door. He could be in his rooms. He could be in the front yard, having a last conversation with Dr. Sam. He could be anywhere.

The images shift, and they become crisp—too crisp. Memories aren't like this, they're all vague and kinda squiggly. This isn't something that's happened; it's an idea.

It shows Jane in our bedroom, with her hands over the place where the door meets the wall. She pulls her hand away, and where once there was a door and a wall and a lock holding them together, there's a hole.

Idea-Jane leaves the room, and does the same to the other bedrooms, freeing everyone. Then she comes to me—

I interrupt that, and send back as forceful a message as I can. I show Irene—and by extension, if she sends it, Jane—the image of all of them escaping out through the tunnel.

I keep Winnie's body out of it, leaving the imaginary floor bare.

I don't relay the rest of the plan. They don't need to know that I'm not going through the tunnel with them. I have to distract Frank so that my siblings can get away safely. I have to do what needs doing.

Jane's response is muted, all washed-out colors and muffled feelings, like Irene is running out of power, but I think it's an agreement. I hope it is. I hope we're on the same page.

But for now, I'm back with my hand on the doorknob of an unlocked room, feeling for all the world as if it is so securely locked that no magic could bypass it.

In the guise of being cautious rather than scared, I press my ear to the door and listen. Frank could be out there, after all. I listen for breathing.

I don't hear it.

It's just me in an unlocked room with an empty hallway on the other side, and I'm still unable to open the door.

"I hate this," I whisper.

*I want to go home,* someone whimpers.

I don't need to turn around to know she's back.

It's me, a long time ago. It's just a memory, I know that, but it plays out before me like a movie.

I turn. She's not alone. She's curled up in a corner, and Frank kneels in front of her.

*I know,* he says. *But this is your home.*

*Where are my mom and dad?*

*They left you, Derry. They were scared of your power, so they left you with me.*

She looks up at him through wet lashes. *Are you scared of me?*

I watch the corner of Frank's mouth tug up into that familiar fatherly smile. I think that was the first time he'd shone it on me full force. I remember how it felt. I remember being confused and sad, but feeling a little bit safer with that smile directed at me.

*I could never be scared of you,* he says, and he and the little me disappear.

"I can fix that," I say.

That little girl really was in a locked room. My first few time-outs came with a locked door, until I could be trusted to not escape.

She didn't have a choice in the matter. I do.

I open the door.

Outside the room, I pause, listening. If Frank's anywhere nearby, he's being very quiet about it. Still, I walk as delicately as I can until I'm at the little twins' room. The door is closed and locked. Shouldn't be surprised. I don't think any of us will be allowed back into that room until he figures out how to block the tunnel.

My siblings start trickling down, Brooke and the little twins first, and the rest a few moments later. Jane nudges her way to the front. She covers the whole doorknob and lock with her hands, closing her eyes.

When she draws back, the lock is gone. It dissolved under her ministrations.

*Ministrations.* Good word.

Before anyone can enter, I sign 'wait' and slip inside. I approach Winnie, pulling a blanket off London's bed as I go.

It's worse, somehow, that he shot her in the face, and that it didn't make a neat little hole in the forehead like in some of the crime shows my parents didn't want me watching but I saw anyway. It left her near unrecognizable. Near. I think I'd have known she was Winnie even if I hadn't seen it happen. If I was taken to identify the body, like in those shows? I'd have seen her intact mouth that I learned the shape of through touch as well as sight, the way her ears point a little, the little scar on her collarbone. I would have known.

"I'm sorry," I whisper. "I should have saved you."

I drape the blanket over her body. It doesn't obscure her shape and there's still blood splatter, but it's better. It's enough.

Only then do I let the rest of my siblings in. I stand back as Brooke opens the wall and they start down the path. Just as Jane brings up the rear, I say, "I'll be right there. I need to grab something."

I don't have a better explanation if she questions me, so I don't give her a chance. I just leave, intending to begin my search for Frank.

Jane catches up with me in the living room. She glares at me. 'What are you doing?'

'Someone has to distract him.'

'No, they don't. You and I could be out already. We'd all be long gone before he even realized we weren't in our rooms. What are you *really* doing?'

No one was ever supposed to know, but if I can tell anyone . . . well. It's Jane. She already knows what I am.

'Stopping him.'

Her expression flashes into something like half a dozen emotions—confusion, realization, sadness, a little anger, and finally, grim determination.

'You don't have to do it alone.'

I do, because I can't let anyone else shoulder this particular burden, but I nod. We can work out the details of who kills who when we've found Frank.

'But before we go look for him . . .' Jane sighs, and points toward the shelf of flowers. "We have to destroy them," she whispers.

There's a sadness in her voice, and I don't know why. She's right, though. I didn't even think of it. Sloppy. If he'd escaped and managed to grab my flower, he could have killed me. Worse, he could have killed one of my siblings.

I pick up my poppy and turn it over in my hands. For years, I've used the color in this glass flower to measure my worth. If it was bright and bold, it meant I was strong.

Seeing it so pale opens a pit in my stomach.

I don't think there's a quiet way to do this, but, well, aren't we trying to find him? If he comes to us, he's found. I take several deep, fortifying breaths, then smash my poppy on the floor.

It doesn't shatter into a million pieces. It breaks into several large chunks. At first I'm not sure if that will do it, but then the red leeches out of it onto the floor . . . and disappears.

I hadn't let myself hope that breaking the flower would give me my magic back. It wasn't in there, not really. It was only a representation of what magic remained in me. Frank has the rest.

When I don't feel a surge of returning power, I'm still disappointed.

Jane and I break all the flowers, even hers, which is still clear. Maybe her connection with it was broken when she was absorbed into the tree and taken to . . . wherever she was. We break Winnie's, and Elle's. We can't leave him with anything to use against future alchemists. I don't intend to let him get that far, but you never know how a plan will go. So we break them all.

Just as I throw the last flower—Olivia's sweet pea—to

the floor, Frank appears. He comes from the hallway, either from his rooms or the basement. Who can say? Does it matter? His gun is drawn and it's pointed at me. His face has gone red with fury and he's breathing hard and ragged.

"Why can't you just fall in *FUCKING LINE?*" he shouts and, without warning, he shoots Jane. She hits the wall *hard,* crumpling. She doesn't move. A moment later, pain flares in my shoulder.

The next moments are all flashes: I realize Jane isn't beside me. Frank is shoved aside at the instant of the gunshot. Pain flares in my left shoulder.

He shot me. He shot us. He really *shot us* and it hurts like nothing has ever hurt in my entire life, and I'm bleeding. I hold my right hand out in front me, as if that could stop another bullet.

Glass crunches under Frank's boots as he steps through the remains of the flowers he's used to control us, and so many others. "I've been generous, haven't I? I've given you so many chances. I've spared you when I should have killed you. You ungrateful . . ." He shakes his head . . . and steadies his aim. "Enough."

I stare at Jane, unmoving on the floor. Everything is going black at the edges of my vision, and I was already so tired, and I'm still bleeding, and Jane might be dead, and I am *not* going down. Not without taking him with us.

A scream rips out of me, wordless and raw. The pain in my shoulder screams with me.

Under our feet, the earth rumbles.

My scream lowers into a snarl and I turn on Frank, who's already staring at me with an expression I didn't think I'd ever see on him.

Now *there's* the fear I've been looking for.

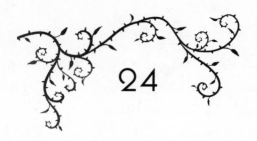

## 24

FOR AS LONG as I've been at the lake house, I've had the same nightmare.

I'm in the backseat of a car. Sometimes my parents are in the front seat, unconscious. Sometimes I'm alone. The car takes a slow headfirst dive into water. I can't move. I try to scream, but it comes out as hard, raspy breathing.

Water fills the car. We sink. They sink. I try to scream again. Something is bleeding at the edges of my vision.

Every time, I wake up unsure of where I am. I don't know if I'm underwater or out of the water or if I'm even real until Jane finds me shivering and soothes me back to sleep.

Now, seeing the fear in Frank's face makes me feel like yes, I did sink with the car. I sank to the bottom and I'm emerging from the water as something new and terrifying.

Frank sees that and he runs.

He runs from *me,* right out the front door.

I check to make sure Jane is breathing, and then the chase begins.

For once, I'm not fleeing. I'm not hiding and cowering and whimpering. I'm pursuing. I'm *hunting*. I don't even feel the pain in my shoulder. All of my focus is on my quarry. *Quarry.*

That's a good word.

Frank disappears into the forest. Stupid. Doesn't he know the forest is a living thing, and living things can play favorites? Doesn't he know that *I'm* the favorite?

By the time I breach the tree line, there's no sign of him. I stop and listen, trying to sense where he's gone.

*"Derry."*

I close my eyes. No. I don't want to hear Winnie.

*"Derry, come on!"*

Something is trying to draw me off the chase using her voice. It even nails her impatience. I can hear the eye roll. I want to run after her voice. I want her to laugh at me for getting so worked up. I want her to tease me and I want to walk home with her, hand in hand.

Winnie sings to me like she used to years ago, before we were sisters.

*"Derry, Derry, give me your answer, do . . ."*

I hear twigs snap under a man's weight, and I run.

The forest greets me, *exultant,* proud of me for passing its test, and my heart swells. Every moment I'm not sure where to turn, there's something to show me the way. Lightning bugs streaming in a line through the trees. Silhouettes in the shadows that look like my parents and Elle and Winnie, all pointing. The forest mimics a hundred animal calls, masking the sounds of my approach.

When I find him, he's doubled over, breathing hard. Stealing our magic can make him young, but it can't make him a runner.

"You okay?" I ask with mocking concern. "You need a hand?"

Frank stands up straight, but shaky. "I'm not the one you need to worry about," he says, all false bravado in his voice. "You're not going to win this fight. You're already injured."

He rolls his shoulders, steadies himself, and takes a step toward me. I bare my teeth at him.

He actually steps back.

It delights me. It *thrills* me. I'm learning so many new things I can do with just a flash of teeth, so many ways to scare the grown man that taught me real fear. Fear of the outside world, fear of being abandoned again, fear of losing the only family I have left, and fear of *him*.

Frank knows how to appear to take up space. He's tall and long-limbed and values the intimidation of seeming to take over a room. He's perfected that skill.

But I am heavier. I have at least a hundred pounds on him, probably more, and on me it is concentrated into a shorter frame. If I dug my toes and heels into the earth, I don't think he could move me.

I am an immovable object, and Frank only plays at being an unstoppable force.

"We can fix this," he says.

"Fix it?" I smile. I show my teeth. "Fix it how?"

"I'll give you back your magic."

I hum like I'm considering it. "Sounds like a lie. I don't think you could give it back even if you wanted to, and you don't."

"Derry, listen, this has been a huge misunderstanding—" He holds out his hands like he's trying to calm a wild animal. Am I imagining his voice shaking? Is he *nervous?* No, what's a better word? Spooked. *Skittish.* Skittish is good.

"Which part did I misunderstand? Was it shooting me and Jane, or killing my sisters?" I tilt my head at him. "You said you'd fix it. Which of those are you going to fix?"

Frank shakes his head. "These were mistakes, yes, but—"

"You taught me mistakes should be punished. Do you need a time-out, Frank, to think about what you've done?"

"I raised you better than this. I know you. You're not a violent girl. I've kept you safe for years—"

I laugh: high, shrill, *hysterical.* I know the history of

that word, I know it's a good word twisted into something bad, something for trapping women away and telling them it's for their own well-being. "You raised me because you *killed my parents!* You killed my parents, you killed my sisters, you killed the alchemists who came before me, and you dress me in their clothes and put me in their bed and you wonder why I'm *violent?* You should have shot me in the head when you had the chance."

Frank took some of my magic, but he didn't take all of it.

He should have. Even some magic is better than none, especially in this forest.

*Some* magic is enough to draw vines out of the ground.

It's enough to lash them out, wrap them around Frank's body, and slam him against a tree so hard I hear the breath burst out of his lungs.

It's enough to stop him.

Frank struggles against the vines. When he looks at me, he smiles. Tries to be that backyard barbecue, tuck us in and read us a story sort of father he always pretended to be.

"Derry." He laughs softly. "This is going a little too far, but we can walk it back." *Come on, kiddo, let's go back to the house. Get some ice cream. Talk it over.* "You don't have to do this."

"No," I say. "I don't."

I press my hand to his chest.

I wish a simple touch could draw my magic back out of him and into me. It doesn't. My magic will come back to full strength in time—but for now, with the forest singing in my ears, I have just enough.

That smile lingers on his face for a moment. He doesn't believe I'll really do anything. He doesn't believe I have it in me. I wait until his eyes meet mine. I wait until they widen when he realizes, too late, what he's done in underestimating me. I wait until he says *please*

and then I dig in.

I will the flowers to grow

out of his veins,

out of his marrow,

out of ventricles and arteries and kidneys and his spleen.

Flowers bloom in his throat,

out of his mouth,

choking.

He bleeds into himself,

and then out of himself,

as thorns pierce his skin from the inside.

His blood flows over my hands, paints my nails red.

I feel it when Frank's heart stops beating. I shudder with satisfaction. A coat of flowers ripples across my skin.

I should feel bad, shouldn't I? The books and movies all tell the same story. I'm supposed to feel bad about taking another life. I'm supposed to be Frank's Good Girl, obedient, toeing the line, and making sure everyone else toes the line with me.

*I'd get the longest time-out ever for this* I think, and it makes me laugh. I clap a hand over my mouth, smearing my face with Frank's blood, mixed with Winnie's.

Frank didn't understand that my whole life wasn't about pleasing him and fearing him. He didn't understand that when he gave me siblings, he gave me something to protect. Everything was to protect them, and this is where it was always leading.

They were never going to be safe if he was alive.

I don't feel bad at all. I look his body up and down, trying to feel something other than pride in a job well done, and nothing comes.

I walk away. I don't look back.

With each step, the adrenaline wears off, and my head spins a little more. My shoulder throbs anew. I'm nearly out of the forest when I'm forced to stop and lean against a tree.

I take a deep breath and grit my teeth before I work up the nerve to look at my shoulder.

I've lost a hell of a lot more blood than I realized.

I faint.

I think it's only moments later when I crawl back to consciousness. I can barely see. My vision is all blurs, both because I'm clinging to the waking world, but also because my glasses were knocked askew when I fell.

I can't tell who's next to me, but someone is.

"You'll be okay."

Elle? I squint through the fog. Blond hair. A pale face. A familiar smile. Hands, hovering over my shoulder.

"This might not feel good, though," she says.

It's an understatement. Before this, being stabbed was the worst pain I'd ever felt. That was bad enough, but knitting a hole in my shoulder back together? What does that even involve? Bringing the flesh back together, skin back together? Are there muscles in there, nerves?

I don't know. What I know is that it hurts, and I'm already so hurt, and it's impossible not to writhe under her. Someone else's hands hold down my other shoulder to keep me steady. My eyes roll wildly to that side, trying to bring the second face into focus. More blond hair. Winnie? No, it shifts dark, just for a moment. Claire. Or—

The pain fades. I'm sweaty and panting from it, but now all that's left is an itchy sore spot where the bullet wound once was.

"See?" Elle says. "Better than Band-Aids."

The other person slips my glasses back on, but before I can see either of them clearly, I pass out again.

When I wake up, I'm alone. No Elle, no Winnie, no Claire. I scramble to my feet. I'm still dizzy, but my shoulder is healed, and after a few steps, my head clears.

The forest doesn't want to let me go. Lightning bugs flit

around me. They're warm and welcoming. One lands on my healed shoulder and its magic sparks into me. The pale remnants of my remaining magic answer. I close my eyes tight to keep from crying.

"They won't understand," Claire says, appearing from behind a tree. The creature I made stands beside her, antlers as magnificent as ever. More so. The roses have grown to be the size of dinner plates. My child is *flourishing*. "You did so good, Derry. You're so strong. But they won't understand."

"You don't know what you're talking about," I say, even as my heart shivers with the fear that she's right.

Frank won't be able to hurt my siblings any longer. He and I could just . . . disappear. Maybe we'd sink into a tree, like Jane and Winnie. Or maybe I'd protect them from afar. They'd never know what kind of monster I am. I imagine myself running wild, my creature beside me, my magic returning, blood-red poppies growing freely all over my body. Maybe I'd live forever out here and become a whispered legend.

I step out of the forest.

Before I return to the house, I stop at the lake. I dip my hands into the water and scrub away as much of the blood as I can. I wash my face and my glasses. In my shaky water-reflection, I think I've gotten most of it. I can't save my ruined shirt, but they won't be able to tell what blood's from Frank and what blood's from my shoulder.

On trembling legs, I return to the house. Dread builds with each step. What will I find? Will Jane have bled out? I don't know where everyone else went after the tunnel. Maybe they're still there. Maybe they came out the other side and got lured into the forest.

Maybe I'm alone.

*God, please, don't let me be alone.*

The front door is still wide open. Through it, I hear voices.

Irene. Then Violet, then London, Irene again. I linger in the doorway, holding my breath.

"I'm going to be fine," Jane says from the living room. She sounds exhausted. But she's *alive*.

I press my hand to my mouth and close my eyes tight, swallowing tears.

Jane is laid out on the couch. London sits on the arm by Jane's feet, eyes red and swollen, cheeks wet. Irene kneels next to her with what looks like every first aid kit we have in the house. She's scowling and wrapping Jane's shoulder. Heh. We match.

"Are you *sure* the bullet isn't in there?" Violet asks, pacing nearby. "On TV they always have to dig out the bullet—"

"There's two holes," Irene says. "One in the front, and

one in the back, which indicates that the bullet went in and went out."

"But—"

"After we have some control over the bleeding, I will look for the bullet myself, but *please* . . ."

London is the first to see me when I step into the living room. She cries out, jumps off the couch, and leaps into my arms. "We thought you were *dead!*" she whimpers. "We thought he got you!"

"Well—"

It apparently wasn't *every* first aid kit in the house, because Brooke and Olivia enter with yet more. I laugh, then remember that we have so many because of Elle and her paranoia, and the laugh becomes strangled.

Olivia gasps when she sees me, then gasps again at the blood on my shirt. The kits drop to the floor and she rushes over to us. "Are you okay?" she squeals. Her shield power flares around me with her worry. "Derry!"

"I'm fine, I'm fine! It only grazed me."

"Lucky duck," Jane says from the couch. I see now that her own shirt is soaked with blood, but she looks okay. Not too pale from blood loss or anything.

Elle would be absolutely losing her shit, though, certain that sepsis would set in at any moment. I smile at Jane, and she smiles back, but it's hesitant. Her gaze roves over my bloody shirt, and searches my face.

"Derry." She speaks slowly. "Where's Frank?"

I look from one sibling to the next, all of them gathered here with me. I'm so worried the forest will be right. I'm so worried that if I tell the truth, I'll never have them around me like this again.

'He's dead,' I sign. Before they can register that: 'I killed him.'

A beat of silence. They try to register what I've said. Brooke tilts her head at me, concern furrowing her brow. Irene's emotions briefly flare into the room — confusion, relief, anger, grief, joy. Violet stares into the middle distance, their eyes unfocused. The little twins look at each other, at me, at everyone else, seeking someone who can show them how to respond.

Jane just nods. I try to read her face. Does she understand why I did it? Does she agree? Or is that resignation, accepting that the hiker wasn't a one-time thing?

Does she think I killed Frank only to take his place as the monster in our home?

'In self-defense,' Brooke signs. She's giving me an out.

I consider correcting her. I consider opening myself up, cracking the ribs, letting them all see the rot inside.

But I killed Frank to protect them, and I can spare them the hardest of truths if it means protecting them.

I nod. 'In self-defense,' I agree. There's a rush of relieved sighs, as if they'd suspected the worst. As if they'd suspected what I'm capable of. Maybe I could tell them the truth—but no. They're smiling, and I don't want them to regret his death for a moment.

I'll carry that for them.

'So . . . it's just us now,' Violet signs. 'What do we do?'

'For now?' Jane signs. 'I think we should let Irene finish up on my arm, get some sleep, and figure the rest out in the morning.'

I'm not going to argue with that.

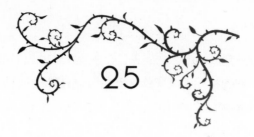

## 25

I WAKE UP the next morning, and Jane is in her bed. I close my eyes, and open them again, and she's still there. She's real.

She's alive.

I fall back asleep to the sound of her snores. I've never felt safer.

The next time I wake up, her bed is empty, and I sit up in a panic, worried I dreamt that she was alive—

She's sitting in the windowsill, holding a mug of what has to be hot chocolate. Jane doesn't like tea or coffee but she loves hot chocolate, even in the middle of summer.

I join her. She offers me the mug, and I take a sip.

"Mm," I say. "Perfect." I nod toward her left arm, which is cradled against her body in a makeshift sling. "How are you feeling?"

"Remarkably better," she says. "I'm not going to be doing any heavy lifting today or anything, but the pain is . . . much less." She purses her lips thoughtfully. "Frank said that alchemists have inhumanly long lives. I wonder what that means for our bodies healing themselves. With Elle around to heal every scrape, we never got a chance to find out."

"I vote for not testing it too much."

Jane smiles, but there's a shadow in it. There's a million reasons for *all* of us to be sad right now, but that's not a reason not to ask.

"What's wrong?"

"It's silly," she says.

"It's not if it bothers you."

"Not fair. I've said that to you a hundred times—"

"And it's just as true now. What's wrong?"

She looks back out the window, and takes another long sip of hot chocolate before she speaks.

"It's the flowers," she says. "I remember each time I bound a flower to one of you. There was another magic in them. Something so much older than any of us, something ancient, and I was the only one of us who could tap into it. I could call to it, and it would answer, and we'd watch the flowers fill up. It was the most profound, beautiful magic I've ever felt. And now they're gone."

"We had to destroy them," I say. "And maybe we can remake them—"

"Derry. Please. This isn't something you need to fix. Sometimes you need to let people be sad. You need to let *me* be sad."

"But . . . if you don't have to be . . ."

"Maybe I do," she says. "Maybe being sad for a little while is how I stop being sad. I know that you want to protect us, and that you think you can do it all on your own." I wince. That's the kind of bull's-eye only a sibling who really knows you can deliver. "Right now, I don't need you to go out and find me glass to turn into new flowers. I don't need you to research ancient spells and figure out how to redo it. I need you to be my sister, and to let me be sad, and to let me lean on you while I mourn. You need to let us all mourn, because there is *so much* to mourn right now, and the only way out is through. Can you do that?"

I don't answer immediately. I want to jump in and say *Yes, yes, of course,* to smooth it over, to make her happy by saying the right thing, but . . . Jane deserves more than that. She deserves a sister who actually hears what she says, and answers honestly.

"I can try extremely hard," I say finally.

She smiles. The shadow is still there, but the smile is genuine.

"And maybe consider asking for help occasionally. You don't have to do . . . *everything* on your own."

There are words left unsaid, hanging in the air between us. I don't have to do everything on my own. I learned that when we pulled Winnie and Jane out of the trees—I couldn't have done that by myself. But there *are* things no one can help me with, and I'd never ask it of them.

I wonder if we'll ever acknowledge out loud the truth we both know about Frank's death.

"Hey, what do you think of *witch?*" I ask. Jane blinks rapidly at the sudden change of subject. "Claire said that the first girls Frank brought here called themselves witches until he convinced them it was bad. Maybe . . . maybe it's been waiting for us to reclaim it."

Jane's smile starts slow, then spreads across her entire face. "I *love* it."

We sit together a little longer. She gives me a few more sips of hot chocolate. When it's all gone, she stands up, and she says, "Right. We have work to do."

Jane, Brooke, and I gather in the living room. Violet and the little twins are outside, enjoying the new freedom. Before almost anyone else was up, Irene was already at Frank's computer, going through his records, learning everything she could.

We are all, perhaps, putting off the inevitable hard emotional work we're going to have to do, but I think we're allowed that respite for a few days more.

'Where do we start?' I ask.

I don't miss Frank. I don't feel guilty or conflicted about his fate, but I do miss knowing that someone else will take care of the practicalities. We've never had to worry about buying food or toiletries. We're not sure if there are bills that need paying, or if Frank found a way around all of that. He kept us off the grid—by necessity, considering he planned to kill all of us—so maybe he kept the whole house off the grid, too. He spent a good chunk of his immortality becoming a technological expert. It's not out of the question.

Jane's the first to suggest going into town. The others immediately protest.

'You saw how often Frank came back beat up,' Brooke signs.

'Did he really get beat up, though?' I ask. My siblings look at me questioningly. I shrug. 'He lied about a lot. He could have faked it—just another way to keep us in line.'

No one knows what to say to that. How far *did* Frank's lies go?

'Either way,' Jane signs finally, 'I think we should go.' Her signing is clumsy with one arm in a sling, and she has to rely on fingerspelling more than usual. 'We'll *have* to eventually, and I think it's better we go before it becomes a need. Scout it out. Get accustomed. None of us knows how to drive, so we'll have to figure that out, but we have Frank's truck. And . . . Winnie.'

Her body isn't in the little twins' room anymore. Before we went to sleep, Irene and I wrapped her in sheets while Brooke took care of the twins, and we put her in the little alcove by the back door. We took on scrubbing the blood together. We expected it to be a hard job, that the blood would have stained the hardwood. Instead, it came up easy. Not even half an hour later and we were sitting back, wiping our foreheads, examining a clean floor.

Not even half an hour, and all the evidence of Winnie's death was gone.

I don't know how to feel about that.

The little twins refuse to sleep in there. They carried Olivia's terrariums into Brooke's room last night to stay with her. Gabriel the beetle got a place of honor by the window.

'We have to bury her,' Brooke signs. 'Next to Elle.'

'I'll dig the grave,' I sign. I won't be able to take a magic shortcut, at least not as easily or effectively as I did with Elle, but we have a shovel. I can dig the hard way.

'We'll work on it together,' Jane signs. 'Then we can have a memorial. For both of them.'

We pull Irene away from the computer, and she and Brooke take turns with the only shovel. I use what magic I can to make it faster. The digging is slow and messy. We end up covered in dirt.

When I talk to the earth, it's not the only thing that answers.

The forest answers, too.

It whispers *Come back* in my dad's voice.

*We love you* in my mom's.

*They know you're lying* in Elle's.

And Winnie, whispering, *The forest made me powerful.*

*Come see what my little poltergeist is now. Come see what you could become.*

I don't listen. I *try* not to listen.

It will have me again soon enough.

It's not easy to gracefully lower Winnie into her grave, but Brooke helps out with a cushion of magic air. We don't really know how funerals are supposed to go, but we each say a little something. None of it seems right or enough. We try to form our sisters out of words, but no words can do them justice.

Violet says that they saw a funeral scene on TV where everyone threw dirt into the grave before it was filled. They don't know what the purpose was, but it seems like a good idea, so we do it. One by one, we take a handful of dirt and throw it into Winnie's grave, then sprinkle a little on the mound of Elle's.

Irene takes up the shovel and she fills the grave the rest of the way.

My magic is still low, but I think there's enough for one last offering. I grab onto that remaining magic, harness it, and ask flowers to grow. For Winnie, a black spiny flower that I invented for her years ago. Elle's favorite flower is crocuses—the colorful little things that pop out of the ground as winter ends and spring begins. It's too late in the season for them, but still they surround her grave, purple and white and yellow.

The next order of business is getting to town. Out of all of us, only Jane has been behind the wheel of any vehicle. Her dad sometimes let her drive around the farm when her mom wasn't home—very slowly, and nine years ago.

'Elle could have helped,' Irene tells us. 'She was so excited to turn sixteen, even though we were still years away back then. She'd watch everything our mother did when she drove and asked a million questions. I never paid much attention.'

Since we don't have Elle or Jane's dad or anyone else, Irene brings Frank's laptop out to the living room and we gather around it. She Googles "how to drive" but it just raises other questions, like, is Frank's truck an automatic or a stick? What does that mean? Jane drove stick on the farm, she thinks. More Googling, then hunting around Frank's truck for the information we need. More Googling. Jane tries to start the truck, but it keeps making a weird noise instead.

I squint at the laptop in Irene's arms. We have a website up—"How to Start a Manual Car: 13 Steps (with Pictures)"—that we've been trying to use to just get the truck *on*.

"Is it in neutral?" Irene asks. "And you have the . . . clutch depressed?"

"That's this pedal thing here, right?" Jane asks. I dutifully compare the position of her foot to the picture on the website.

"Yeah," I say. "So, keep that down, then turn the key."

This time, the car jerks forward, making us all shriek, and then does nothing else.

"Okay, let's take a break," Jane says. "This will be easier once I'm out of the sling anyway."

Irene returns to looking through Frank's records, but leaves the laptop with us. Jane and I settle on the couch with a video about driving a stick shift. We're hardly three minutes in when there's a knock on the door.

For the first time, I regret that Frank isn't here. Frank always knew what to do with anyone who came to the house. He always protected us. He—

No.

We have plenty of ways to protect ourselves.

"Dr. Sam," Jane says. "Right?"

It hadn't occurred to me he'd come back. "I could scare him off," I say. "A little magic show?"

Jane shakes her head. "No. We need him. We need access to a doctor, and we need to keep track of him."

After a beat, I understand. "He knows too much." Jane nods.

The knock comes again, and I go to the foyer. I pull the magic up until it tingles my right palm. I open the door.

Dr. Sam stands several steps away, as though he'd been about to leave.

"Derry," he says. He smiles, and runs a hand through

his hair, looking sheepish. The magic in my palm flares in irritation. "Is Frank around?"

I shake my head. Then, plainly, I say, "He's dead. It's just us now."

His eyes go wide, and he stutters. "O-Oh. I . . . how d-did he . . ."

He looks at me, and I stare back.

He doesn't press the subject.

I knew he wouldn't, because that's the thing with Dr. Sam—if it's too hard, he'd rather not know about it at all.

"I wanted to apologize," he says. He doesn't say *to whoever happened to be in power when I arrived,* but I hear the words anyway. If Frank had answered the door, he'd be apologizing for getting caught by me. Since I'm the one standing here—

"I shouldn't have left," he continues. "I should have helped you."

"Yes," I say. "You should have."

"And I'm sorry."

"Good."

His mouth works, goldfish-like. He obviously doesn't know what to do.

He obviously expected Frank to answer.

He takes a step forward, as if to enter. Of all the choices he could make. I slam my tingling palm into the doorframe to block him. I grow thorny vines out of the wood. My forehead sweats with the effort, but Dr. Sam is hardly observant enough to notice, not when he's scared, and oh, is he scared. He looks from the thorns to me, to the thorns, back behind me into the house.

"Derry," he says. His voice shakes. He clears his throat and says again, "Derry." This time he says it in that soothing doctor voice, the one he used when he gave us our shots, the one that said *This will only sting a little* even when it was going to sting a lot. "I can hardly just leave a group of children all alone here."

*Why not?* I want to say. *You did for years.*

But Jane's right. He knows too much, and we need him.

"You're right," I say. "We could use your help."

His face brightens at that, and he tries to step in again. My fingernails rake against the doorframe and the thorns get a little bigger.

"At *our* discretion. Do for us what you did for Frank. Come when we call, stay away when we don't. Don't ask questions. Don't tell anyone about us. Can you do that?"

He hesitates. "You know . . . Frank used to pay me for my services."

I roll my eyes. Yeah. That makes sense. Why else would someone who so clearly considers himself a generally good guy do what he's done?

Money.

"Yeah, fine. We'll match his prices," I say. "And we're

343

going through his records right now, so, don't worry, we'll figure them out on our own."

"Of course," he says. He smiles, and it's like I can see him absolving himself of everything else. If he helps us now—even if it's just for money—wouldn't all his other actions be forgiven? He definitely thinks so. "Of course. In that case, I can help. Do you need anything right now? Food, or . . ."

I'm about to say no and send him on his way, but I stop. "Actually," I say. "I think you *can* help us."

Ten minutes later, Jane's in the driver's seat of Frank's truck with Dr. Sam beside her, teaching her. Violet and Irene lounge in the back. No one says it out loud, but no one thinks it's a good idea for someone to be alone with Dr. Sam.

His presence has reminded me of something else. Dr. Sam isn't Frank's only ally. Frank had psychics he went to see. There were people who gave him the locations of the witches.

Will they come looking for him? Was he a customer, or a friend?

I think we have to make sure there's nothing to find, and Frank's body is still in the forest.

I have an idea for what to do about that.

While driving lessons go on, I ask Brooke to do me a favor.

'A bonfire?' she signs, making sure she got it right.

'A big one.'

She twists her mouth to the side, then asks, 'Why? And tell me the truth.'

I hesitate. I wasn't going to tell anyone until it was done, so there wasn't a chance for anyone to stop me. Brooke just waits. She'll know if I lie. I don't know if she'll do something about it, or if I'll be met with that resignation I thought I saw on Jane's face when she found out I killed Frank. Like it's confirmation of who I am.

I don't want to be the kind of person who lies this much to her siblings.

So, I tell her. When I'm done, she sighs, and rubs her eyes.

'I don't know.'

'I think it would be good for us,' I sign. I bite my lip, then add in slow, jerky motions, as if it's being forced out of me, 'but if you think it's not a good idea . . .'

'Then you'd do it in secret?' she asks.

'No, no,' I sign, not sure I'm telling the truth.

'You want my honest opinion?'

'I really do.'

'I think we need to be discussing this with *everyone*. It can't be on us to decide. And if the majority vote is no . . .'

I nod. 'Yeah. I understand.'

We wait for Dr. Sam to leave before we gather everyone.

I tell them my plan, just as I told it to Brooke. It seemed like a better idea when it was just her. With all these other eyes watching me . . . it seems gruesome. It seems like an incomprehensible thing to suggest to my siblings, including a pair of eight-year-olds.

Irene's all in, immediately. Violet is much less sure about it. Olivia and London have a lot of questions, and I can't answer all of them, but I try. Jane . . . I'm not sure. She's taking it seriously. She's considering it. I don't know which way she'll vote.

I only need three of them to win, technically, but I want all of them. This needs to be for *all* of us. I argue my case as well as I can.

Still, when the vote comes down, it surprises me that it's unanimous. Even Brooke agrees once she realizes everyone else wants it.

So, a little before dusk, I return to the forest with a big blanket from Frank's bed—the better to drag his body with.

The forest is happy to have me back. It floods me with warmth and magic enough to make my eyes sting with the threat of tears.

It'll come back. He said it comes back. I'll have this much magic again, and it'll be all mine.

The forest wasn't as kind to Frank's body as it was to Elle's. The animals have already been at it. I remember the word for it — *predation.* I like that word. They've taken his softest parts, and it's not a pretty sight. My stomach roils, but I don't flinch away.

I could just leave him here to keep rotting and rotting into nothing. It would be easier. But I want to be rid of the evidence, and I think it would do us all good to get the kind of closure I'm planning.

I also don't want the forest to have him. It's already spread farther, past its borders. I'm not sure how much taking his body will help to stop that, if at all. Maybe the surge of power at his death was all the forest needed.

Or maybe the forest can drain him slowly, like he was going to drain us.

Maybe it isn't animal predation on his body. What animals are there to do the predation? Lightning bugs? My creature?

I'm not sure what to think about that — if something I made fed on Frank.

My magic isn't strong enough right now to get the vines to pull away from his body. That's okay. I brought a knife from the kitchen just in case.

"What do you want?" I ask as I saw at the vines. Claire rounds the tree with her familiar crooked smile, my creature beside her. "You have a new best friend, huh?" I ask it, a little accusingly.

"Just checking in," she says. "You don't have to worry

about that, you know." She nods toward Frank. "The forest will take care of him."

"Oh, I know." Once one vine is cut, the others go quickly, like they've remembered who I am and want to help. "But I have to take him back."

"What use could you have with him? At least we'll use all the parts."

I sigh. "We need this closure," I say. "My siblings and I. We all need to see him and *know* he's gone. Otherwise we'll be kept up nights, imagining him running around out here. You lived with him. You *died* with him. Surely you can understand that."

She doesn't respond. With Frank's body free of the vines, I clumsily lower him to the blanket. I wrap him in it as best I can. I straighten up, brushing my hands on my skirt. I turn my attention back to Claire.

"Considering all I've done for you," I say. *All I've killed for you.* "Could you tell me the truth? Are you really Claire, the witch who died here decades ago, or are you just the forest wearing her face?"

Her smile returns along with that curious, owlish tilt of her head. "I still don't see why you have to make that distinction."

"Yeah." I shake my head. "That's what I thought you'd say."

I drag Frank through the trees. The shadows of my parents and my sisters walk on either side of us. Just before I'm out, Claire appears in front of me.

"See you again soon," she says. I follow her with my eyes as she walks around me, and stands next to my creation. The giant roses on its antlers are dripping with a black ooze. Something like . . . ichor.

*Good word.*

When Claire smiles, she has too many teeth.

The sun is down by the time I return. Brooke didn't skimp on the bonfire—I can see its glow from the tree line. I worry that everyone's minds will change when faced with the reality of Frank's body, even wrapped in a blanket, but when I haul it over, they only watch with solemn faces.

I need Irene's help to get him into the fire.

My siblings and I make a circle around the blaze. We join hands.

The magic we perform doesn't have words. It is felt. It is the roots beneath our feet. It is the strings connecting our fates to each other and to the rest of the world. It is the life-giving water, it is the power in ourselves.

We watch Frank burn. We make our wishes. We wish for peace. We wish for clarity. We wish to be able to let our past go, to grow, to move on.

We wish and the sparks float into the air and we wish harder.

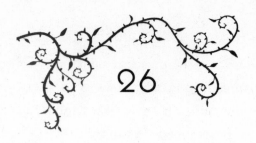

# 26

IT TAKES LONGER for Frank to burn than I would have thought. The blanket goes first, of course, and I expect the rest to be fast.

It's not fast.

It's almost two hours.

The others go inside before the flesh begins to melt. I stay. I watch his body melt and collapse and pop. I feed the fire to keep it hot enough, even though I'm not sure what *hot enough* entails when it comes to cremation.

It smells terrible. Metallic and dead. In my peripheral vision, the forest is full of lightning bugs.

I stay outside long after it's dark, until all that's left of Frank is bone.

I didn't expect so many huge pieces of bone to be left over, either. I'll have to bury those. They don't require near as big of a grave as a full body, and I'm able to dig one myself. It's not easy to find a place both far from my sisters and far from the forest, but I do.

When I finally sleep, I don't have any nightmares.

A few days later, Jane's able to take off the sling. Seems she wasn't far off about the possibility that we have rapid healing alongside a long life. Her mobility in that arm is still limited but she can drive, so we go to town for the first time. Only Jane and I had intended to go. Other than the fact that Jane's still a little nervous about the driving thing, we also don't want to draw attention to ourselves. From what Irene's found online, it seems that Frank vastly overstated how much the outside world cares about witches. They don't seem to believe we exist at all, much less want to kill us. I was probably right about him faking all those attacks.

But what if?

The little twins won't take no for an answer. The others stay behind more willingly. Irene has her research, and Brooke and Violet just aren't ready. I'm not sure I am either.

So Jane, the little twins, and I pile into the truck. Jane mutters the steps to herself as she starts the truck. It only jerks a little as she steers us forward.

We drive down the same road we watched Frank disappear down so many times. The road passes through the forest, but the trees don't encroach close enough to worry me.

The car crests a hill and we're out of the forest and I can't help it—I gasp.

I knew our forest and our lake weren't the whole world, but the scenery before us is like a punch in the gut. The road dips in and out of view as we pass over hills, and on the passenger's side there's a drop-off. Jane swears under her breath the entire way, taking the turns as slow as she can. And the *trees*. Miles and miles of trees. More trees than I remember ever seeing.

These huge swaths of trees aren't familiar, but the dip in my stomach when we crest and descend each hill? That is. My stomach rises into my throat and dives back down, and I'm nine years old again in the backseat of my parents' car, blissfully unaware of the future to come.

At the top of a hill, I look back to our forest. It's cut off from the rest. On the side I can see, there's a significant barrier of what looks like dead, barren land.

I wonder who did that. Who found out what our forest was and cut it off from spreading? I'll have to take a look at that border. Maybe we can build something like it around the house.

It's twenty minutes to town. I don't breathe between getting out of the car and walking into the store. Even with everything Irene found to contradict Frank's stories, I still imagine someone grabbing us and throwing us into a fire. What if any of these people knew that hiker? What if they can smell his blood on me, weeks in the past?

But no one cares. As far as they're concerned, we're just people passing through. They might know Frank, but they don't know that we're his.

That we *were* his.

We aren't here because we need anything. We just want

to dip our toes into the water of the world, ease our fear. But we do have some cash from Frank's wallet, so Jane still grabs a basket. The little twins' eyes light up the moment they see the candy aisle, and they drag Jane, laughing, into a chocolate and caramel and nougat heaven.

I wander on my own. I walk through the pharmacy section, trying to understand the medicines and kinds of bandages we may one day need. I wander through aisles of scented toiletries I'd never imagined.

I find myself at a display of nail polish.

It's nothing Frank would have ever allowed, but there's an old memory. My mom. Her hand holding mine, her other hand gracefully sweeping the brush across my nails. Both of us blowing on them.

I choose a shade that says CHERRYLICIOUS on the bottom, and when I rejoin my sisters, I put it with the pile of candy and cheese puffs and other snacks Frank rarely bought us that they shove onto the counter.

The drive home is made in high spirits. I twirl Cherrylicious between my fingers, and Jane tells the little twins to wait on the candy until we're home, even as they dig into the bag.

Once we're home, the little twins abscond with the candy and snacks. Jane rolls her eyes and goes off to supervise. Irene is still holed up in Frank's rooms. Violet and Brooke are deep into some kind of redecoration plans.

I take the time to sit on my bed and paint my nails. The result is amateurish and messy, but I love it.

If anyone asks, I won't tell them I chose red because it reminds me of Frank's blood on my nails the night I killed him.

With dry red nails, I go downstairs to find my siblings, and I meet Jane in the hallway. She's standing outside the big twins' and Violet's room, a piece of paper shaking in her hands.

"Irene's gone," she says. "She'd been in Frank's rooms forever, so I went looking for her, and she wasn't there. So I looked up here, and . . ." She blinks back tears, and holds out the paper for me.

*I hope you'll understand that I have to go find my peace somewhere else. I'll come back one day if I can.*

*I've left everything I found of use on Frank's desk. You should also know that he hoarded cash — you'll find all of it in his office, too. Well, most of it. I took a little for myself. Trust me. There's so much you won't miss it.*

*I love all of you.*

That's it.

In Frank's rooms, we find what else she's left — summaries of what she learned, paths to useful files on his computer, and more cash than I've ever seen or would ever know what to do with. I pick up a piece of paper on one stack.

*I can't find records of where he kept disappearing to*

*when he left us alone, but these are all the contacts I found.*
*And, if you're interested, he kept journals on his research.*

All this information, all this money, but no goodbye.

"Why?" I ask Jane. "Why didn't she talk to us first?"

She looks at me with that shadowed smile. "Because she needed to go be sad."

We split up Frank's notes, and Irene's notes on his notes. I read about his attempt to figure out if magic was caused by our biology, or if our biology was changed by the magic. I learn that our aging will slow down sometime in our twenties, around when everyone else's speeds up, and given the chance, we could all live to be two hundred years old or more.

I learn that Frank was much, much older than that.

Violet waves their hands to get our attention. 'He kept family records,' they sign. 'On all of us. There's records on what happened to our parents, and on immediate family — anyone who might come looking for us.'

I stare at the notebook in their hands. *What happened to our parents.* I know we saw similar notes in the old profiles we looked at days ago, but right there, in that notebook, is all the compiled information on who was abandoned and whose parents are dead.

I still don't know which would be worse.

'Can I see?' I ask. Violet hands it over, and I flip through. We each have a page, front and back. There it is — my confirmation. My parents died in the lake. I apparently have an aunt somewhere, but she and my mom were estranged, so Frank wasn't worried about her. I hold my breath as I turn to Winnie's page. I know she can't feel the hurt anymore, but I also know how badly she wanted to go home.

It shouldn't be a relief to know her parents are dead, but it is. It says right there that they thought they'd just come to get help, and when Frank tried to keep Winnie, they resisted. He killed them.

Winnie's parents wanted her.

I look up to find my siblings watching me. I set the notebook down. 'So. Who wants to know?'

The little twins and Jane don't. 'Maybe later,' Jane signs. 'I'm not ready.'

We learn that Violet's parents also died, but Brooke's left her of their own free will. We also learn that Violet and Brooke are the only ones who have surviving family that Frank had any concern about. Violet, especially, has a *huge* extended family—aunts and uncles and cousins for days. Brooke has a grandmother and uncle who Frank found poking around, but were redirected.

In the end, it turns out that Irene's departure is just the beginning.

After days of discussion and uncertainty, Brooke and Violet announce they want to find what family they have left. They take their time preparing to leave. There's research to do and bus tickets to buy and emails to set up so that they can always contact us. They have Frank's cell phone number, too, and they'll call when they can.

We don't hold a going-away party because that would make it seem permanent. We aren't willing to admit it's possible they'll never come back. They'll find their families, and we want that for them, but they'll come back eventually. Even if it's just a visit.

One morning, Jane drives them to the nearest bus station.

It's *not* goodbye.

Now it's just the four of us—me and Jane and the little twins. The house abruptly feels impossibly big and empty.

"I don't suppose you're planning on leaving, too?" I ask Jane. It's the day after Violet and Brooke left, and the weather is gorgeous. We're lounging on a picnic blanket while London and Olivia chase each other around the lake. "You can, of course." I try to mean that, but I don't. If Jane left, it'd be too much.

"I'm definitely staying. I have plans for this place," Jane says, a smile on her face.

"Plans?" I ask.

"There are a lot of magical children out there," she says. "Some of them don't understand their powers. Some of them really are being abandoned by their parents. We have this big house, and Frank has records of up-and-coming witches. We could find them and *ask* if they need or want the kind of home we can provide. We could teach them. We could grow our family."

It's brilliant, and it's incredibly *Jane*. She's been back for weeks and I still keep being hit with how much I missed her while she was gone.

"Tell me everything," I say.

Jane dives into the plans with a passion. She wants to make the house worthy of being a school and a home, which means getting rid of the division between the main house and Frank's rooms, adding more windows, and remodeling the time-out room. She wants to take advantage of the huge yards and expand our garden. It's a lot of work, but Jane is obviously excited, and she'll have all of us to help her.

When the little twins crash onto the blanket, worn out, we tell them the plan.

"Promise we can get a cat before we get kids," Olivia moans. *"Please."*

*"Pleeeease,"* London adds.

"I'm sure we can make that happen," Jane says.

Satisfied, the little twins run off to decide if they want a different room than they have now before anyone new comes to claim the best one.

Everyone has plans and goals for what to do with this new life.

Why am I so unsure of what I want?

Jane glances toward the forest before following the little twins inside. She's never talked about what she experienced in there, and I don't push. She'll tell me when she's ready. If she's ever ready.

I fold up the blanket, but before I go in, I walk toward the nearest tree. I did go visit that barren land, alone, because no one else wants to go into the forest, and I don't want them to, either. I'm still not sure how the barren circle was achieved. Someone burned and salted the earth, I guess. We'll have to figure it out soon. The forest hasn't slowed its approach.

I place my hand on the tree.

The magic still sparkles, but now I feel the darkness in it more keenly than ever. It's been weeks since I killed Frank, but my own magic hasn't returned completely. I'm worried it'll never recover entirely.

The forest could probably restore it. In fact, I'm sure it could. I've been good, though. I haven't been sneaking out at night, even though I want to, so much that it hurts. I miss my creature. I miss Claire's gravitational pull.

But every time the urge to go cover myself in fireflies feels impossible to resist, I remember all the soft spots chewed off of Frank's body by animals that don't live in the forest.

I remember Claire's crooked smile and her too many teeth.

I press my palm more firmly against the trunk. I push back the magic it tries to flow into me, and send out my own.

The forest is in me. I don't think I'll ever get it out. Maybe it'll take me over, bit by bit, a virus eating its way through every cell.

That doesn't mean I can't make sure there's a piece of me invading the forest.

Irene is off to find her peace. Brooke and Violet are seeking their families. Jane is building a school and a home. The little twins are preparing themselves to be mentors for new witches.

They're all finding their way, figuring out who they are, and I think I know what my role is, finally. I'll do what I've always done. I'll keep protecting my siblings. I'll try to accept the times I can't protect them, and I'll try to ask for help when I need it. But that doesn't mean I can't focus on the protection I *can* provide, doesn't mean I can't hone that skill. No more accidental casualties, like the hiker. That was panic. That was badly placed instinct. I'll always regret that. I'll always wonder what I took out of the world when I killed him. But I know there are going to be other threats. Even if Frank was lying about how much everyone hates witches, I don't think Frank can be unique. He can't be the only person looking to exploit our power.

Someone else came out of the forest the day I killed

Frank. Someone with a purpose outside of fueling another person's immortality. Someone who knows what difficult things need to be done for the safety of those she loves. Someone who will do it.

That's the witch I have to learn to be.

# ACKNOWLEDGMENTS

When I was young, acknowledgments might as well have not existed. As I got older, they became a little peek into the author's world and the people who helped them. As a debut, they became study material. And now, as the person writing them, they're a place to make my friends and family cry.

Thank you to my incredible agent, Thao Le, who believed in this book and believed in me, and who always has my back.

Thank you to my editors—to Nicole Sclama, who saw what this book could be. To Lily Kessinger, who became my guiding light to release day.

Thank you to the entire team at HMH, who put passion and love behind my book—Helen Seachrist, Mary Claire Cruz, Alice Wang, Samantha Bertschmann, Anna Ravenelle, Zoe Del Mar, and Taylor Navis. Thank you to Kim Ekdahl, the artist who brought Derry to life for the cover. Thank you to my sensitivity readers, Isabelle Felix and D, for their insight and honesty.

Thank you to Ian, who came into my life around the same time as the idea for this book, and never doubted that I'd make it this far. Thank you for loving me, and thank you for distracting our terrible cat sons when I need to write.